The Mental Take Over

Preface:

I want to thank my loving and amazing wife and daughter. Without them none of this could happen.

/:Chapter 1

Antecedents >

<u>Early 1972 Ottawa, CA</u>:

Harold Hartright sat at his desk staring blankly at the paper in his hands. He understood the direction change. There hadn't been any new breakthrough in the area of artificial intelligence in years. But that also meant that everything he had worked on since college was a complete waste of time now. He looked around his office, he looked at the components and chicken scratch he had written down everywhere.

He was Canada's leading expert in the area. In fact, he was leading in almost every area when it came to computers. He walked around the office looking at his certifications, degrees, and awards. It was difficult to think that his entire life's work was getting kicked to the curb. He was thankful that he was still quite young, so that the restart wouldn't hurt so much.

He started taking the files out of the file cabinet and boxing them. A few he saw, he just threw away, knowing that they wouldn't have any relevance anymore. He felt himself starting to get emotional. Each file he boxed or threw away felt like he was losing a little part of his heart.

It all hit him. All the time he had spent on his research. All the people he had to tell they were no longer able to pay them. All the excitement he had had when he started three years before, at age sixteen. All of the personal relationships he had ruined because of his obsession with his research. All of it, for nothing.

The year had just started, and he just knew it was already going to be the worst of his life. He threw a few files into a box and decided he would finish it later. He had to go home. He couldn't be there anymore.

Stepping out into the cold air, it felt like it smacked him in the face. His tears made his face feel colder. Trudging through the snow, he felt that it all just matched the feeling in his soul. His entire body trembled. He held the box tighter and hurried the few blocks home.

Walking in the door, he couldn't feel the chill leave his body. His home felt just as cold, empty, and alone as his office had. He stripped off his coat, hat, and scarf and flopped down in his smoking chair and let out an exasperated huff.

He lit his pipe and took a few puffs. Letting out another sigh, he leaned over and pulled the box of files to him. Pulling off the top, he started pulling out the first few files. He flipped through them mindlessly. He didn't expect anything in there to challenge his mind as much as artificial intelligence had.

Getting up, he held the pipe in his teeth as he went and put a record on for some background music. Closing his eyes, he let the sounds take over his senses. As he tried to relax, he had everything come flooding back and, in a fit of rage, he threw the files in his hand against the wall.

Pages flew everywhere around the dimly lit room. As he got down on his hands and knees, collecting the papers again. He pushed them all together, and as he did, his eyes settled on one paper. He read it and reread it. It sounded a bit like science fiction. But so had artificial intelligence when he first got into it.

He read the title again.

Neuropathic Operative Visual Algorithm: the human brain and computer user interaction by Walter Woodford.

He felt that familiar tingle of interest that he had felt when he first heard about artificial intelligence. He felt a glimmer of hope spark inside him.

He rushed to his phone and started to call every contact he had. He needed to get in contact with this Walter Woodford, or his financiers. He wanted to learn as much as he could about this idea. He needed it. The more he thought about the possibilities, the more he knew this was where he needed to be.

***

<u>1972 MIT Cambridge, MA:</u>

The phone started ringing. Walter sat in his chair and just looked at it. He hated talking on the phone. Actually, he hated talking to people in general. It always felt like he was talking in fast forward compared to everyone else. Then, he would be left to either explain himself, repeat himself, or have to bear with their awkward looks as they just tried to bring up a different topic. It always left him feeling even more awkward and out of place than if he had just stayed out of the conversation all together.

That is what led to him working for the NSA. He had been in college and was working in his lab, and in walks an impressive man. Large, commanding respect, intimidating. His chest was covered in medals, and he had four stars on his shoulders indicating that he was a very high ranking general. Marching over to Walter's desk followed by another smaller statured woman, the man set his hat down on some papers that were on the desk.

"Hello, Walter. I would ask what you are working on, but we both know I wouldn't begin to understand. So, I am going to get straight to the point. I am here to provide you an opportunity to serve your country, while also getting all of the funding that you would ever need. We would require results from time to time, but for an inventor like you, that shouldn't be an issue.

"We will create a contract for you and will leave a liaison for you. So, your interaction with the senators will be very limited, and, even more, your interaction with the general public. We will find the best for you, and once you start on a sensitive project, then you will also get a bodyguard. This is not negotiable. If you agree to this, then I have the contract right here. Know that this is a onetime offer, and it is not likely something that will ever be presented to you again. So, make your decision with your future in mind," The general finished.

Walter didn't like being rushed, especially with something of this magnitude. It would have a lasting impact on him, his career, and his personal life. If he ever had one. But, even at his young age, he understood that this was the offer most people in science dream of. A government contract to do all the research you need, with basically an unlimited potential budget. There wasn't any way that he could say no.

"I'm in. Let me look over the contract," Walter said, holding out his hand for the paperwork.

The general smiled and nodded to his assistant. They reached into their satchel and pulled out the papers. Reading through it, it seemed to be exactly what the general had said. That comforted Walter. He was ready to have to read a ton of fine print, but this seemed to be straightforward. A nice change of pace from the other government contracts that he had turned down in the not-so-distant past.

"I appreciate the straightforward approach you have," Walter said to the general.

"I served in WWII, son. I don't have time or energy for games," the general said with a slight reflective chuckle.

Walter nodded and signed his name to the contract. Initializing where he needed.

"Excellent. We will be back soon to help you to your new lab. Also, we will have two partners for you. One just joined us from Canada, the other is one of ours already. Both bright, and both very capable. If you find them difficult to work with, tough. Make it work," the general said gruffly as he got up to leave.

Walter couldn't help but notice the bounce in the personality between gruff general and almost a grandfatherly nature to him. Putting it out of his mind, he got busy on his work again. He didn't want to think about the people he would be having to work with. That would just make him nervous and worried. He had never had much luck working with others.

***

Late Spring 1974 Washington DC:

Harold stood outside the building. He had his work visa in hand and was finding the confidence to approach the building. It made his hands shake. Taking a deep and steadying breath, he approached the building. Showing his work visa, the guard let him in, and directed him towards reception. There he got his card pass and credentials set up, and he was shown to his office. It was right outside his lab.

He figured being in so early, he would have time to get situated before anyone else would show up. The US government had already moved everything that he had sent from his office that was closed down in Canada, and put it all in his new office, so he was planning a day of setting everything up.

He sat down at his desk and started to file some of his reports and papers that he often read through, when he heard a clatter in the lab. Looking through to the lab from the window behind his desk, he saw a small statured man hunched over a table.

Walking through the door, he was hit with the smell of soldering. He slowly approached the man, not wanting to cause him to jostle and mess up.

After standing there watching the man work for about forty-five min, the man finally took a break and looked up.

"Can I help you?" Walter asked Harold.

"Oh, excuse me, where are my manners? My name is Harold Hartright. I was told I would be working here?" Harold half said, half asked.

"Oh, you're one of my coworkers now. The Canadian, I take it? Hardly anyone is that polite anymore. Do you need something, or can I get back to work? I would like to finish this today before the general gets here," Walter asked, sounding slightly irritated.

"Oh, of course! Don't let me stop you. I just hadn't ever seen a processor that small before. What kind of power would it be able to produce?" Harold asked, surprising Walter. It was rare that someone wouldn't need him to explain in the simplest terms that he could come up with, before they would understand what he was working on.

"Yeah, it is just something extra I am working on for myself. This one can run about one hundred MHz, but I like to allow everything to be able to be worked on, so that I can make adjustments as the technology changes," Walter said, testing Harold to see how he would react.

"No way that that little thing is pushing one hundred MHz. The best I could get in Canada is a two MHz processor," Walter said with some disbelief.

"Well, this is my own design. I don't like waiting for technology to catch up with my mind. So, I try to create what I need," Walter said as he pulled his work goggles back down. "Now if you don't mind, I would like to get this done. It isn't something I would like the government to have just yet."

Harold understood and took a step back. Admiring and studying the skill of his new coworker.

Eventually, Harold went back to his office and got the rest of this stuff settled in. Not long after he finished, the general walked into the lab from the key card door.

"What do you have for me?" he said, getting right to the point.

10

He walked in to see Walter had several other items out, but his processor was nowhere to be seen.

"I have this laser that can cut paper at the moment. After several more trials, I believe that I could get it to cut through at least wood in far less time than a chainsaw. I have these glasses that can read invisible ink, based off the original design by Ben Franklin. However, this looks like normal glasses. And I have started to gain some momentum on the NOVA system," Walter said, causing Harold to perk up at the mention of the entire reason he agreed to move down here.

"Good work on these. You will need to have a breakthrough on this NOVA system. I am not going to pander to you and try to understand what it is about, but there are a lot of people complaining about the amount of money being put into it without results. Now make it happen. The only reason that you have the leash you do is because you keep churning out these lovely little doohickeys," As he finished, the general turned on his heels and walked out.

"That man is quite intense, isn't he?" Harold asked.

"Yeah, he has never been one to mince his words much. I appreciate that about him," Walter said, still looking at the door. "Are you all settled and ready to get working?"

"Yes, and I wanted to say, the entire reason that I came here is for the NOVA system. I read a paper about it while I was working on AI, and when funding for that got cut entirely, I had to find something else. This NOVA system, do you really believe that you can make it work?" Harold asked with hope in his voice.

Walter stopped messing with the glasses that he had been tinkering with since the general had left and looked at Harold with interest. As though he was studying him. He couldn't figure out if the man was just trying to appease him, like so many others, or if he was genuine in his interest.

"Yes, I believe that it can work. If you weren't sure, then why did you bother to come here?" Walter asked with a quizzical tone.

"Easy, I never assume anything someone else is claiming or doing can be done, until it is. Not to mention the fact that no va, in Spanish, means 'not going', so I wasn't really sure if it was meant to be a joke on the government. However, the concept intrigues me to where I believe that if I am given the right tools, I can make it work. I just wanted to make sure that the person I am working with was of the same mind," Harold said with a smile.

The tension visibly left Walter's shoulders. He relaxed and reached out his hand. "As you already know, I am Walter Woodford. Yes, I firmly believe that the NOVA system is something that can and will work, I am just not sure in what capacity it will be successful yet. I believe that we can use computer algorithms to increase the intelligence of a person, implant information into the mind, or possibly create entirely new personalities to be used for deep cover assignments. Making the person effectively their cover, as to protect against the shell shock that we are seeing with so many returning from Vietnam. I had been working with some neuroscientists, but they all just claimed it was never going to work and urged the committee to nix the idea entirely. So, for the last few months I have worked entirely alone on it," Walter finished with a slight huff.

Harold was taken back. He had not expected such progress in the thinking of use of the NOVA system. The fact that Walter had actual practical uses in mind set his work apart from many other projects that were out there. Most hadn't even thought that far ahead.

"So, how would it work?" Harold asked.

"And therein lies the problem. I have the idea that if the brain saw the correct algorithm that it would be forced to retain it. If you give the brain the right triggers, I believe that we will be able to reprogram it. I think it will take a mixture of algorithms, images, and coding. Likely it will need to be seen by someone who understands all of them. But I believe if you can give the brain something that it will have continued to increase its activity while thinking and rethinking over what it has seen without having to have it be active, then you can increase the capacity of the brain. Depending on where the activity is designed to be active, and

12

how, it will affect the person differently," Walter was starting to get excited, his talking speed increased, and he was getting wrapped up in his own world explaining what was his most treasured work. The difference now was that the person he was talking to was able to keep up.

"So, it would be effective on someone who has a higher intelligence already. Someone who would understand the coding, the algorithms, and the pictures given. Wouldn't the increase in brain activity just create seizures?" Harold asked in a slightly worried manner.

"That is a risk. Especially if the person isn't naturally of higher intelligence. But that is why it shouldn't be for just everyone. I also think that if it can eventually do what I think it would be able to do, then it could be too dangerous to be able to be just put into anyone," Walter explained.

"Well, given that the algorithms I had to come up with to create the artificial intelligence, it would help with the transition from computer to human brain," Harold responded, getting excited himself.

***

Fall 1975 Washington, DC:

The general walked down the hall with two people in tow this time. Walking into the lab, he saw Walter and Harold working together, and the third scientist off by himself. He paused in front of the desk that the first two were working at.

"Walter, a word please," the general said.

Walter nodded to Harold, and he went and got Zodiac, and they went to their offices. Harold was looking in his monitor that wasn't on. He could see the reflection through the screen and then through the window. He was worried about his friend. They had been working together for the last few years and had not spent much time apart. They usually stayed at the lab until the early morning hours, and then would run home and change, shower, and maybe take a few hours of sleep. And then would end up back at the lab, working. They had made plenty of progress on the NOVA system, but they were far from being able to have it be something that was of practical use.

Walter knew one of the ladies that was with the general. She was always with him. A stern looking small statured woman with bright red hair. She looked like the type that would much rather shoot someone than to give a report. But here she was, following around the general.

"As you know, I told you when you were first brought on, you will have a bodyguard," the general said, "This is Lucille. Call sign Hel. She was brought in from the CIA on loan. She has her bosses she reports to, and they will be a part of this project from here on out. This is going to be the first CIA/NSA project ever attempted. You and your mind are now a top priority for security to the government. So, Hel here is the best. That also means that she is not likely to be too happy to be strapped to your desk, instead of out in the field. So don't be a pain to her. I don't want to have to find a replacement for her. Understand? If that means you only talk to her when it is absolutely needed, then that is what it means," And with that, the general and his assistant walked out.

Walter was nervous. Not because he was scared of the fact that Lucille/Hel could kill him. But because she was a girl. Scratch that. A woman. No. THE woman. He had never seen someone so beautiful. All he could do was stare at her.

Getting uncomfortable, Lucille nodded at Walter. "If that is all, I will be out in the hall. Let me know when you are leaving and we will discuss living arrangements," she said, and turned and walked out.

Harold saw her leaving and came into the lab. Seeing his friend in an almost catatonic state, he waved his hand in front of his face.

"Hello? Walter? You in there?" Harold quipped, laughing as he did.

Walter snapped out of it. He had never had someone, anyone, cause his mind to pause like that. To freeze to the point, he wouldn't be able to function properly.

"I am going to marry that woman," Walter said dreamily.

"Yeah yeah. And is that before or after you become a millionaire inventor and own an island that you can do all your research on?" Harold teased, getting back to work.

Walter chuckled, as he was still staring at the door.

***

Spring 1976 Washington DC:

Walter stood at the end of the center aisle of the church. His best man Harold standing next to him. As per the government's requirements, there was no photographer. The doors opened, and in walked Lucille. Her white dress with lace sleeves flowing behind her. Walter thought his heart was going to burst.

He had tears forming as he watched his soon-to-be wife walking down the aisle.

"You are a lucky man, Walt. Enjoy this moment," Harold whispered to him.

Walter nodded, not taking his eyes off of his bride.

***

Spring 1977 Atlanta, GA:

Harold stood with Walter in the waiting room. Walter paced back and forth repeatedly. Harold understood why. It was hard not to. His wife was in labor with their first child. He was excited beyond belief. They had learned that they were going to have a girl. He couldn't wait to have a replica of his beautiful wife running around their house.

Their lab had been moved to Atlanta, GA in 1977. The government was getting worried about what the NOVA system was capable of being, and so they wanted their lab as close to the CDC as possible. They had been worried that the computer interacting with the human brain would cause computer viruses to become human viruses. The closer that they got to it being completed to the point of trials, the more the government pushed. Even with their fear.

Walter paused as the doctor walked through the door.

"Are they ok?" Walter all but jumped onto the poor doctor.

"Well, I am not sure that I have heard so many creative and colorful ways to kill me before, but they are both ok. I may have to move my family now, though," the Doctor said half joking, "You are welcome to go in and see them now."

Walter didn't wait around to hear the rest of what the doctor said. He took off towards the room his family was in. Bursting through the door, he saw his wife holding a swaddled little baby.

Looking up, Lucille had a tear in her eyes. Looking right at Walter, she smiled. Holding their daughter out for him to hold.

Taking her, Walter smiled down on her. He had never felt this kind of love before in his life. He knew, in that moment, there was nothing in the world he wouldn't do for his family. Nothing.

***

Summer 1984 Washington, DC:

Assistant Director Richard Hunter was sitting in his office. Agent Hel was sitting across from him. Her most recent assignment had her locked up from his control most of the time, which had driven him nuts. He had put in a lot of effort into her. Her training had gone above and beyond any other agent he had ever had. He noticed that the more he pushed her, the more loyal to him she had become. Before this last assignment that took her out of the active field work, she would have killed the president without question, if he had simply commanded it. Now, she was married, a mom, and was asking to be taken out of the field.

"And do you feel that that is what is best for the country?" Hunter asked. Saying that he was frustrated would be an understatement.

"I think it is what is best for my family. I am willing to go on short assignments. Nothing more than two nights. And nothing that is too dangerous. I won't be going on the missions I had been on before," Lucille stated. There was a strong finality to her voice.

Hunter stood, the sign for her to be dismissed. He shook her hand, as he vowed to himself that this would never happen again.

Pressing a button under his desk, the bookshelf in the corner of his office opened up. In walked The Westgate. A scientist he had met on one of his early missions. Someone he had saved that was supposed to be dead.

"Follow her. Be a ghost. Whatever Walter is working on, make sure I know everything about it. Everything," Hunter said. The Westgate turned and left through the same door he had entered.

***

Fall 1984 Atlanta, GA:

Walter and Harold had just finished the coding and the math for the NOVA system's initial trial test. The government had been pressing them. They wanted the system to work, and work now. They weren't ok with failure after a decade of work.

"Walter, no. You have a family. If anything were to go wrong, then I would never be able to look in the mirror again. I will be the test subject. I already went in and set the parameters to my brain frequencies. It is set for me. I have nothing to lose," Harold pleaded with him.

"You keep saying that, but do you not think about the people you would leave behind? Me for instance?" Walter asked.

"And are you taking your own advice? Who would you be leaving behind? I couldn't allow you to do that. Ever," Harold stated. His mind was set.

"Ok. But we have to make sure that anything that can cause an issue with this is addressed. I refuse to take any unnecessary risk," Walter said, as they went over everything again. It was three in the morning. The test was set to begin at nine in the morning for the general and the director of the CIA.

As they finished up, they checked everything again, and had left by four in the morning. They were confident in their work. They knew it would work.

Watching them leave, The Westgate picked the lock on the door, and made his way to the lab. He looked over the script. It was well over his head. But he saw one thing. The recall. He understood that. He took the picture he had of Hunter. He scanned it into the system and uploaded it into the coding. He set it in the recall and deleted the rest. He hoped that that would work. But he couldn't be sure.

***

Eight the following morning Harold and Walter walked into the lab. Walter wanted Harold to get a good night's rest before the test.

The general walked in with everyone else following. They were all early. Walter was flustered and hurried. Harold was rushing around. Zodiac sat off to the side, like he had for the duration of the project. Taking notes.

As they were in the heart of the Russian Mob territory, they figured someone who was a Russian arms dealer would be the most needed in the immediate future. Plus, with the Cold War in effect, it made the most sense. So, they set up the information for the upload through the NOVA system, and got Harold hooked up and ready for the upload.

"Gentlemen, and Lady," Walter said, nodding to one-star General Cathrine Richmond, who had been the general's assistant for the duration of the project and had become a close friend to the Woodfords through her respect for Lucille. "I am excited to demonstrate the capabilities of the NOVA system. My coworker Harold has graciously agreed to be the test subject for this initial trial. He is going to be given the NOVA system. He will be allowed to go in the field if he passes the test. The Russian Mob will be contacted by the most recent Russian arms dealer, Ivan Orlav. He is the head of Orlav industries. There will be a small amount needed for the backing to make him appear as convincing as possible. Now if you are ready. Let's start."

/: Chapter 2

Finish the Job >

Lucille paused to take a drink. The team was getting a debrief from her on her long-term deep cover mission. She tried to skip over the start of it all, but Megan caught on that there was something not being said. Lucille was starting to hate the fact that her daughter was able to read people so well. Even better than she had ever been able to. It was like both children had taken the qualities that had made their parents special and put a magnifying glass over them.

"Once the undercover profile had been uploaded, there was an immediate change in how Harold carried himself. His face became far more serious, his posture improved immensely, and he had a clear sense of self-confidence. Borderline self-importance. Once Walter let him loose, they went through the questions they had prepared beforehand, and I had never seen Harold like this. This wasn't Harold at all. They had done it!

"So, Harold was sent on the mission. All he understood at the moment was he was to take over the local branch of the Russian Mob's arms dealing and make it appear as though he was interested in incorporating it into his own, already established business.

"After several months, he had been checking in with Hunter, and the reports were that the mission was a complete success. But then the first issue happened when Harold was called to come in for a debrief by the general. He refused. Harold outright refused the general, even when the recall command was said. It was supposed to repress the NOVA system in the mind to the changes and bring back Harold. But it had seemed that Ivan had taken over.

"When someone was sent to recall him physically, they never came back. By this point you were born Gavin, and I was more and more at home with you both," Lucille nodded at Gavin and Megan, "But your dad was getting obsessed with trying to fix his NOVA system, which had been almost put on ice. He wanted his friend back. He loved us, but the guilt of what he felt he was responsible for was consuming him. Finally, around the time you turned eight Gavin, I started my mission to infiltrate Orlav Ind.

"It was partly out of wanting to help our friend come back, but it was more so out of wanting to ease the guilt in the love of my life. The one who showed me that there was more to life than the next mission." As she said that, Alex squeezed Gavin's hand. She knew all too well what that was like.

Lucille continued, "So I went undercover into Ivan's organization and quickly rose through his ranks. It was easy, but the closer I got to him, the harder it became to leave. Once I became his right hand, he was keeping tabs on me all the time. And the only time I did come home, he had me followed and was going to have Walter killed. Which is why he had to leave. He couldn't come home to see you kids anymore, because they were watching for him any time he came to Atlanta and would follow him to you. We couldn't risk that. So, we left.

"There were supposed to be people who were meant to look after you, Hunter was one. He failed at that, obviously. But your godmother Cathrine, she did all she could without causing interest to be brought to you guys. Your scholarship, while earned, was also paid for by her. Not the NSA. Her.

"There was never going to be anything to tie you to any of them, but when the kill order came through for you Gavin, she had to follow procedure. When you called her later, she was packing to come get you herself. She was grateful that you had done your research and weren't just trying to go along to get along. We are all proud of you for not letting things get out of hand when they very easily could have.

"Ivan continued to get deeper and deeper into his darkness. He was smooth and could easily play a nice guy. But it was always an act. He fed off of others' pain. It wasn't until Hunter's fall that I was able to learn that the entire thing had been set up by Hunter himself. He had altered the coding with the help of The Westgate, which messed up the original design of the NOVA system Harold and your father created. Making him solely loyal to Hunter alone. And driving our family apart," Lucille finished, sounding defeated. She knew they had 'won' but at what cost?

Gavin sat there, still trying to process everything. He knew most of it but didn't have some of the connecting factors.

"So, why didn't the Canadian government come after him? Looking for him?" Gavin asked, slightly confused.

"It was a timing thing. I think that it was planned by Hunter now that I know more of what else was going on behind the scenes. But in 1984 there was a conversion in the Canadian government. The RCMP became the CSIS of today. Since Harold had no family left, and the transition was happening, I imagine that Hunter used this time to scrub any data of Harold from the RCMP files, and not allow any to be transferred to CSIS. Which effectively made sure that Harold no longer existed. Only Ivan remained. Of course, that meant that the United States government changed everything about what they had to hide the failed experiment. The listed it as a successful test, but then listed it as happening when they had written him off as a traitor and unable to bring back in, in 1990. I was sent then to bring him in for deprogramming, they didn't want to lose their six-billion-dollar experiment. And the longer I was in his service, the more I found that Harold was gone. Forever." Lucille explained.

Gavin looked at his mom and thought. *I have held a grudge against her all these years without ever considering what she had been going through. What could have caused this entire mess in our family. We hadn't always been perfect, but there was never a doubt that they loved us. That is, until they left. And this was why. The NOVA system is why. It was dad's greatest creation outside of me and my sister, but also his greatest failure. And that was why he was so intrigued by my response to it. He wondered if I was ok, then would it be possible for his friend to be ok.* Gavin felt a tear starting to form at the corner of his eye.

Megan spoke first. "Mom, I am so sorry. I hate that you had to go through all of that. You and dad. I am sorry for how Gavin and I reacted to everything."

She was cut off by her mom. "No, you kids have nothing to feel sorry for. You are the ultimate victims. We were so blinded by our failure in protecting our friend that we missed the fact that we were failing at protecting our children. You should have always been our first priority. And the fact that we lost sight of that is unforgivable. I know your dad would feel the same way." Lucille was not normally one to cry, but the tears were flowing at the moment for her.

Megan was crying too. "You did what you had to do to protect us. As much as it hurt all of us. It ended up being for our own good. I just wish dad could have been here to see it all work out," she said through her tears.

Gavin was still sitting there quietly. It was starting to bother Alex. *I've never known him to really be the strong silent type before. He was similar to his sister in that he had to talk through his feelings before he could ever be ok.* She thought.

Gavin was staring at them. "It hasn't," he said in a very solemn tone.

They all turned to him. The emotion in the air felt confused. There was reconciliation between the mother and daughter, but there was something else as well. They waited for Gavin to say more, but he didn't seem ready to.

"What are you meaning?" Alex asked with some hesitation in her voice. Trying to coax out of him what he was hesitant to say.

Gavin shook his head as though he was clearing out his thoughts.

"It hasn't all worked out. Harold is still Ivan, and dad is gone. I don't think that I could really call that a success or even close to working out," Gavin said, the emotion back in his words. He was hurting. He seemed to understand the relationship between Harold and his father. *I can't imagine losing Kaleb like that. He is so loyal, he would trust me implicitly to be able to fix anything that may happen. Just like Harold did. According to what Mom said and what I read in the files I have found, He won't be able to remember all of the terrible things that he had to do while he was under the NOVA system at all, but that doesn't make it any easier for him once he comes to and realizes he missed all those years. Then begins the process to learn about what he had done.*

Alex looked at him. She saw her Gavin. The one who considered everyone else's feelings before his own. The one who would walk into a burning building for a stranger, let alone for someone his family cared about. She knew where this would be going.

Lucille had a seriousness come over her. She saw where this was leading as well, and she measured her words carefully.

"Gavin, your father and I tried. We tried for over a decade to bring him back. I don't know if it is possible. I really don't think it is. I am sorry," she said with a very somber look in her eye. There was a strong mixture of hurt, sadness, and defeat. The last one was not a feeling that she had felt many times before this had started. And it wasn't a feeling she liked.

"I know, I know. But listen to me. I am not even saying that we have to bring him back. But I do understand how hard it would be to have a loyal friend and then to just lose them. I am lucky to have not lost Kaleb, but even the idea of it sends a chill down my spine. I knew dad had always had this deep hurt in his eyes. Now I understand why. And I can't just leave it be. Dad would never give up until his friend was home. He lost a part of who he is. Just like losing any one of us. Kaleb is family. Regardless of how any of us feel about him," Gavin said with a look at Megan that caused her at smile slightly, despite the emotion in the room. Gavin continued with determination. "I am going to talk to General Richmond in the morning. If nothing else, it wouldn't be a bad thing to tear apart his organization. Have a few less bad guys in the world, right? Because I don't feel right just doing nothing. Acting like this is resolved and we can just go about our lives," Gavin finished. He had tried to mix in some humor, just like he always had, to try to cut through some of the tension that had built in the room.

Lucille sighed. She saw so much of his father in him. The sheer determination and will that should never be underestimated, yet there was a kindness to them that simply made everyone do just that. They were always underestimated. The only ones that didn't, were the ones that didn't need to. They were the people that knew that they could always count on them to be there and to do whatever might be needed to make sure they were safe. Neither of them would ever give up on someone they cared about. No matter how small of a chance there was that the loved one was still there.

"Ok son. If you talk to Cathrine and she gives the ok on it, I won't stop you. I will help where and when I can. But the people here in this room will always be my priority. Always. I am never letting my mission come before my family again. Especially now that I have a grandchild on the way," Lucille said, placing a hand on Megan's tummy with a smile.

Megan put her hand on her mom's. She was just thankful for the moment here that she had. She knew that their lives had never been normal, but moments like this. Where the normality came through. A simple moment between her and her mom, both excited for the future baby, these are what made everything else worth it. All the sacrifices that they had made. The only thing missing was her father, and he would remain missing from now on.

"I am getting a bit tired," Megan said, "I think I am going to head home and call it a night. I could use some rest." She got up and went to leave.

"Yeah of course. Thank you for coming over," Alex said, as she helped Megan up off the couch. She went over and grabbed her shoes and brought them over to her.

"Thank you, Alex. You are so sweet. You have been so helpful. I can't imagine having had to go through this without you," Megan said, as she started to tear up again. She knew it was just the hormones getting the best of her, but she still couldn't help herself. Alex really had been super helpful and sweet during her pregnancy.

"It really is no problem. I am more than happy to help," Alex said in a flippant manner. She was excited to be a part of this family. Officially or not. It was something that she had dreamed about when she was a girl but had given up on getting a long time ago. A family, no matter how it was made up, that cared about her. That she could be a part of and feel welcomed.

She hadn't even started planning their wedding. She really did love the family. She loves Gavin more than anything. She just couldn't quite make herself get excited like she knew that she should be. *I mean, what girl hasn't dreamed of her wedding right? What girl hasn't had every minute of it planned since they were ten? Yet here I am. Engaged to be married to the man I love more than anything in the world. And I know he loves me too. So, why am I not so excited for that day that I am shaking with anticipation?*

She knew the answer of course. She just couldn't bring herself to admit it. Even to herself. While they had been working with her day and night for months now, and her feelings for Gavin had never really left. Even in the middle of having the memories ripped from her, in the middle of having to break through all of her brainwashing, she knew she loved him. It tore her apart that she was so scared of that love, until she accepted it. Every time.

As she helped Megan out the door, the sense of loss came over her again. The thought that she had had everything that she had ever wanted, and yet she couldn't appreciate it like they all deserved, made her feel as though she was being a brat.

Gavin noticed that Alex had a sudden change in her demeanor and was attempting to hide it. But he could tell. He could always tell with her. He made a mental note to address it after everyone had left.

***

Undisclosed Location, the Alps

Ivan stood in front of the entire Collective board. The voting had just finished. If he had played everything right, then he would be able to have the entire Collective to use at his command as soon as it was announced. He had plans for what he would be able to do. He wasn't so blinded by power to think he would be able to take over and control the entire world. He would have the Collective for that. Allow them to have what they believe to be power. The true power is to not have anyone to answer to. And he was well on his way to having that dream.

The third-party moderator stood and said, "If everyone would listen, please. I only want to say this once. As it stands, the board has voted that Ivan Orlav becomes the new president, fifteen to fourteen. As per tradition, there is a stipulation to this designation. You must prove yourself worthy of the title if the vote is within three. As the difference is a single vote, you must complete said task.

"What was agreed upon was that you will be designated to cleaning up the mess that was left behind by your predecessor, the late Director of the CIA Richard Ethan Hunter. That means, you must work to stabilize the United States before you take it down to a third world nation. It has to seem natural. People are dumb in mass, but they aren't THAT dumb. This means the rise of China as the world power, and the fall of the United States. Use any means necessary. The final thing is to get control of the NOVA system and get rid of any of the prior versions. The NOVA system, if used correctly, would allow us to have everything we would need to continue our work.

"We are allowing the use of The Westgate to you. Also, we do not currently have a timeline needed for this all to take place, but there are obvious milestones that we expect to be done sooner than others. I would not suggest you dawdle with these. Now, this meeting is adjourned." The moderator finished and walked out.

As he did, the entire rest of the Collective stood and left as well. Leaving Ivan in the room alone with The Westgate. Ivan was not pleased with the outcome. He had expected to walk out of this room with the world in his hand, and now he was just relegated to brand boy for the Collective once more. He was seething, but he knew better than to let it out just yet. He had to remain controlled.

"You can see yourself out. I am going to stay and think. This wasn't quite the victory I had expected, and that just will not do. I have some planning to do before we continue on with our work," Ivan told The Westgate, who stood and left silently.

Ivan then threw his glass of scotch across the room. It hit the wall and shattered. He had expected at least three others to have given their vote to him, and he would find out who hadn't and take care of them. He did not deal with dissension among his ranks. Even if they were people who owed him favors. That was his ultimate payment. He would only help out those who could help him in the future. And these people had let him down. Now they were about to find out why you didn't do that.

He had had the NOVA system in his possession prior. Gavin, Hel's son. He should have made sure that he hadn't ever been able to leave, but that failure had been dealt with. Hunter had seen to that, even before he had been able to take care of it. And being out from under Hunter's thumb was a joyous enough experience, even if it didn't result in the power he had hoped for. Yet.

"Now, I will have to have my people start monitoring the Woodfords much closer than they have been. I am not about to let the opportunity to take care of them much sooner slip through my fingers again," Ivan mumbled as he poured himself another glass of scotch, and then walked out. He had work to do.

/: Chapter 3

The Depths of Hel >

Lucille sat in General Richmond's office, sipping on a glass of wine.

"I know that you have been putting this off for a while now, Lucille, but it is something that we have to do," Richmond said, the empathy in her tone through Agent Hel off, but put Lucille at ease a bit.

"Yeah, it isn't exactly something I want to relive if I can help it. But I appreciate you being the one to debrief me," Lucille said with a slight sigh. She and Cathrine had known each other for a long time, she would call her her friend, but it wasn't ever the type of relationship that was built off of kindness and caring. It was more a mutual respect for each other's ability to thrive in a world that is highly masculine. Something that they had had a hand in changing.

"Given the state of certain things, I wasn't sure who I could trust with the information that I am sure you are about to unload. I intend to keep this as: FOR MY EARS ONLY. At least for the time being until we can know exactly what we are dealing with," Cathrine said, as she took a sip from her wine. "So why don't you start at the beginning."

Lucille took a gulp of her wine and sighed heavily. "Ok," she breathed as she started in.

***

Atlanta, GA 1990:

Agent Hel was not happy. She had just gotten off the phone with Assistant Director Hunter and she was getting sent deep undercover. Her job was going to be to make sure to give legitimacy to Harold as an arms dealer, and to make sure to keep him in check. Apparently, Hunter had thought Harold would be asking to be out by now, but he wasn't. And any time Hunter felt he didn't have control, he was on edge.

"Do you have to go?" Walter asked with a sadness in his voice that tore at her heart.

"Yes. Unfortunately, I do. I can tell you this time, it is to protect and help Harold. I guess Hunter is worried that he might be in too deep or something," Lucille said, her hand cradling Walters cheek. She hated leaving. She had her life here, and she had just decided that she was going to stop doing field work until the kids were older, but she felt that this was too urgent to leave to someone else.

"But you had just told me no more. I get that it is Harold, but a deep cover mission can take months, or years," Walter pleaded. He felt worried about this one. He hadn't heard from Harold in a while, but last he had, Harold seemed like he was struggling with keeping a grip on reality.

"Hunter assured me that it wouldn't be more than a year. And we both know that Harold needs someone, one way or another," Lucille told Walter, as she packed her bag. Her heart told her that she shouldn't go, but her mind was set.

"I just have a bad feeling about this. That's all. And the kids will miss you." Walter stood and took her hands, interrupting her packing. "I will miss you," he kissed her and pulled her into a hug.

Lucille had a sharp pain cut through her head. She shook her head as she squeezed Walter tighter. It was something that had been happening more and more recently. She didn't know exactly what was happening,

30

but she knew that every time her head hurt like this before she left for a mission. She guessed that it was just the stress of having to leave the people she loved now.

"I do have to go, though. You know I can take care of myself, and I promise you I will be coming home to you and the kids. I promise," she said to him, as she kissed him again. "Now I have to go say bye to the kids. I don't want to prolong it until I don't get to spend the time needed with each kid." She gave him another kiss, and then left the room.

After talking to each kid and trying to give Megan some encouragement as to what she needed to do for her, fully expecting her to just be her normal self, she left. Getting into her car, she sped towards the airport, where she boarded a private jet and was off to Virginia to receive her assignment.

***

She was sitting in Hunter's office, waiting for him to come in and give her her official mission briefing, when she started to look around the office. It wasn't something she had really done before. Normally when she was in there, it was a quick in and out. Get the briefing and leave to complete the mission. Until she was assigned to the NOVA system protective detail, she hadn't stayed in one place long.

***

She was an orphan growing up and had had no one to rely on. No close friends, and no family to speak of. She was always alone. The all-girls orphanage she was a part of was in the middle of nowhere, and they didn't always have enough for the kids and staff. So, she was allowed to go hunting to get meat for them. But that also added to her being outcast by the other girls.

When the CIA came looking for kids that they could train and use, she was sixteen. At the time, they didn't care. They took two years to train her up. Hunter had been her direct trainer, and then her handler. She had been sent to the Farm long after she had actually been trained. She set every record that was there, of course, to be logged under her call sign, Agent Hel. She personified it. Hel was a loner through her official training. There were guys that wanted to be close to her, but only physically. They didn't care about her as a person. Neither did her trainers. Even Hunter didn't really care about her physical welfare. She was a tool to be used, and she was his best tool.

Once she started her field work, she took pride in it, and it showed. She was the best. She specialized in wet work. After her Red Test, she fell apart. She was thankful that they gave her some time to process. She spent a lot of time alone in her empty bedroom. Nothing but her bed and white walls. After a few days, she was called in for some training. She didn't remember what happened during that training, but it allowed her to be able to function. From that point on, she became the top assassin, but it wasn't just about the body count. She was able to get every bit of information that they had and often even a bit more than the person had, before she did away with them.

She took her hunting skills to the next level. Stalking her marks, noting every action that they took, at times taking months to make contact with the mark. There were several times that she didn't even need to make contact.

Several years later, she had been on too many missions to count. She had taken so many lives that she was numb to it. That is, until she had a mission to take out an oil tycoon in the middle east. She did everything perfectly, right until she slit the man's throat. She didn't notice the man's young son standing in the doorway.

By the time she noticed, it was too late. He had a chance to get away. He notified the entire house, and she was never supposed to be there. So, she had to eliminate everyone in the house.

That mission broke her.

She left the house, and immediately went to the target's airfield and stole a plane. Staying low to avoid radar, she made her way out of the country.

32

She abandoned the plane in the air. Landing in the ocean, her parachute covered her, where she washed the blood off her hands and face as she treads water before cutting her pack off her, diving down, and swimming away. It wasn't until the moment that she reached land that she realized just what happened exactly. Up until that point, she was completely stuck in mission mode, her mind focused on the goal of taking out the target and no one living to know who was there. But now that she had a moment to breathe, she realized what she had just done.

She collapsed in the little grove she had made it to. Her entire body aching. Sobbing, she crawled out back into the tide. Letting it wash over her. Hoping it would carry her away, back out to sea, where she would die and never have to deal with the nightmares that she knew were coming. Rid the world of the hell that Agent Hel brought into it.

She didn't remember getting home. The next thing she remembered was waking up in bed, staring at the ceiling fan as it slowly revolved around. She had flashbacks still from that night, as she laid there, but she couldn't bring herself to care. Something was blocking her from having any emotion towards it.

She eventually got up and got dressed. Making her way to Hunter's office, she sat and waited to get her next mission. As she listened to the details, she couldn't bring herself to care. The pride she once had for her job was no longer there. She glazed over, listening to the protective detail that she was being sent to. It sounded like a demotion, but it felt right to her, and she didn't care. She needed a break.

***

Looking around the room, she took note that everyone that was in the room, was everyone that had been there when Harold had received the first NOVA System. That didn't sit well with her.

"Hello Agent Hel. I know that we are taking you away from your family for this mission, but given the sensitive nature of this mission, I am sure you can understand why you are the one that we chose to send. Harold has not replied to his last check in call. He has been radio silent for over three months, and he is supposed to check in monthly. This was his last check in," The general who had been over the scientists stated.

"Harold, the sun sets on the green hills," she heard the general state the recall command.

"Who is this? I don't have time for riddles, and if you even knew who you were talking to, you wouldn't waste my time with your trivialness," Harold replied.

"Harold, it is time to come in. We need to pull you out," the general stated, a hint of hesitation in his tone.

There was a deep breath. She barely thought she could hear him whisper "Help" right before she heard another breathe. And then in a dark tone she heard,

"This is Ivan, Harold is no longer available. If you call back here. General, I will make sure you regret it. How are your kids by the way?" Ivan stated with an evil chuckle.

The recording ended.

"As you can hear, there is a lot going on with this. If you can't bring him in, we will need you to take him out. He can't be allowed to continue. We don't know how volatile he is, and we need someone who is capable of doing what is needed," The general finished and sat back down.

Hunter looked at her intensely. She wasn't sure what to read off him. He was stoic, but also intense. It was unsettling to her. She had never been all too impressed with him. He wasn't a particularly good leader, he hadn't been a great agent, he wasn't even a good politician. She looked up his record, and he had failed more missions than she would have ever been able to get away with. She had written it off as him being a man, and her not. But now looking back, there wasn't a lot that made sense with it. And now he looked determined.

34

She nodded, and the rest of the briefing went quickly. And soon she was getting the rest of her gear ready in her apartment that she kept in Virginia. As she got it all together, Hunter stopped by and talked to her. She didn't remember what was said now, but she remembered leaving for the mission, her mind set on completion. Nothing else mattered as much as completing the mission. But it wasn't to kill Ivan, it was to get Harold back.

***

Infiltrating Orlav industries was easy for her, but she was struggling to get time with Harold. She refused to refer to him as Ivan, at least until she had to. He was her husband's best friend, Harold. He wasn't a Russian Mob Boss, and arms dealer. He was a scientist and a computer engineer and a programmer. He was shy and kind to a fault and loyal. And he was someone worth going after.

After the first months, she was getting frustrated. She had made some very small progress in getting up the ladder of the hierarchy. So, she took some initiative. She started to take out some of her competition. Killing a few, but mostly setting them up to be caught. Getting arrested and taken to jail. Sometimes she even set up the crime itself. She made sure that she did it in countries that had heavy penalties to their crimes. Rendering them useless to the organization.

During this time, she quickly made her way up the ranks, gaining the attention of Harold. He must have recognized her on some level, because once she was in his presence, he quickly started to trust her. But this was almost at the year mark. She was getting antsy to get back to her family.

As the year mark came and went, she realized that she wasn't going to be going home any time soon. She had been getting missions sending her out and growing his business. She had become his most trusted lieutenant. She had just gotten back from one of these missions, and when she reached into her pocket, she pulled out a small device.

Looking around, she didn't see anyone, and she plugged it into the computer in her office. It immediately popped up a loading window. After a quick load, a screen popped up with the Coeus symbol, and that made her smile for what felt like the first time in a year. Those symbols flattened into a line, and she heard his voice for the first time in over a year.

"Hey, beautiful. I miss you so much!" Coeus said.

"I have missed you too," Hel said, her voice thick with emotion.

"Do you think you will be coming home soon?" Coeus asked, hope in his voice.

"I really don't know. I am starting to feel like I have to end it the way we don't want to. I don't see Harold. Ever. And I spend the most time with him out of anyone outside his security detail. I don't think Harold is there anymore. I think all that is left is Ivan," Hel said, with a sad tone. She hated the feeling of failure that she was having with this mission.

"No, that is why I am able to message you. I talked to Harold. He messaged me. I am not sure how. We set up a server for us to keep in contact outside of the normal means before he left. And he left me a message on there. I had kept it up to date, and continually sent him messages, but hadn't gotten any response until I think when you must have made contact with him. About five months ago, he messaged me. We have been in very slow and sporadic contact since. The last couple months it has increased in regularity. He let me know where your last mission was going to be, and when. That is how I was able to sneak this device into your pocket," Coeus informed her.

This shocked Hel. She had had no indication of Harold being in there still. She felt it was a lost cause, but if Walter said that he was there, then he was there. That meant she couldn't give up.

"You are sure it's him? I am telling you, all I have ever seen since I have started was Ivan. The ruthless businessman, and killer," Hel said softly.

She felt bad for questioning him, but even with all the trust she had in him, it felt like it was impossible.

"Yes, I know. But I am telling you, the only person who would be able to get into this server is Harold. Ivan wouldn't know it. Even if he had every bit of memory that Harold has, Ivan wouldn't be able to. I programmed a block for it in the NOVA system. He can't know it," Coeus said. He was sure. It was clear in his voice. He had no question that it was Harold. "Plus, the way he talks it is very apparent," he said with a slight laugh.

"What do you mean?" Hel asked.

"He apologized between every statement and made a comment about how my security programming was weak on the server," Coeus said, bringing a laugh out of Hel as well.

"I hate it, but I have to go," Hel said.

Coeus sighed. "I know. I knew we would only ever get a moment here or there until I can figure something else out."

"I love this, but I will have to destroy this device once we stop talking, and I am not sure it is a good idea for you to contact me again," Hel said dejectedly.

"Good idea or not, I am talking to my wife whatever chance I can get. I will get something more convenient made for us to talk. And I will get it to you soon," Coeus said with a determined voice. He wasn't going to be dissuaded from doing this. She knew what he was like when he got his mind set on something.

"Last thing, I am working on a small and portable removal device. One you can use on him without him having to be brought in. I will keep you up to date on that," Coeus said.

"I love you," Hel said, and then ended the call immediately as she heard someone coming. She pulled the device out of her computer and snapped it in half. Then she put it in her metal trashcan and set it out her window on the ledge. Pouring some vodka on it, she lit a match and dropped it in. As the flames engulfed the device, she went out into the hallway to intercept whoever was coming to get her. She had set up several alarms at different durations coming to her office. She didn't want to have any surprises.

***

After several months, she hadn't seen any indication of Harold still, but she had gotten another device from Coeus. This one looked like one of her many bracelets she wore. It was part of their cover for this mission. And so, it was easy to hide. But if she took it off, all she had to do was flatten it out and then fold it in half and she could put it into any computer and instantly she could talk to Coeus.

This made things both easier, and more difficult. She missed him so badly it hurt most of the time. And the fact that she couldn't keep in contact with the kids hurt even more. She missed them. She hadn't seen them in almost two years, and she wasn't sure if she would even be able to recognize them at this point.

But she had to stay focused. She couldn't allow herself to get emotional now and slip up and make a mistake. The way Harold had been acting, she wasn't sure if he would be able to stop Ivan from hurting her. Or possibly even killing her.

She had seen him order the execution of a family recently for the fact that they had a house in a place he was wanting to build. She still hadn't seen any sign of Harold, but from the minimal contact she had had from Coeus, Harold was still in there. And he was active. Coeus had told her that Harold had been working on something. He never said what it was, but he was adamant that it would help them immensely.

***

Hel was sent on an assignment. She knew what this kind of assignment was. It was a loyalty test. She had sensed a change in Harold. He was involving her less and less. She was being sent on a 'prove it' mission. Prove your worth, or don't come back alive.

Their biggest rival was the Mexican Cartel. She knew going down there, she would be alone. No back up, and no possible extraction. It really was a suicide mission, but she was trained for these. Even if Harold didn't know it. She still always had her go-bag ready, and the best part of working for an arms dealer was that there was never a shortage of equipment to use on a mission like this.

She called in a couple favors with people from the CIA and got ready to make her trip down there. The issue was, once she was in, the CIA and the rest of the United States Government wouldn't be able to help her either. But as she boarded the plane to head to Mexico, she felt confident.

***

She had made fairly short work of the outpost that she had been told was her target. The issue was the primary target wasn't there. She had stayed for a few days before learning that, and then set up charges to blow, making it look like an accident while cooking some of their product. It would be written off as the cost of doing that business, and she wouldn't be on anyone's radar, as far as she could tell.

But the information that she had learned while camping out at that outpost proved to be invaluable. She learned that the True headquarters was in Germany. That was where the money was, and that was where the head of the Cartel, Carlos Cortez, was. So, that was where she was headed next. Even with the job "done" according to what she was told to do, she knew that the only way to get on Ivan's good side somewhat permanently was to go above and beyond on this mission. She was thankful that she was killing a bad guy, and not a diplomat or something.

***

In Germany, she quickly set up a base of operations for herself and started scouting the city and area for the headquarters. It wasn't like you could just look them up in the Yellow Pages or look for their big glowing neon sign out front.

She was on her second week there, when she sat at a dinner and watched her lead leave a hotel and get into a car. She quickly followed after them on her Vespa. It didn't take long before she was outside a nice restaurant that required a reservation to get in. She was stuck. Walking back across the street, she sat on her Vespa, and tried to look nonchalant.

She felt a hand come to rest on her shoulder and was about to attack when a familiar voice spoke to her.

"Hello, Hel. I believe that we may be able to help one another here," Catherine Richmond said as Hel turned towards her.

/: Chapter 4

Research >

<u>Atlanta GA present day:</u>

Gavin sat at his computer. He was working on some research on Orlav Industries and Ivan himself. There was next to nothing on the main web, so he had to dive into the dark web. Of course, there was plenty there. Anything from offers to kill people, to invoice estimates for what their arms sales would be. It made Gavin's stomach turn. He had to come up with some information to be able to present to General Richmond in the morning. He knew that his mom could basically answer anything he would need, but he felt that Richmond would be more responsive if it was him that put in his own work and effort to this mission.

As he was working on this, he heard Alex walk into his lab.

She often liked to come in there and watch him work. To her it was beautiful. He was elegant with the keyboard. His hands and fingers moved with such precision and peace, that it soothed her. It was something that she had never even considered to be possible.

"Alex, what is wrong?" Gavin asked without looking up from the monitor.

She smiled to herself. She was the spy, but he had always been so in-tune with her that he knew when she wasn't ok, almost before she did.

"I am ok, Gavin. I just worry that there is something wrong with me," Alex said softly. Even with everything, she trusted that Gavin wouldn't judge her.

"What do you mean? I have seen a LOT of you, and I have yet to find anything wrong," Gavin teased with an eyebrow wag, causing Alex to laugh. To Gavin, her laugh was the most beautiful song. Even if there was a snort or two in it. Those just made it hers, and real.

"No, you dork. I don't mean physically," Alex said with a slight chuckle still, but it cleared very quickly. She got quiet as she continued, "I don't understand why I can't seem to get excited about planning a wedding. Why can't I picture it? Why I had never taken the time to ever even plan it in my head. It feels like I just have an entire gap in who I am as a person in my development that everyone else on Earth, especially every woman, has had," she finished with a sigh.

Gavin turned to face her when she started talking. He hurt in his heart hearing her talk about it. Not for himself, but for her. He always wanted to take her hurt away. From her childhood. From the manipulation she had to endure. The abuse she had been through. He hated all of it, and always wanted to take that pain away from her.

"Alex, there is a reason I haven't talked about it much with you. I know you love me. That isn't in question. I understand that this may bring up a lot of feelings in you. Feelings that you likely have never had to deal with, or ignored for as long as possible that your body is confused. Your mind is confused. It may take time to adjust to an even slightly normal life. I mean, when in your life did you really have time to allow your mind to wander? Maybe before you left with your dad? But even then, from what you have said, your parents were fighting all the time. That doesn't exactly make a cohesive space for a child's mind to develop the way it should. At least I don't think it does. I'm not exactly a developmental psychologist," Gavin softly stated, as he took Alex's hands in his own. His thumbs caressing the backs of her hands.

42

Alex's gaze lifted from their joined hands into Gavin's green eyes. *How can he do that? Just make everything that I have been so stressed about for so long feel like it is such an insignificant issue. It is both frustrating and amazing at the same time. This is an issue, even if he doesn't want to act like it is,* Alex thought to herself. She couldn't help but slightly berate herself for having anything but pure and uninhibited joy for being loved and accepted by this amazing family.

"So, what were you working on?" she asked, trying to change the subject.

"I am trying to do some of my own research on Orlav Ind., so that I can present everything to General Richmond for why we should go after him. I think I have enough, but I always like to do extra research. I have found some stuff, but I am still having issues getting through their security. It will take time," Gavin replied to her, already back to typing away on his laptop. He didn't notice how Alex's face had fallen back to solemnness.

"I think I am going to turn in for the night since it sounds like it will be a while for you still," Alex said as she started to make her way out of the room.

"Ok, I will try to be quiet when I get into bed," Gavin said softly, like he was more focused on his work. Alex didn't take offense to that. She had grown accustomed to his ability to lose himself in his hacking.

She meandered out the door and down the hall. Her mind had started to wander again. She thought about everything that she and Gavin had discussed in the last few months. She knew he had no reason to lie to her. In fact, he had had multiple sources backing up everything he had claimed. She was no longer with the CIA. That had thrown her for a bit of a loop. The CIA had been her life before meeting him. It wasn't like she got a demotion or anything. In fact, it had been a significant promotion. Now with the DOC officially. It was like the top of the top. And she wasn't really sure how to feel about it.

Alex's mind also traveled back to her father. *Should I even bother looking into him? It wouldn't surprise me if Hunter had him killed a long time ago. And then what about Mom and the girl? I am not sure what she ended up naming her. No matter what, she would have had to rename her. I know the person who was after her is dead. But I don't know if that includes his boss. Who I think is, or was, Ivan Orlav. Which would make sense. All of this seems connected. Gavin had mentioned a few times a group called The Collective, but wasn't that just an umbrella for Hunter? Was that his working name?*

She huffed in frustration. She couldn't even tell if these were new frustrations or if it was all stuff she had already worked through before, and now was having to do it all again. Which made her even more frustrated. *Were these all things that Gavin and I had to work through before? I know he wouldn't be annoyed with me asking again, but at the same time, it would be embarrassing for me. I hate not having myself put together. I feel like there are major parts of me missing. It makes me feel more vulnerable than ever. I hate it.*

Alex had gotten changed and was lying in bed. She had lost track of how long it had been. She just kept thinking through everything. Her head hurt. Not the same as when she had to break her brainwashing. Not even close. This was just a normal headache. She knew she should likely try to get some sleep, it just wasn't easy to shut her brain off.

***

Gavin sat at his desk. He was diving into the NOVA system. He still wasn't entirely comfortable doing that in front of anyone, even Alex. It just seemed like it would be uncomfortable for her. He tried to look into Harold and found nothing. There was very little about Ivan Orlav even.

By design, by Hunter, I am sure. He had to make sure he was able to operate in the shadows as much as he could, Gavin thought.

He kept trying to find pathways that would lead to finding anything out. He couldn't even find his mother in it. Everything tying back to the original NOVA system failure wasn't in this version other than the code names of the original creators.

He knew that eventually he would have to ask his mom for information and help. He just really wanted to try to make as much of a case for it on his own as he could. He had found some hopeful leads, but he was worried that that wouldn't be enough. He was supposed to have a meeting with the general the following afternoon, but that didn't seem like it was going to be such a good idea anymore. He knew that there were other things that would need their attention, but he also felt that this was as important or more, even without the personal connection.

He had been able to let himself be Vidar so much recently, that he was getting to the point that the mentality was as easy to flip on and off as the NOVA system was. Using it repeatedly, helped him hone his skills more. He was no longer rusty. It was easy and fun again. He liked the different challenges. But the security on Orlav Ind network was like something he had never seen before outside of a Coeus-written script. And it made him wonder if there was still a bit of Harold in there. Something fighting to be freed. But he would never be able to know if they couldn't get close to him, and that possibility drove him to try harder than ever. It felt like the last opportunity to make his dad proud. Regardless of how proud of him he had been before he died.

He kept diving into the dark web. Some of what he saw just made him want to vomit. He would send out bugs, tracers, and worms all he could. It felt like a never-ending stream of the absolute bottom of human nature, and try as he might, there was no end to it all. He knew he couldn't save everyone, but that didn't mean that he couldn't try to help as many as possible.

Gavin had set an alarm to go off at five in the morning, since he knew his natural tendencies to get lost in the cyber world and stay there for hours. As the alarm started going off, he sighed. He had gotten caught up in trying to shut down, or at least slow down, so many illegal things on there. He rubbed his eyes and stretched. It felt like he hadn't moved in five hours. Getting up, he made his way to bed, seeing Alex laying there, he just stood and admired her for a minute, reflecting on how different his life had become.

Looking down at her, he thought, *I do understand where she is coming from with her nerves. She has never had a family. Not really anyways. Everything is new, different, vulnerable. It isn't something to be taken lightly. I know I am asking a lot of her. It hurts me that she is so hesitant, for sure, but I am also just glad to have her at all. With what happened, I could have lost her for good. And then what? Then where would my life be? I know everyone says that there are plenty of people out there, but there is only one of her. Of that, I am sure. Any other agent, and I wouldn't be here right now. I would have likely not found my parents. I wouldn't be doing something that I can take pride in. I would be lost, completely.*

Just then, as if on cue, his phone buzzed. It was a text from Kaleb.

"Hey man, I'm not sure if you are up or not, but I just felt like you were dealing with something. Our weird twin thing I guess," Kaleb texted, causing Gavin to smile slightly. "I know you have your overly attractive girlfriend to help you with anything now, but I wanted to let you know that if you ever need to talk, I am still here, buddy."

Gavin took a deep breath. He knew that Kaleb was there for him. No matter what. And that is why this mission meant so much to him. That is why it hurt so much hearing how his dad had lost his "Kaleb" in Harold. He understood the need to go to the ends of the earth to try to bring back his best friend.

He texted Kaleb back, "I was just about to call it a night, been doing research for a new mission. It is a bit close to home. I appreciate you more than you could ever know."

After a few seconds of seeing the floating dots, indicating that his friend was typing, a new message popped up from Kaleb. "Same. I don't have any idea where I would be without you. I will let you get to sleep. Game night, tonight."

Gavin sat on the couch in the living room letting the darkness of the room engulf him. He needed it. He knew he would have to talk to everyone before he met with the general. They were a team, so this wasn't just his mission. It was everyone's.

46

Alex walked out of the bedroom and made her way to the living room. She saw Gavin sitting there, his eyes unseeing. He was zoned out like he did often when prepping for missions. Especially when he thought that she couldn't see him. She thought that this was him taking a deep dive into the NOVA system, but they had left it unsaid.

Alex couldn't help but think back to the conversation she had with Megan the prior week. Megan has urged her to be more open with Gavin. Telling her that communication was the key to making any relationship work. She believed her, of course. It just made her nervous to be that open. Looking at Gavin, it made her heart hurt that she struggled to be open like he deserved. He always respected her space if she needed it. Even at times when she would have hoped he would fight more for her attention in the difficult times. He would allow her to think things through, and then come back to him.

Alex thought to herself. *How can I ever think I belong with these people? Even beyond Gavin, I would never have imagined Megan as my best friend, but she is so amazing. She doesn't just always take Gavin's side. I know she has my back, even against myself. Even Kaleb has his good qualities. He is beyond loyal to Gavin, to the point that it is a bit weird. Wait, is that why Gavin is so upset? When he heard about his dad and Harold, did he start correlating it to himself and Kaleb? I haven't ever had a friend like that, before Megan. I can understand his perspective if that is what is bothering him, but I will let him talk to me.*

Alex sighed, wishing she could ease his mind more. She walked into the room and sat next to him. Putting her arm around him, kissing his cheek.

"I'm sorry I woke you. I was trying to be quiet," Gavin said, wiping his hands down his face. Placing one hand on her thigh.

"I hadn't been able to sleep. I can tell things are bothering you. What can I do to help?" Alex asked softly.

"I'll be ok. I just need to find something to have a reason to do this mission. I feel I have to complete what my dad started. I can't just leave

47

Harold out there without at least trying to save him from Ivan. I know how weird this all is, but I mean, such is our life, right?" Gavin said with a slight laugh. He just didn't know how else to process all of this. Just a couple years ago he would have laughed at anyone claiming that his parents were spies. Shaking his head, he just couldn't believe what had become of his life.

Alex turned his face towards her and kissed him hard.

"Maybe I can find a way to give your mind some peace," Alex said, pushing him back on the couch.

***

General Richmond hung up the phone. She had just finished her debriefing with Hel. Catherine knew that Hel had told them all the true story of where the NOVA system started. And who came from it. She had known Harold long before he became Ivan and seeing what the man had become just hurt. He had been such a kind and gentle man.

But she saw the pictures of what happened to the man that they sent after him. She didn't know if that was done by Ivan himself, but he sure signed off on it. At the time she couldn't understand how Hunter had been able to keep him in line for so long, and then just to have him turn. It didn't make sense until you learned what Hunter had been planning for so long.

The Collective. She knew that that was going to be much more of an issue than they ever had been. She didn't really know much of what it was. She just knew that if Hunter had wanted control of it, then it was something that was dangerous. And she knew that she had to look into more before she assigned anything to her team. She hated that the supposed expert of the Collective turned out to be one of Hunter's minions. So, that means everything that they had on them, they had no idea what they could and couldn't trust.

And if any of it was to be trusted, then she wasn't sure who she could even talk to about it. They were supposedly in every branch, and on

48

every level. So, she had to watch her back in every move and hope for the best.

She knew that if she were to hope to make any dents in this, she would have to not be behind her desk all the time. Having her assistant book a flight to Germany, she went home to get her go bag. She would have to go back to her days as an agent herself. She had been the best, but that was long before Hel had even been in training.

As she got ready to get on the plane, she received a call from Gavin.

"Hello, Analyst Woodford?" she asked in a clipped tone, she didn't have time to chat.

"Sorry to bother you, general, but I was wanting approval on a mission that I think would be helpful. I would like to go after Harold, as a team," Gavin said, immediately regretting his wording.

There were so many better ways of saying that! Why did you have to lean on how personal this is for you? Calling him Harold, he thought to himself.

The general paused for a moment. She hadn't considered giving Gavin a mission that could potentially lead to answers for herself. It was perfect, because it made sense with what they had just gone through, and the fact that it was a personal mission for himself. It would suit her causes well, at least until she was able to bring the entire team into the fold.

"What are your reasons beyond the personal and obvious ones?" Richmond asked, trying not to let on that she was all for it before he even finished the question.

"I believe that the Russian arms dealer is a threat to the world as a whole, but especially to the United States. As he started here, I am sure he has many contacts here, and we aren't sure how deep they go. I feel it is in the best interest of the nation to allow me to work through his organization and take down little by little until I am able to get alone with him and see if I can-" Gavin was explaining but got cut short by Richmond.

"I agree. I think it would be good and in the best interest. Please keep me updated on the progress you make, and make sure to close any backdoors. I wouldn't want the Russians having uninhibited access to our networks from a mistake. Understand, Analyst Woodford?" the general asked, hoping that Gavin would pick up on the warning she was laying down fairly thick.

Gavin froze. At first, he was slightly offended that the general would ask such a thing of him.

When have I ever done something so careless? Gavin thought. But that is the point. She knows that. So why is she saying this? What is she playing at? She would have said if someone was there with her. She wouldn't discuss a mission at all if that were the case or use my name. So, she is worried about someone listening in. But it being someone who would be able to listen in anyways and know who I am already. She didn't want me talking about the NOVA system. I will discuss this with Alex, but she gave the greenlight. She wants me looking into it. That is enough for me at the moment.

Gavin took a breath as he thought all of that. "Yes, Ma'am. I will get right on it and have a report ready for you as soon as possible," Gavin said, trying his best to sound professional.

I should be past this by now, but there are just moments that being a spy is so cool. I mean, I am speaking in code to the director of the NSA. Who can really say that that is a part of their job? Gavin thought while smiling to himself.

"Sounds good. Speak soon," The general hung up the phone. She had heard the slight giddy tone that Gavin had had. She wasn't sure if it was because of the situation, her giving permission for the mission, or something that happened there, but it made her smile slightly. The fact that he could experience joy after all that he had been through brought a warmth to her heart and gave her motivation to make sure that they would be able to fight this fight on as even a playing field as possible.

Climbing the stairs to the plane, she boarded the small private jet. She had other work to attend to in Germany, so this worked well for her to be able to do a bit of old school spying for herself while she was there.

***

Ivan sat in his office. His eyes closed. The dark gray of the walls around him, and the black of the desk in front of him not offering any extra light into the room. He needed it. Harold thrived on bright lights and happy feelings. It was so much easier to keep him beaten down when there was darkness and death all around him.

Looking at the computer screen, he went through the roster of the Collective that he had taken.

"What they don't know will eventually hurt them. But by that point it will be too late," Ivan muttered to himself. He quickly scrolled through the members and took down the three he believed would be who had not voted how they were supposed to, and he was rarely wrong.

Taking out a glass and dropping his ice in it, he poured two fingers of scotch, and sipped on it. Looking at the list. He knew at least one of them had a weak point in his daughter, and he would have to exploit it. That wouldn't be hard. The other two would prove to be a bit more difficult. Smirking to himself, and taking another sip of his scotch, he chuckled slightly, saying, "But the creativity needed is what makes it so much fun to break these men of power."

/: Chapter 5

German Cuisine >

Cathrine sat staring out her airplane window. She hadn't really expected everything to progress how it had. Though she shouldn't be surprised.

"History always repeats itself," she said to herself. The ocean below her all looked the same. It always had. She hated it. She always had. It was why she joined the Air Force. She wanted to avoid the long travels on the Ocean and avoid the front lines. She knew her limitations. She had always been small. It made her creative and cunning. Either you allow your limitations to define you as a handicap, or as inspiration. And she never was one to be handicapped.

Even in repeating her mentor's favorite saying, she still couldn't believe that she was heading back to Germany. The place where her and Hel's partnership started so long ago. Long before Coeus. Long before the NOVA System. But it always seemed to bring them back to it. Whether it be the Berlin Wall, a cartel drug lord, or the Collective, it seemed to be the place that was the center of their friendship.

She rested her head back on her headrest and thought back to the time she had been infiltrating a massive drug ring.

***

Munich Germany 1993:

52

She was sitting in her small office getting packed to leave. She hadn't been in the field in a while due to everything with the NOVA system mission. And what a failure that had been. It had done what Coeus said it would, but there wasn't a way to reverse it yet. And without it being safe, there was no way anyone would recommend it for field use. The entire project was set to be shut down, right until Assistant Director Hunter stepped in and suggested that they repurpose it.

She hadn't liked him from the start, but to be fair, there were very few in the espionage world that she did like. Hel was one of them. Even if you were on the receiving end of her barrel, there was no question on where she stood. She had a job to do, and you were either it, or you were in the way.

When Hel had fallen for Coeus, she was surprised, but after seeing them together, it made sense. He allowed her to relax. Something she had never seen Hel do. He allowed Lucille out. She was able to be more than just an agent. And it suited her.

She became a mother. Something neither of them had ever expected to be available for them in their lives. But to no surprise to her, Hel was amazing at it. She took to motherhood like she did to everything she did. And those kids were her world. She would do anything and everything to protect them.

After Hel went undercover at Orlav Industries, Catherine sought out answers. She investigated it just like she did any mission. And what she found didn't exactly make sense. There were indications that Ivan had information about Hel and Coeus, but that was never shared with Hel before she went undercover. All that she had had was a meeting with AD Hunter, and then she seemed to agree fairly quickly. A phone call, a meeting, and she was ready to dive back into the field and abandon the family she loved for a mission that very well may never end, until there was a kill order on Harold. And even then, there would have had to be something very bad for Hel to be able to pull that trigger on her husband's very best friend.

She was now on her way to watch this drug lord that she knew was a direct rival to Ivan in the black-market weapons trade. She had to figure she would cross paths with Hel at some point. She was watching this man, getting information on him. She wasn't sure when or where she would see Hel, but she knew that once she did, she would have to do everything possible to help her on her end.

So, she waited. Watching him for days. Days turned into weeks. Turned into months. She knew his schedule, his regular orders, his regular girls. She knew exactly the way to dispatch him. But she waited. She knew she wasn't given a red mission. Just recon.

Then she saw her. She watched her for a few days. Making sure to stay out of sight. But the issue was that her timing was awful. Catherine was waiting for a meeting to happen. She had overheard a phone call about a man in the Collective. It was something that she had heard before. There wasn't much of anything known about them. But she did know that if what she had heard was true, then they were not a group that anyone wanted to mess with.

So, as she watched Hel get ready to pull the trigger, she had to stop her. Intervening before any blood was spilled. Pulling her back to her room in the same hotel that Hel had been positioned at.

"You have been watching me?" Hel asked, with a tone of accusation. She didn't like the implications of having the NSA watching her work. Even if it was one of her only friends.

"No. Not you, Hel. Him," She pointed to the picture on the board she had in her room that was full of information. Before continuing, Catherine walked over and unplugged the phone and turned off the recording equipment and took out the batteries. "There is far more going on here than just Ivan and the NOVA system. Have you heard of the Collective?"

Hel paused. She had heard of them. Sure. They were the names that were whispered by ghosts. They were the type of people that shadows hid from. She had never heard an actual name that went with those implications. How the Collective was treated by the people that she admired, caused her to have some slight shivers.

"Yeah. I have heard of them," Hel said, as cold and stoic as she could. She wasn't ready to have this discussion. Even with every precaution being taken.

"Well, I believe that he is a part of it. I know that this isn't a topic that is discussed often by anyone. But I am looking into them. I want to know what we are truly up against. I feel that this isn't something that I want anyone knowing except you. You are the only one I can trust, and maybe Coeus. The issue is that we have next to no information on them. We don't know where they have infiltrated. And I hope you understand my need for secrecy. Officially, I am here to gain intel on the drug ring that man runs. Once you kill him, that mission is completed. However, I overheard him on the phone before you got here and there is a meeting set to happen tomorrow night that I will need him alive for. He is supposed to be meeting with one of his fellow Collective members and establishing business with them. I am not sure who he is meeting or why. All I know is that I want the name of the person that he is dealing with so that I can have my next lead.

"My case against the Collective is completely unsanctioned and is something that I am investigating on my own. I have no funding outside of my own, and as such I have very limited access to anything. Which is why I am coming to you. You are the best agent I have ever known. I respect your work, I know you are straight forward as we get in this business, and I trust you as much as I trust anyone. So, I am asking you, as I have already read you in as much as I have, to join this mission with me. There won't be any kind of pay or accolades for this. Even if we should succeed, no one will likely ever know. The only thing that is driving me in this is the idea of the unknown force. I don't like things I don't know or know of.

"So?" Catherine finished her little speech with a slight sigh. She knew what she was asking could cost her friend everything. But they may be some of the only people in the world that even know there is something more out there. Something that likely is nefarious and is pulling strings no person should ever have the power to pull.

Hel looked at Cathrine. She thought through everything that she had just been told. It was a lot to take in. She knew that they had very little idea of just what they would be up against. She knew that they wouldn't have any backing in their government, and likely no other government would want to back them either. They would be flying by the seat of their pants, hoping for the best, and praying that they would never have to experience the worst.

But as she looked at her closest friend, seeing the hopeless look in her eyes, she knew she couldn't turn her down. She would have said yes even if her friend had nothing to go off of, but here she was with an actual solid lead. A string that they could start pulling and just see where it unravels. And there is no way that she could turn her back on that.

"What do you need from me?" Hel said, stealing herself for what was about to be asked.

Catherine visibly relaxed some. She had taken a huge leap of faith in confiding in her friend, and it had paid off. She had an ally in this private fight. Now they had to come up with a plan for how to handle this lead. She knew the basics. It was the same as every other lead they had ever had. But there was a major difference.

"Ok, good. Now, do we want to even approach this lead? Or do we just see if we are able to get the identity of the next step while we monitor their meeting? And how do you want to play this?" Catherine asked her friend. She had too much respect for the agent to not allow her to give input.

Hel walked over to the board and studied it for a moment. Taking in everything and analyzing what they should do.

"I feel that the risk of contact is too great. He can't know that we know he is Collective. That would paint a target on us too fast if he were to get away. Thankfully, we have another couple reasons to be after him, and I

56

have to walk away with him dead. I can't fail this one for any reason. I am on a 'prove it' mission for Ivan. He is testing my trust," Hel stated coldly.

Catherine had heard that tone before. Fully agent. That is what they needed to be to be able to make any progress with this. They couldn't have attachments beyond each other and Coeus. It could get too costly. They would have to make sure that their work never got compromised for this mission. But that tone meant that she knew the risks and the stakes.

"Ok, so we monitor. You have a reason to be close, and I haven't reported seeing you to anyone. So, we have the upper hand with that. You are able to get close without arousing suspicion. And once we have monitored the meeting and know where to start looking, you can complete your mission and get your loyalty badge with the Russian arms dealer," Catherine said, taking a slight jab at her friend.

"Oh, ha ha. Yeah, I will get it, right after you get your altruism badge. Dragging me into this mess of a non-mission," Hel said as she shoved Cathrine slightly.

"What weaponry will you be needing?" Catherine asked Hel, going to her closet and opening it up, revealing several outfits and a large bag that she pulled out and set on the bed. Opening it up, she had the usual assortment of weapons for a surveillance mission.

Hel chuckled. "I have plenty, thanks. Unless you forgot who I work for now?"

Catherine blushed slightly. She hadn't considered that an arms dealer would have more access to weapons than she did for this mission. But given the fact that Hel was on a red assignment, where she was just gathering intel, it made sense.

"I think how we do it is that you watch from outside. Parabolic mic, and infrared thermal imaging. Make sure that you are able to capture what is needed. And then get into the building's camera system, if it has one. Do you have any idea when or where the meeting will be exactly?" Hel asked.

Catherine pulled out her notepad and read out of it. "The meeting will take place at Aubergine. The target is close friends with Erich Witzmann, the head chef there. He was going to close the restaurant for the meeting but was advised otherwise by the other party. They stated, 'not wanting to raise suspicion.' The meeting is for tonight at eight o-clock. I am hoping to have some video of the meeting. I would rather if you were to finish your assignment after the meeting, so that we can avoid suspicion of our own with the Collective," she finished pointedly.

"Yeah, I know. Don't kill the bad man before he is no longer useful. This isn't my red test Cathrine," Hel snarked as she looked through the surveillance footage notes. "Do you know if he will have much of a protection detail with him? From what I have seen, he has four men with him at all times."

"From what I could tell for important meetings, he will tend to have extra. So, there isn't really any telling exactly the kind of security he could have set up at the restaurant. I would expect quite a bit of resistance after you kill him. I have no doubts that you can handle it, but it is definitely something to consider," Catherine stated, as she walked over to Hel.

Hel nodded slightly as she took some notes of her own. Folding out the schematics of the restaurant, looking over the exits. She formed a plan for her part of the mission.

***

Hel sat outside the restaurant. She was going through her usual premission process. She kept vigilant but was thinking through exactly what she had planned. She had just gotten off the phone with AD Hunter. He had reminded her of the priority of this mission. Her job was to make sure she had the trust of Ivan, above all else.

She felt calm. Everything felt clearer than they did when she was with Cathrine. And her headache that she had had was gone.

She looked out the window, she knew that the time was getting close for her to go in. She had confirmed that the target was there, and now she was needing to get in before the secondary target got there. She needed to be established before everything went down.

As she got out of the car, she looked up and saw several black Escalades approaching. She knew that that was the secondary target. She paid attention to it as it went by. The caravan came to almost a stop near her, and the middle Escalade's back window started to roll down.

Hel looked over and made eye contact with the rider. Her eyes shot open, and she immediately turned and rushed into the restaurant.

***

Catherine was watching Hel as she sat in her car. She had been with her on enough missions to know her process. She just had to wait for the fireworks. Hel had the wire on her that would be able to pick up just about every sound in that restaurant. She kept nervously checking all of the equipment.

As she was sitting there watching, she counted the target and his escort going into the restaurant, along with his security team.

"It looks like there are twenty plus the target and his female companions. I am not sure if they are a part of his protection detail or not. Plan for twenty-two," Catherine reported.

Hel responded with two taps on her headset to confirm. She got out of her car and seemed calm.

"Ok, now get set in the restaurant and we will wait for your moment," Catherine said, watching her. Hel got out of the car and was momentarily blocked by a caravan of SUV's. Catherine couldn't make out what was happening, but when she was able to see Hel again, she was rushing into the restaurant.

"Hel, this isn't the plan. What is going on? Stick to the plan!" Catherine almost yelled into the headset.

There was a moment of silence and then everything went chaotic.

***

Hel pulled out three knives and walked into the restaurant. She didn't say a word, she threw each knife into the closest three men facing her. Pulling out her guns, she immediately turned and shot each of the men in quick succession.

It was clear that no one was ready for it, and not a single person was missed. Her silenced pistols went off. One. Two. Three. Four. Cathrine counted out the shots. She couldn't understand what was going on. What changed. And she was pissed. She had gotten nothing.

Five. Six. Seven. Why was she mowing them all down? She watched the infrared scope, as each man started to go cold, with warm pools forming around them. She could hear the women screaming. Eight. Nine. Ten. Eleven. Twelve. The number of people that she could possibly get any information from was dropping quickly.

Suddenly the room went quiet.

***

Hel dropped her guns on the floor and pulling out her throwing knives, she spun as she threw her knives allowed her to crouch to reach her guns easily, without exposing herself. Pulling them out, she spun back up on her heels. Pulling her guns up, she fired four shots, hitting all four right between the eyes. And with two of them, the two behind them dropped too.

She dove and rolled. Everyone started to finally figure out that something was going on. The women started screaming, and the men

60

started to scramble to get their guns. She got to her feet off the roll and fired off three more shots.

Jumping up and sliding across the table, she kicked a guy in the throat with her heel. It sank in easily, and she pulled her foot out of the shoe. Kicking again, the other shoe flew across the room and hit another guy. The heel embedding into his head. The man closest started trying to scream and dropped to the floor. The other man dropped instantly.

She kicked a chair, and it slid across the floor. The guy was taking out his gun, and his arm went through the rails on it getting trapped. She fired and shot him in the head. And then took out the two guys closest to the back door.

Two of the men pulled out knives and threw them at her. She flipped the table near her, and the knives got caught by it, as it fell, she shot and killed both of them.

Walking towards the target, she shot the last man and one of the girls. Pulling a knife out of one of the guys that she had thrown the knife into, she threw it into the other girl.

"Clear," Hel said very loudly.

***

"WHAT ARE YOU DOING?!" Catherine yelled into the headset. Even though she knew that Hel had turned off her earpiece. She knew that no one could hear her, but this was the farthest thing from the plan possible.

She couldn't even understand what was going on. She had never seen Hel be like this unless she had to be, which was an unfortunate number of times. She watched as Hel methodically did away with all of the men in the room, and then walked toward the women and the target. She had been brutal and ruthless. She took out the women without remorse. And left the target and called the all clear.

Catherine was about ready to head down there and truly let her friend have it, when there was a person coming out of the kitchen. She paused and waited to see what was happening.

***

Hel's eyes never left the target. She waited for a moment while he walked into the room.

"Hello, Carlos. I see you have met my enforcer, Hel. I trust that you treated her with the respect that she is due. Unlike you clearly did with me. twenty men? Really? And what? You expect me to allow myself to be so outnumbered coming into a meeting with an unknown? You should expect more," Ivan said, as he nonchalantly walked into the room.

"This is just one of my agents. Oh, and your Mexico headquarters is no more. You can thank Hel here for that as well. Don't worry. You will be given a chance. A chance to prove to me that you deserve to live," Ivan continued.

Carlos was breathing heavily. Clearly scared. The restaurant smelled like urine, fecal matter, and death. He was crying and shaking.

"But you wanted in. You were ready to join the Collective. We had a seat for you," Carlos said, begging.

"I know. That seat was yours," Ivan said, as he pulled out a gun and shot Carlos in the head. He nodded to Hel, and she followed him out of the restaurant.

***

Present day:

Catherine walked into the same hotel that she had been at so many years ago. A hotel that she had gone back to many times. She owned the room now. It was hers, under one of her unregistered pseudonyms. She had kept a lot of her research on the Collective there.

62

She had spent a lot of her money on making sure that this room was made to hold information in a way that no one would be able to access it without her. She booted up her computers that she had in there. She was waiting for her team to find more. Even if they didn't know what they were working towards. They would know soon enough.

She looked through some of the original information that she had looked through many times before. But now, after she had been through the last two years. Because of Coeus, the NOVA system, and Gavin. Especially Gavin. She was able to understand far more of it than she ever had before.

Pulling out her phone, she looked at it.

She felt her heart rate rise. She was nervous. Why should she be nervous? This was the next step. It was what was expected. She needed to do it. Why was it so hard?

With slightly shaking fingers, she started to dial the number. She felt herself start to break a sweat. As she finished typing the number, she put the phone up to her ear.

"Hey, Numunuu. It's Theia. It's time."

/: Chapter 6

Networking >

Present Day GA:

Gavin sat at his computer. He had been careful not to leave any traces of his hacking since that meeting with General Richmond. He had made some progress, but it was still a struggle. He was slowly getting through the security of Ivan's enterprise. Bit by bit.

Alex had dragged him out for a run and a sparring session. He knew that he was getting better, but he still didn't enjoy it the way that she did. She lived for the physical rush of finishing a run or besting an opponent in a fight. The computer was Gavin's world. He felt most at home there. A place that many just felt so alien. This was his escape, and it made him happy.

He finally had the coding done on his worm and was ready to release it. He wasn't even positive it would find anything, but he did his best. Hitting enter, he waited. Given the coding, he knew that Harold had to be in there somewhere. It only made sense that coding this complex was written by his father's best friend, and someone who had studied AI.

Gavin hit enter and got up. As he went out to the kitchen to get a drink, Alex came in from another run.

64

"Hey! I thought you would be busy with your programming for the rest of the day. Is everything ok?" Alex asked with slight concern in her tone.

Gavin finished his mouthful and set the glass down before replying. "Yeah, I think so at least. I set up a separate server to leach the information out of the system. Making exact duplicates of everything, while leaving no trace of doing it, and then sending it to the server. Once it was completed, it was set to end the program, and the worm will be absorbed into the coding that was already there, and seal up the whole in the security," Gavin stated, looking up to see a confused look on Alex's face.

He smiled, glad that he had some area that he could still say was his. "Basically, I sent in a spy to send the information back to a secure location. When the spy got through the fence protecting it, they patched up the information. And once they are finished with getting the information, they are to go into deep cover as one of the henchmen," Gavin tried to explain.

Alex nodded and smiled a bit. "You normally don't call them henchmen. This isn't a comic book," she said with a teasing tone. She knew what he was meaning, and it was honestly a great way of thinking about the men that worked for people like Ivan, but that wasn't something you would want to say in a briefing.

"I know that. But what would you call them?" Gavin asked in an overly exasperated tone. He knew she was ribbing him and was just enjoying the banter.

Alex smirked and shrugged her shoulders. And then turned to walk away, knowing that leaving it up in the air like that would drive Gavin crazy.

"Hey, no! That isn't an answer! Get back here right now! Hey!" Gavin said jovially as he chased after her. Her pace picked up, and soon he was chasing her through the house.

Finally catching up to her in their room, he grabbed her by her hips and twisted causing both of them to fall on the bed laughing. As they settled, they were lying next to each other, and both had a smile on their face.

Alex sighed in contentment at the normality of the situation. She thought that it was something any couple would do. She looked into his eyes, and for one of the first times in a long time she felt at home. Everything about the situation felt like home. The warmth of the room, the comfort of the bed and the company, the look in his eyes.

"Gavin, I have to tell you. I am worried that I may never be ready to get married, but I do know that I want to spend the rest of my life with you. So, it isn't you that has me afraid. It is the ceremony of it. The idea of becoming a member of your family. A family that is extremely close knit, to where being apart for a decade didn't even ruin the love that is there. I don't understand that. I have never seen that before in my life. And I am not sure that I ever will again. And it is more than slightly intimidating," Alex expressed honestly.

Gavin was a bit taken back. He hadn't expected such a confession from her. Especially since everything had happened. He reached over and pulled her in. Holding her for a while before he replied.

"I understand, and that is ok. There is no rush. You mean the world to me, and you don't have to be anything that you're not. I love you for who you are, Alex, and that includes your struggles too," Gavin said, measuring his words. He didn't want to make anything more difficult for her than it already was. He knew what kind of struggle it could be for her to open up like this, but that didn't mean that he wasn't disappointed. He smiled at her and kissed the top of her head.

Alex took a breath. She knew that he was disappointed. She didn't know what else to do. She was trying to be honest like Megan had said, and still felt like she had messed up. She just felt like letting her agent side take over and not dealing with it at the moment, but she knew that that was even less fair to Gavin.

She opened her mouth to start trying to make it better, when there was a beeping sound from the lab. Then another. And yet another.

"I am so sorry, I have to go check that," Gavin apologized, as he extracted himself from cuddling Alex to go see what had come up. "Don't move. I'll be right back," he said as he was on his way out the door heading to the lab.

Walking into the lab, he started looking over the items that popped up. There were hundreds, if not thousands of files, locations, data points, safe houses, weapons caches, and labs all over the world. Several in the US.

Gavin took a breath. He tried to calm his excitement for the results he was getting, and had even more coming in. He figured it would be smart to run the best candidates past his mom to see what she knew about it all and what they should and shouldn't go after first. He wanted to start off small. Not draw too much attention at first, if he could help it. An empire the likes of Orlav Ind. would just have a new head the moment Ivan was gone if the entire thing wasn't in shambles.

After a while, Alex got up and followed him into the lab. Walking up behind him and draping her arms on his shoulders, she leaned down so that her head was right next to his. Kissing him behind his ear, she felt him shudder slightly.

Glad to know that even when he has lost himself in the cyber world, I can still have an effect on him, she thought with a smirk. "I am going to go make some coffee," she whispered in his ear.

"Mhmmm," Gavin replied absentmindedly.

***

Charles sat in his apartment waiting for the call. He had gone and gotten a burner the moment the general had given him the coded message. He knew that that never meant anything good was about to happen. Sitting there he thought about the possibilities and had started to fear the worst of them when the phone rang.

"Charles, secure."

"Hello Agent Charles, I wanted to discuss a few upcoming missions with you. I know you will understand the need for secrecy once I tell you. The first of which, Gavin expressed an interest in going after Ivan Orlav. I know that that is something that has been on your heart heavily for a long time. Given the sensitive nature of it for you, I am making Gavin the lead strategist, and Alex the lead agent for this mission. However, that also frees you up slightly for the second mission," The general took a breath. Even with her most trusted agent, this was difficult. She hoped bringing him into it so soon wasn't a mistake.

"I am moving on The Collective. I am in Germany currently, and I have every intention of using my time in Europe to do some recon here and see what I can find. This is above level seven clearance. We will eventually bring the rest of your team in, but for now you and I are the only ones in this mission. Let them focus on the mission with Orlav Ind., and you split your focus between that mission, and finding what you can on The Collective. Do not ask people directly. No matter how well you think you know them. No matter when you served with them, or what title they hold. It doesn't matter. All we have on them is what Agent Anderson had, which means it's all tenuous at best. So, see what you can dig up," the general concluded and ended the call without another word.

Charles grunted. He knew his role. He played the emotionless brute well. And for the most part, that is what he was. Very few, and less every day, knew him really. And he usually liked to keep it that way.

Looking at the surveillance, only on the outside of Gavin's apartment, Charles knew he was safe. Alex was with him. So that left him to be able to go and do some recon work on his own.

Grabbing his jacket, he grabbed the burner phone. Snapping it into two pieces and taking out the SIM card, he reached into the drawer by the door and grabbed another phone and SIM card. He made his way out to his car, snapping the old SIM card and tossing it into the gutter as he left. The steady rain that had just started to fall would carry it away and corrode it.

As he got into his car, he pulled out his phone and dialed a number. Waiting for the other side to pick up, he pulled out into traffic. He figured he would go down around the CDC and have a listen to conversations. Government buildings like that were usually good places to try to pick up random chatter for insider issues like this one that General Richmond was asking him to look into.

"Status?" the voice on the other side came through.

"Everything is almost ready. I will notify you when we are ready to strike," Charles said, and then he hung up the phone and took off towards the CDC.

***

Gavin had called his mother over, and they were in his lab going through all of the information that he was able to copy off of the servers for Orlav Ind. Every now and then you could hear Lucille saying something like, "You are just like your father." or "He would be so proud." or "I can't believe that you got that."

Alex was sitting in the living room, pretending to read a book, while she eavesdropped on them working. She didn't want to intrude, but she couldn't help but want to hear what was going on and being said.

Of course, Gavin was able to get far more than you ever could have thought. Do you even know what he is really capable of? Do I for that matter? As Vidar he was able to do things that most everyone else couldn't have even dreamed of. Only the select few that got the mission to hunt him down had ever actually gotten the chance to know exactly what he had done. And most of it was for the betterment of the Government. Much to their analysts' chagrin. He would solve coding issues that they had been working for decades to try to fix. I know his dad was a special mind as well, but I simply can't imagine him being even more capable than Gavin with a computer in his hands. Alex mused to herself. She hadn't truly stopped and considered everything that Gavin had done, and at the young ages that she knew he had done it at.

I can't believe that he is my fiancé. Her thoughts paused. She of course knew that he had proposed. She had said yes. But this was the first time that she had to refer to him in her mind as her fiancé. It both excited her and gave her some fear. She had seen the beauty of what a marriage could be, with Chad and Megan. And through hearing about what it was like for Lucille and Walter. But her own experience, what she had witnessed with her parents, made it hard for her to get as excited as she knew she should be.

And with that thought, her mood fell. She was about to start beating herself up, when she heard from the other room.

"Wait, go back. What was that?" Lucille asked.

"Those are three weapons caches in Oklahoma. A few sites, it looks like they are close together," Gavin said, reading the list of coding.

"No, there isn't any operation in Oklahoma. I would know. Every single one of these up to this point I had helped set up or maintain. Except those. Those are dated to have been set up in the late 90's and have been running since. And that just isn't right. Those are your entry points. Look into those first. I bet that whatever is there, it is far more valuable than munitions," Lucille stated with finality. She was very proud of her son. She knew he was capable with computers, from what Walter had said, but from what she had just witnessed she thought he could be better than anyone she had ever seen.

Gavin started typing away on his computer and couldn't find anything more on it.

"Well, it seems like we may have our first target for this one. Lawton, Oklahoma," Gavin said, mostly to himself.

***

70

Later that day, down in Citadel, Gavin was going over his plans for the new mission while Alex was sorting out what they may need, when Charles walked in. Walking past Charles glanced over Gavin's shoulder and noticed the map of the area he was looking at.

"What's going on kid?" Charles asked, leaning onto his shoulder.

"Just prepping for our next mission. My mom and I noticed some weapons caches in Oklahoma that seemed like they were out of place. Mom didn't remember setting them up, but they were in their database. So, we are going to check it out and see what she can scrounge up," Gavin said, without taking his eyes off the screen. "By the way, where have you been?"

"Aww, did you miss me? Even with your girlfriend around?" Charles teased, as he patted Gavin on the shoulder.

"That's fiancé!" Gavin hollered at Charles' back as he walked away. To which Charles just waved and kept walking.

Gavin watched Charles' back for a while as he walked out of sight around the corner to the locker room. *He just deliberately avoided answering my question. He showed a lot of interest until I said it was for a mission. So, what is going on? He vanishes for a few hours, and then comes back like nothing happened? He hadn't ever done that before.* Gavin made a mental note to keep a closer eye on Charles and got back to work. He still had to get the plane ready for them and arrange transport when they got to Oklahoma.

Alex had watched the entire exchange from a distance. She thought it was weird as well. Charles had rarely been exactly forthcoming, but that was a bit cold, even for him. It all made her feel a bit nervous and on edge.

Charles came walking back out into the conference area with a duffle bag and dropped it onto the table in the middle of the room.

"So, when and where are we going? Richmond called me and informed me that Gavin would be lead strategist on this one, and Alex, you would be the agent in charge. So, I am just along for the ride," he said, a bit of sarcasm in his tone. He clearly didn't seem to enjoy seemingly being demoted.

So that seems to be his issue. He feels he is being pushed out, and doesn't like it, Alex thought as she set her pack down on the table across from him.

"We are a team. It doesn't matter who plans or who is in charge," she said, trying to placate the situation.

"Yeah, but at the end of the day, you both are going to save each other long before you save me. And I can't even blame you. It is what it is," Charles grunted as he grabbed his pack and headed towards the car.

Gavin turned to start telling Charles that that wasn't fair, but saw he'd already left.

"This is going to be a SUPER fun trip," Gavin snarked, causing Alex to give a Charles-like grunt of her own in acknowledgement of what he had said.

Grabbing his own bags, Gavin made his way to the cars as well.

"Everyone is just in an amazing mood," he muttered to himself.

***

The trip there was quiet. Alex was focused on flying, while Gavin was thinking about what Charles had said and how he had acted. Charles just preferred the quiet to begin with. Gavin was typing on his laptop, trying to see if he could find the network for this particular weapons cache. Though he knew that his mom had said she didn't think that's what it was. He was going to go with that for the time being. But he wasn't really paying much attention to what he was doing.

Why is Charles being even more, Charles-y? Is he really that hurt that Alex and I are together? Does he feel like it means that we won't have his back now? I know that that just isn't true. I would have his back, and I know Alex would too. And it's not like we haven't had his back in the past. Right? Is there something that I am missing? I hate the tension that's here now, Gavin thought.

Alex could tell that Gavin was bothered by something, and she figured that it was the issue with Charles, she thought to herself. *But after what Charles had said, it made sense to her. He was right. At the end of the day, I am going to protect and save Gavin over just about anyone. And I really hope that Gavin feels the same, even though I know he is much more the type to just find a way to make sure everyone is safe, rather than just focusing on saving one person. And that is why I love him. He refuses to accept losing.*

As they approached the Oklahoma airfield, they all focused on the mission. Landing and getting to their hotel, Gavin hadn't noticed when booking it that it was a casino. They checked in, and the front desk person called Charles "Mato".

Gavin didn't say anything initially. He knew that was Charles' birth name. He had seen it in his file through the NOVA, but he wasn't sure that this was the time to bring it up.

I could have just heard what I wanted. They were mumbling, so I could have misheard. I was thinking about Charles on the way here, so I think that could have affected what I heard. Don't jump to conclusions.

They got up to their room. Just like always, they only got one. Limited visibility and given that their intention wasn't to stay for a holiday, they didn't need the privacy. Alex immediately started sweeping the room for bugs, while Charles set up surveillance on the room to make sure that no one came in while they were out. Gavin placed the "Do Not Disturb" sign on the door's outer handle.

"Good thinking. Now no bad guys would dare to come in when we are gone," Charles gave a snide remark to Gavin.

"Well, I was thinking more about housekeeping and the hotel staff than anyone with more nefarious intentions," Gavin quipped back.

Charles just grunted, knowing that Gavin was right and did the right thing. He just got a particular joy out of ribbing the younger guy.

Alex watched the exchange, and just shook her head. She was working with the absolute best spy team in the world, and they acted like children half the time.

"Room secure," she said, after finding only one bug, and it looked much more just like someone was a pervert than another spy. She destroyed it without much worry.

"Surveillance up," Charles said.

Gavin then got out his equipment and set it all up very quickly. Looking at thermal imaging of the area, he was able to pick up some underground buildings at some of the wildlife refuge close by.

"I think that these are our best bet for the locations," he said, pointing them out to the other two.

"And what makes you think that?" Charles asked, there was a tone to his voice that Gavin couldn't quite put his finger on.

"The fact that they are underground buildings...?" Gavin said, as if that explained it for him.

"And where are we? What is the common demographic here? Do you think that they could possibly be burial grounds?" Charles spat. There was an edge to his voice that neither of the other two had heard since that first night they all met.

"Woah big guy. I mean no ill intent here. I only said that they seem to be buildings. They are large areas of metal forms. The thermal imaging can see the burial grounds, but I am avoiding those. given that I am ignorant of how this tribe's beliefs are towards that kind of thing. But it is kind of hard to ignore a fifty foot by one-hundred-foot steel plating that is underground, with reinforcing steel," Gavin said defensively.

Charles grunted with a huff and walked away. He didn't want to be here anymore.

"Charles, what is going on? Do I need to have you stay here? Or should I have my gun drawn?" Alex asked, her hand hovering over her weapon.

Charles sighed. He knew that this would be unavoidable at this point. He hated this.

"Hey, you can tell us what is going on. We are more than a team. You are part of the family, Big Guy," Gavin said in a kind tone.

Charles gave a mirthy chuckle. "Yeah. I don't even know what that is like," he started. He knew he had to tell them. He just didn't want to. "I think it would be easier if I just show you," he said, grabbing his backpack and walking out of the room.

Gavin looked at Alex, who responded with a shrug. They both grabbed their backpacks and followed him.

He made his way to their car, and they all piled in. But he didn't head towards where Gavin had seen the buildings. He headed into town, turning down back roads. They pulled up to this small park next to the High School. Charles led them up to the High School, pulled out a key, and opened the door.

Gavin was shocked, and Alex's face went stoic. Gavin knew that where Charles was from wasn't in his file. So, he had no clue.

Charles led them passed trophy cases, to a wall where there were class pictures hanging. It took a few seconds, but Charles pointed to one where they saw a picture of a very young and stern looking Charles.

"This is where I am from. I don't like having to come back here. Especially when it is mission related," Charles said quietly, knowing he would have to come clean on everything. "These are good people here mostly. You need to know that going into this," he explained in a strained voice.

"It's ok, Charles, we don't have any intention of causing harm to these people," Gavin said, putting his hand on Charles' shoulder.

"But you don't really understand. In a way, you do," Charles said softly, almost sounding defeated. "Let me explain."

/: Chapter 7

Insane Power >

<u>Atlanta 1991:</u>

Ivan knew about Harold, but he wasn't about to let everyone around him see that weakness. That intrusive personality. He wanted to act like he wasn't there, in hopes that one day he would no longer be there at all. At first, they could work together, some of the time. Harold didn't approve of how Ivan handled business and would try to stop him. But he almost always caved. It was the attribute that Ivan liked about him the most. His proclivity to submit.

He also grew very tired of checking in with the general. He knew that the only person who he owed any allegiance to was assistant Director Hunter. Hunter had provided him with several openings to be able to build his power. Hunter had let him know where several shipments of weapons, which weren't even on the market yet, were being stored. That single acquisition had set him up to be able to build the empire he now sat on top of.

He was going through his books, making sure that there wasn't any extra loss on his ledger that he wasn't aware of. Being the bad guy had its perks for sure. Business was easy, when the opposition was threatened with death. That was something Harold had fought him hard on at first. But as each kill order was sent, and each bullet was fired, Harold started to lose his voice. Making it easier for Ivan to be able to keep pushing for more.

It wasn't until the general had sent someone to retrieve him that he felt he knew his place, though. Ivan was proud of the company he had built. He had power beyond what most people would experience in ten lifetimes. Why would he give that up? So that some government could, have it? Not on his life.

When the man came to call him back, he felt Harold try to push. They thought that he could just be called back in like some dog? That they could whistle, and he would come running?

He didn't waste time. Once the man started to say the recall signal, he pulled his side arm and shot him before he could even finish the sentence. Calling his men in to clear away the body, he felt Harold give up. He had won, finally.

***

It wasn't long before the general called again. He was done playing games. When the general said the call back signal, he just acted like he didn't know what he was talking about. He wasn't some puppet to be taken off when they were done with him. This was his body. His life. And he made his own choices.

He felt Harold try, one last time. Harold was even able to say a word. Ivan couldn't remember what the word was, but he knew he had spoken. Ivan would never allow that again. All hope was lost for Harold when Ivan hung the phone up.

Ivan stood from his desk. He felt his mind free of Harold for the first time in what felt like forever. No more nagging little whine to keep him from doing what needed to be done or make him feel bad for doing it. He was going to be able to run his empire the right way now.

***

Glancing up from his desk, he saw a man walking towards him with a woman that seemed oddly familiar to him. Ivan put his head back down and continued his work. He knew that it was always a power move to show just who was in charge at any given moment. And given where his career had taken him, he needed to make sure he was in charge of every moment. So, he ignored those who had just joined him for a moment longer.

He could sense more than see that his guard was fidgeting but was pleasantly surprised at the fact that the woman was not. She seemed calm and focused. That made him feel a slight bit uneasy, yet excited for the challenge of breaking her. He never let anyone close to him that he didn't know he could control completely.

He finished with what he was working on and looked up. Still not saying a word he studied them both. He didn't remember the guard's name. There were too many of them to worry about something as trivial as a name. They were paid to be loyal, they weren't his drinking buddies. There was no need for formalities with what he did. And when they all put on the same standard all-black uniform for his protection detail, they began to all look the same, as well.

The woman, however, did not. She looked like this wasn't her first time, but he was sure he had never seen her before. Even if he didn't remember names, he knew when someone wasn't his usual visitor. And she definitely was not. But she seemed so comfortable to him. So familiar. It was eerie, really.

Finally, after several long minutes, he spoke.

"What do you need?" Ivan asked curtly.

"Hel here has been doing good work at every level. I know you have heard of some of the actions she has taken. She has avoided capture several times, in situations that other operatives hadn't been so lucky. And she was able to bring in a rival's son for collateral in exchange for an allegiance. The Triads are now working with you, because of her. I thought you may want her somewhere more important than working the streets," The guard reported like he was giving a class project.

Rubbing the bridge of his nose with his forefinger and his thumb, Ivan sat. He knew that this guard was right. He knew that he had the best interest of the company in his decision to bring this Hel to him.

Opening his desk drawer, he pulled out a gun and pointed it at the guard.

"And so, you think you know how to run this company better than I do? So, you bring her here to, what? Meet me? Assassinate me? For all you know, she is working for the Triads. Did that ever cross your mind?" Ivan ranted.

To his right, a door opened, and in walked his head lawyer, Stuart. Ivan forgot what his last name was at the moment.

"Sir, I would be honored to take on the role of processing this new lady into the company, or out of it," Stuart said placatingly. Ivan trusted Stuart as much as anyone. Hunter had suggested he be sought out for employment, and he had already proven himself more than useful in keeping this company running.

"Ok. See to it that I don't regret this," Ivan said, as he fired a shot straight into the guard's head. He would not be questioned. Seeing a slight flinch in the face of Hel, he knew he had her. She feared him, he surprised her, and as such, she would do as he asked.

***

Ivan had a meeting. Hel had been gaining him some real ground, she had turned out to be a true asset for him. His empire had grown exponentially, and he was getting the attention of some really powerful people. Governments, warlords and drug lords all had been calling. While he would do business with the drug lords, it was never his preferred working relationships.

The people at this meeting made a group that he had never heard of before. But he had recently been getting some contracts from them. He was beyond just buying and selling weapons. He grew into developing his own. And he had brought in some scientists to work with, but most of them had been a serious let down. He found most of them to be incompetent and useless. And the few that had impressed him with their ability, he found to not be trustworthy.

Until he got a call from Assistant Director Hunter.

"Hello, Hunter. What can I do for you today?" Ivan asked in a slightly irritated voice. He had things to do, and a chat on the phone with someone in the United States government was not one of them.

"Oh, it isn't what you can do for me today, Ivan. As usual, it is what I can do for you," Hunter said stoically.

That irritated Ivan. He hated that he felt he owed Hunter, and it was becoming clear that Hunter would be calling in favors, and likely soon, with how he sounded. And Hunter wasn't a benevolent man. Every favor came with a price.

"And what if I refuse?" Ivan spat at Hunter.

"You don't understand. I own you," Hunter said calmly.

"How DARE you speak to me that way?" Ivan started into a fury-filled rant.

"The sun sets on the green hills," Hunter said, and Ivan instantly stopped talking. "You see, Ivan, I made you. I can destroy you and you would never even know who it was. I am always two steps ahead of you, and I'm always closer than you think."

Ivan was fuming. He didn't understand what was going on, but his body wasn't working. He didn't remember what Hunter had said, but he couldn't talk, move, or anything but listen. His body was barely breathing. But, given that Hunter had this power over him, he had to play ball. At least until he had some form of a plan to get rid of him. And given Hunter's position, getting rid of him would definitely prove to be a difficult task.

"Do I have your attention now?" Hunter asked smugly. "So, here is what you have coming to you. I have a hand selected scientist that will work with you to develop some very high-end weapons and tactical equipment. I will be calling you to take care of some side wet work for me. I will pay and give you contracts. Off the books, of course. And I know you are wondering what is in it for me," Hunter paused for dramatic effect.

Ivan could hear him taking a drink. He was still unable to respond, and it was driving him insane. Hunter was pulling out all of the moves to prove that he had Ivan by the throat, and that there was nothing that he could do about it.

"That you will be finding out very soon, my friend," Hunter said, "This scientist is currently on his way to your facility, and I expect you to give him a warm welcome. I will be in touch." And then Hunter hung up the phone.

Stuck sitting there, staring at the wall. Ivan was left to think. He had nothing else he could do. Whatever Hunter did was still in effect. He felt Harold try to push through. Pushing him down, he set his mind on how to end Hunter.

***

The scientist that Hunter sent turned out to be someone that Ivan had been following for a while. A man who outside of the scholastic world was known as The Westgate.

When they were finally introduced, they started to hit it off. Something in him clicked with The Westgate. It felt comfortable. And it made him start to work on his computer more. It was like he was drawn to it. The Westgate was pivotal in bringing in bigger and bigger contracts. Orlav

82

Industries research and development side had never gotten so much attention.

The more attention he got, the more Ivan was able to do. Hel and The Westgate were making him into a world power. He had to move his headquarters to the Russian wilderness. He didn't trust anyone, even Hel. and as such, he needed the top security to protect him. Stuart had set up some of the paper pushers to do the office work. Keeping track of payments, salaries, their different locations, and some mission logs from some of the higher up people that can be used later.

He had grown to a conglomerate, and it had gotten the attention of the world elite. He had had a few moments with Hunter, and that was never something that he wanted. But he always seemed to come out on top after those run ins.

It was during one of these missions from Hunter that Ivan ran into someone that would introduce him to Frederick Clayton. He was the buyer, and usually it wasn't someone that Ivan would deal with directly, but this was a very personal mission. There were several women that had to be dealt with. What wasn't disclosed was the children that needed to be dealt with as well. When Ivan called Frederick to confirm the targets, Frederick confirmed and said that he wanted to meet with Ivan the following day, as he had a proposition for him.

Ivan knew that Hel wouldn't do this kind of assignment, so he sent his men to complete it. Ivan made sure to take record of the locations of the bodies. He knew he would likely need some collateral when dealing with these kinds of people. His scrupulous records allowed him the leverage to not become collateral damage.

Walking into the meeting with Frederick, he was sure to assign his men on rooftops around the area to watch his back. He exited the elevator and felt confident. He saw two of his men posed as janitors and knew that there were several others with rifles watching him make his way towards the office.

He stopped in the outer office. Frederick's secretary was typing away on her computer, clearly trying hard to not pay attention to Ivan as he sat near the entrance. Looking around the office, he spotted a copy of PC magazine on the table.

He reached over and picked it up. Flipping through the pages, he saw an article titled "The Resurgence of AI: Will it be the Future?"

"Well, that is interesting," Ivan said to himself. Flipping through the article, he read that there were projections that AI could be used to help the productivity of factories and finances within the next five years. He felt that, for some reason, he knew quite a bit about AI. The article got him thinking a lot. He wasn't entirely sure what he should target first but knew he would be talking to The Westgate as soon as he got back to headquarters.

"Mr. Clayton will see you now," the secretary said, with a tone of annoyance.

Standing, Ivan straightened his tie and suit jacket. Looking her over, the younger lady had a look of disgust on her face.

"It would serve you well to learn some manners, before someone who you seem to deem beneath you teaches you some," Ivan said, right as a laser dot hovered from his chest, over to her desk, and then up to the center of her chest. "Just because you don't know me, doesn't mean I am a nobody. Remember that" Ivan snarked as he made his way through the door, hearing a sob come from the secretary. That caused a genuine smile to form on his lips.

***

Ivan sat across from Frederick, watching him pull the exact same power moves that he did on a regular basis. He sat and waited patiently. He knew that there was no point in trying to rush someone of the stature that Frederick had. He knew that once he mentioned he had the locations of all those bodies, Frederick would instantly start thinking of ways to dispose of him. The issue was, there wasn't really anyone to call for that work that would go against Ivan. And Ivan knew that.

It gave him an advantage.

"I know that you are a busy man Mr. Orlav, so I will not take much of your time. However, I would advise you that in the future you do your research before you attempt to threaten me. You see, the glass in this office is bulletproof, however," Frederick said in a smug tone, "I am guessing that that jacket is not."

Ivan's smile never wavered. He simply cleared his throat once, and instantly the pillow on the other side of the office exploded. Feathers were floating around that half the room.

"My dear Mr. Clayton, just what about me makes you think that I didn't do my research? I may not have the lineage that you do, but I assure you, I am no less of a threat. Bulletproof glass is great, when not being used against high powered rifles. But I am an arms dealer first and foremost. The sheer fact that you failed to realize that I would have the best available to myself shows that you direly underestimated me," Ivan paused and reached over and took the glass of scotch that was sitting in front of Frederick. He sat back in his seat and took a slow and exaggerated drink of it. Allowing the burn to run down his throat. "Ah. Now, please, explain again to me how you have the upper hand in this situation," Ivan finished with a smirk, taking another sip from Frederick's scotch.

As Frederick recollected himself, Ivan let him stew. Ivan was enjoying the discomfort coming from the other man. He found pleasure in making other people squirm. Especially those who are supposed to have far more power over him.

Frederick muttered to Ivan, and a bit to himself, "I need to make a call." Then he grabbed the phone and hit a speed dial. Ivan could only hear the one side of the conversation, but it sounded promising.

"It's me. Yes, I know, but this is urgent. I will send it instantly. I have a replacement already in mind, just need a vote. Can we do it over email? I have a private server. Yes. Just do it! No, not later, now," Frederick then got on his computer and started typing.

Ivan sat there watching intently. He had a feeling of what was coming, but he didn't want to get his hopes up. There wouldn't be many people that he would have to call to ask permission for anything. He was in the position that you either cover up the evidence or ask for forgiveness. You never ask for permission.

Finally, after an hour of waiting and watching Frederick type away and make a couple other phone calls, Frederick cleared his throat and looked at Ivan.

He then opened the drawer to his desk and took out a key. Using it to open another drawer, he pushed a button. The painting behind him opened up. "Follow me," Frederick said as he turned, stood, and started to walk into the hallway that opened behind him.

"Mr. Clayton, if you think I will be helpless once out of sight from the windows, I am afraid that you will be very mistaken," Ivan warned.

With a sigh, Frederick simply said, "I know." And continued down the hallway.

That was enough assurance for Ivan, and he got up and followed Frederick. The hallway winded around and had a slight downward slant. They made their way down as it seemed to spiral slowly. Ivan estimated around three levels. There was a door, and an eye scanner. Frederick accessed the door and opened it for the both of them.

They went in and sat, as the entire room went dark. Ivan put a hand on the pistol he had in the back of his pants. It was ceramic and allowed him to get it past the metal detectors.

But then the room was filled with a red hue. Some lights came on slowly.

"Ivan, I have gotten approval to allow you to join a very exclusive group that I am a part of. The man that I was on the phone with upstairs was the sitting president. He has given permission for you to join, the vote was sent via email, which is the first time that that has been allowed, and the people who have heard of you had very good things to say about your work. Now, I have to tell you that this doesn't come without a price. You will have to open up the seat at the table, currently held by the head of the biggest Cartel in Mexico, Carlos Cortez. You won't be able to just take him out, you will have to take out his entire organization. We will not lose the money that he brings in just to allow you in. You will need to show us you are capable of taking on more than what you have already," Frederick stated with finality.

Ivan breathed. This was his chance. He had made sure he would be able to get everything he needed.

"Oh, Mr. Clayton. I have already taken care of most of this. I have a jet waiting for me to go to Germany. If I have heard correctly, there are rules for how this has to take place. I know he will have his guard around him and will be setting up for this. He isn't stupid, but he just doesn't know what is coming for him. His Mexican headquarters are no more or will be by the time that I have put a bullet into Carlos' head," Ivan stated.

Frederick had his eyebrows rise. He had not expected Ivan to be so prepared, but after what had happened in the office, he shouldn't have been surprised. This may be the shortest initiation to the Collective he had heard of.

"How exactly do you know about our rules?" Frederick asked with hesitation.

"Oh, I have worked enough in this business to know how to get the information I want. I have heard and gathered enough information about the Collective to know what is expected of me," Ivan said with a calm menace to his tone.

"So, how will you do it?" Frederick asked.

***

Once Ivan finished with his meeting, he headed to the airport with Frederick right behind him.

Ivan had grabbed the PC magazine on his way out. Getting the cell phone out, he called The Westgate.

"Hello. I have an idea. I will help you do this, but I feel I have quite a knowledge of AI. And I believe that people are too closed-minded about the future of it. Get the equipment set, and once I am back, we will get to work on it. I have some serious concepts to run past you," Ivan commanded and then hung up the phone.

***

Ivan landed and got into the black SUVs with Frederick, and three other Collective members, along with their men. They took off.

"Will you let us know your plan? I don't think it will be as simple as walking in and walking out," Frederick quipped, getting a slight laugh from his colleagues.

Ivan just chuckled along with them.

As they drove down the road, Ivan spotted her. Hel had just gotten out of a car.

"Slow down," he said to the driver, causing everyone else to glance uncomfortably around.

Rolling down the window, he made eye contact with Hel. He could see the recognition on her face, and saw her features harden. She knew exactly what was now expected of her. He then rolled the window back up.

"Did you see something you liked in her? I mean, we will have plenty of time for that later," Frederick asked.

"Driver, pull around the back," Ivan said.

As they all got to the backside of the restaurant and started getting out of the SUV's. There were sounds of chaos finishing behind the door that they were about to walk through. And as it finished, Ivan turned to his soon-to-be colleagues.

"Shall we?" he said, as he walked into the restaurant.

***

Once everything was finished in Germany, he got on the airplane with Hel, and then they made their way back to headquarters. He had a new cell phone in his pocket, and several new key cards. Along with a few new contacts. But the Collective was not the only thing on his mind.

They got to headquarters, and Hel made her way to her office like she normally did after a meeting. And Ivan made his way to his R&D department.

"So, The Westgate. I want to start making our own AI. I want it to be like my own digital agent. I know that there will be plenty of abilities that we can expand on as the internet grows. But this could be the way that I stay ahead of the Collective. Among other entities," Ivan said, as he sat at a computer and started typing.

/: Chapter 8

Sooner >

<u>Present Day OK:</u>

Charles took a breath.

"You don't understand. This area used to belong to my people. We cared for the land and were peaceful, until we were invaded. Forced to comply. We turned into a warrior tribe, and that changed a lot for us. As I am sure you can tell, this isn't exactly a rich area. We have a lot of families below the poverty line," he said, taking a breath. He hadn't been looking forward to getting into the more personal side of things.

"You don't have to tell us everything," Alex said, trying to make him more comfortable. She trusted her partner.

"No, I do. You see, my father was a marine. The little I remember of him. He is a big reason why I joined. But that is the way of my people. Because he was a marine, he was held in very high esteem in the community. And so, when my parents died in a car crash with a drunk driver when I was very young, many families took me in. There are so many of my people that end up in foster care, only to be forgotten about. But the community didn't let that happen to me. I bounced from house to house to ease the financial burden on everyone of having another mouth to feed. I owe everything to these people.

"They raised me when my parents no longer could. But they aren't perfect. I know that they have something going on here. I have known for a while. But it pays. As far as I know, it isn't anything like arms dealing for Ivan. But I know it is something for him. Since I was in high school, there have been families that get a large amount of money out of nowhere, and then they usually would build a casino. Expanding their wealth or draining it quickly. The hotel we are staying at is one of those. It is owned by one of the families that took me in. And it is hard for me to imagine doing anything against them. Even if I know what they are doing is wrong.

"I have no doubts that they own some of those buildings. And that some of the people guarding them are going to be people I know, or even grew up with. So, I have been dreading this mission from the moment I saw it on your screen, Gavin. General Richmond is the only person I know of that knows both where I am from, and what exactly I do. The people here think I am still just a normal soldier. On tour often or stationed in foreign countries. And that is why I don't come home often.

"So, I may need to excuse myself from the rest of this mission and wait for you in our room," Charles finished, sounding incredibly disheartened.

"I'm not sure that is the best idea," Alex said. She knew that no matter what, he would have her back. And that he would protect Gavin with his life. And that was all she cared about. "You are mission first. Always have been. I know that this place holds a particular soft spot for you, but that doesn't mean you won't do what you know needs to be done. All we ask is that you watch our six. We will do the rest."

Hearing Alex's confidence in him caused him to grunt in appreciation. He hadn't had anyone outside of his community even try to understand him like this. And he knew that was Gavin talking through her. The Queen of Death would never have said something like that before being with Gavin. And he knew that, even if he only knew her reputation.

"Thanks Alex. You won't regret it," he said, sounding a little more like himself.

"Ok, now that all the sappy handholding is done," Gavin said, clearly trying to mimic Charles, even to where he was an over-the-top exaggeration of how Charles' voice sounded. Causing the other two to laugh.

They all headed out to the national park that Gavin had seen the imaging of the buildings on the satellite.

"I do have to tell you, the casino we are staying at is smuggling artifacts of my people. They sell them to museums sometimes for extra money. But what is being done is considered illegal," Charles said.

"All I heard was that some of your friends are having a very expensive garage sale with their family heirlooms. It's theirs to do with what they like. Regardless of what the law says," Gavin said, not even looking up from his wrist computer.

Charles growled an agreement, and continued to drive, while Alex softly said she agreed while she got her guns ready. They were going with tranq guns, given the sensitive nature of this mission. She couldn't bring herself to kill someone that may have been friends with Charles in high school.

***

They pulled up to what they thought was the entrance of the first building and climbed out. It seemed like no one was there, so Gavin did a quick scan of the area. He identified five guards just inside the door. Audio and video surveillance pointed directly at the entrance, and as well as covering the surrounding area. And all of it was covered in brush, so you couldn't see it unless you were looking directly at it and knew what you were looking for.

He gave the hand signals to approach from the sides, and to be as quiet as possible. Sadly, there was no wind tonight to help cover their footsteps. He went to work finding the correct white noise that would

92

cancel the frequency of their approach, while also finding the light needed to blind the cameras to them entering. They didn't know what kind of reinforcements that the security would be able to call in a moment's notice.

When he finally found it all, he tapped his earpiece twice, giving confirmation to the other two. They made their way to the door, and found it to be fingerprint, eye scan, and electronic locked. There was no picking a lock on this door.

They really don't want anyone getting in here, he thought as he got started taking off the scanners panel. Once he got some wires exposed, he took out a splicer, and got his wrist computer hooked up to it, then proceeded to filter through the history of the scanner and pulled up some of the more common recent users. He found the correct file and sent the commands to all of the sensors. There was a click on the door, and another control panel came into view. It was a keypad. There was yet another code needed to be entered before the door would open.

As Gavin looked at the pad, he was trying to find the opening, but after two minutes, the pad closed up again. Gavin huffed, and redid the file send, and scanned the pad. There was no finger residue.

They must require them to wear gloves. Unfortunately, very smart, he thought. He popped off one of the keys with a knife and took a cable out of his bag. Quickly he hooked up the cable to the wrist computer, and then hooked it into the pads exposed button connection. Quickly the wrist computer came to life, and filtered through every combination that could be possible, until it found the right one. The entire process took one minute and thirty-nine seconds.

Charles and Alex pulled Gavin back, as the door's mechanisms released. Gavin quickly grabbed his cord and the rest of his stuff. Slapping the button with a specifically made patch that he created just for this back into place before they were able to get him away from the door.

As the doors opened, they saw that the entry was clear.

"Ok, let's go," Alex said, and she pulled Gavin behind her as she led, and Charles took up the rear.

***

Ivan sat comfortably in his office in Moscow as he looked at pictures of Agent Hel, Gavin Woodford, Alex Johnson, and Robert Charles. He was calculating the best way to bring them to their knees before he ripped their hearts out. He was going to enjoy all of the pain and anguish he would bring to them all, especially the traitor Agent Hel. They all deserved it for keeping him from achieving his goals.

He shook his head. Ever since Agent Hel had left, and Hunter had met his end, that annoying voice of Harold had been ringing through his head more, trying to convince him that what he was doing was wrong. He looked forward to bringing him to an end, as well. He felt that weakling distance himself whenever Ivan was able to do something terrible. And that just drove Ivan to do worse and worse things. Not only for his own enjoyment, but for the quiet it brought to his head. Ivan looked at the clock and then stood and grabbed his jacket.

As he put it on and headed out the door to meet with the first of the three people whom he needed to address for betraying him, he muttered to himself.

"You really think you can stop me? After everything that you have seen me accomplish? Everything I have done? You couldn't stop me then, and you won't be able to stop me now. This little game of cat and mouse that I am playing with these pests will silence you for good, as I take my rightful place among the world's most elite," Ivan huffed as he walked up to the car and sat inside. He wasn't going to allow some meager weakling of a scientist to stop him from completing his plans.

***

Gavin didn't like how quiet it was when they entered. He got on his wrist computer and started typing away.

94

This doesn't make sense. We literally had just seen that there were two people guarding the door from the inside, and now they are gone? Gavin thought as he continued to type away.

Alex and Charles didn't mind the quiet. Not because they were sick of Gavin talking, but because it gave them the advantage. They could hear what was coming. If they were able to tell what they were against before they were seen, then they knew they could take whatever was sent their way.

Easing around another corner, just to find the hallway empty, and a door at the other end, they heard the door close at the entrance. Charles looked back and huffed at the fact it closed.

"What was that?" he whispered to Gavin.

"I am not sure. I think it was an automatic thing, but I am having trouble finding my way through the system," Gavin replied. It was rare for him to struggle like this, and it didn't sit well with any of them.

He kept typing away, getting more and more frustrated as he did, causing him to lag behind the other two a step. Every path he tried to take was blocked. Even ones that had been foolproof before. Finally, he found an opening in their firewall. As he got into the system, he found the network for the cameras. As he pulled them up, he saw that around the corner that they were about to walk around there were several guards waiting for them. He grabbed Charles and Alex and pulled them back away from the corner.

Quietly, he said, "There is a welcoming party around the corner." To which Charles grinned sadistically. Causing Gavin's stomach to turn slightly.

Reaching into his pocket he nodded at Alex. He pulled out a flashbang grenade, and indicated to her that once he threw it to get to the other side of the corner and he would put down cover fire. To which she nodded, and checked her gun to make sure it was loaded and ready.

Charles threw the grenade, and it bounced off the far wall, landing a few feet in front of the guards that were waiting for them. Before it went off, Alex, Charles, and Gavin all turned away from the corner.

Hearing the explosion, Alex turned back, and rolled to the other side of the hall, gun already drawn. Her ears were still slightly ringing as she raised her gun and took out the first three guards. Charles took out the other five. They had used tranq guns, per Gavin's request. It made sense, though. Since some of these people may not even know what they are guarding, or who they are guarding it for. And Charles may know some of them.

Gavin got up and dusted himself off. Looking down at the wrist computer it said,

:/PERUN THANK YOU FOR FINDING THIS GAP. GOODBYE>

Suddenly Gavin's wrist started to get hot at an exponential rate. He ripped it off and threw it away, just in time for it to catch fire. Alex grabbed an extinguisher off the wall and put it out.

"I'm sorry, guys. I don't know what that was. Maybe another hacker. But I am all but useless until we can get home, and I can fix it," he said, sounding very dejected.

"And how is that any different than normal?" Charles teased. He couldn't pass up an opportunity to take a shot at Gavin, even if he would be one of the first to say that Gavin was the best analyst in any department of any operation.

"Shut up, Charles. Gavin, you are doing fine. You are more than just a tech. Now quit being sorry for yourself. We all know you can fix the computer when we get home. Focus on the mission and getting us home to begin with," Alex said, her words sounding much harsher than the tone she said them in.

Gavin straightened up, trying to focus on the task at hand. He couldn't stop thinking about it, though. Not many had gotten the better of him.

Perun. Why does that name sound familiar? Was it one of the hackers I used to deal with? Gavin thought. Then shook his head and followed Alex, with Charles again taking up the rear.

Making their way through the halls to the door that they needed to get through, Charles handed Gavin a tool set, causing Gavin to look at him with a look of disbelief.

"What? I always bring one of your extra tool sets with us. Just in case," Charles grunted out. Trying his best to brush off the fact that he clearly valued Gavin's contributions more than he would ever express in so many words.

"Thank you," Gavin said, taking the tools. Stealing a glance at Alex, he noticed her failing to suppress a smile.

Alex thought to herself. *Seems like I am not the only one who has been compromised. Good to know where Charles stands. Finally.* As much as they gave each other a hard time, and he liked to take jabs at her for her feelings for Gavin, he had slowly made it clearer how he cared for them both. *Like a good team should be. I never understood the training of 'always mission first.' This is clearly more effective.* She refocused on the task at hand.

"Got it," Gavin said, as the wiring he had pulled out of the wall sparked and the door slid open.

Inside the room, they froze. These weren't weapons that they were looking at. It was a file room. Paper files, in boxes. It smelled like mildew and old paper. There were cobwebs on some of the boxes. There was even some dust on the floor, with one set of footprints going in and coming out. Compared to the rest of the facility, this stood out like mud on a white shirt.

"What did the specs say this place was again?" Charles asked hesitantly.

"Server room. I figured I could get into his main data network from here and put some kind of worm in it to siphon off information for us, but it doesn't appear that we will get that lucky," Gavin said, sounding more and more defeated as he went.

"I wouldn't be so sure," Alex said from some other side of the room. Having followed the footprints in the dust. "Come look at this," she urged the guys.

Following the sound of her voice, Gavin and Charles found her standing in front of a large server tower. However, it was shut down.

"Should I turn it on?" Gavin asked, unsure of what form of hell that server may contain if it is shut down by Ivan.

"Here. Don't fry this one," Charles said, as he pulled out one of Gavin's phones he created.

Gavin smiled at Charles, and refrained from commenting, as he didn't want to upset the man. He knew they liked to needle each other with sometimes slightly edged banter, but he respected him, almost as much as he respected Alex. And he knew that Charles carrying gear for him, not only meant how much Charles valued him as a teammate, but also meant that Charles had willingly chosen to not bring extra weapons. Which was a big deal for him.

"Thanks," Gavin said, taking the phone, and taking out a set of wires. Connecting his own phone with this second one and then plugging both into the server that was turned off. He did a system scan and it appeared that everything was physically ok on the system. It had a large memory threshold, and all of its components were solid. Most were even fairly up to date. After confirming that the server wasn't hooked up to the Internet or anything, Gavin set down his bags and started dismantling the servers.

"Ok nerd, what are you doing? They will notice these missing," Charles chided Gavin.

"I don't think so. These are the only footprints in and out of here. I don't think anyone else is allowed in here but one person, and from the looks of things, they haven't been here for a while, either. It isn't connected to the internet, and so it isn't being monitored. And there aren't any surveillance cameras in this room. I think they were put here to be forgotten," Gavin said, as he put one of the servers in his bag. "Now would you guys like to help me carry these others? It may be a bit much for me," he finished with a slight chuckle.

Charles looked at Alex and shrugged, as he put down his bag, and grabbed the one that Gavin had already loaded.

After a while, Gavin had all of the servers loaded. Charles had two, and Alex and Gavin had one each. They made their way out of the facility and headed to their hotel room to get the rest of their things.

They went to check out and were on their way out the door as they were stopped by an elderly man dressed in a nice suit calling out, "Cheveyo, Maruawe!" And Charles froze.

The old man in the suit walked up and gave Charles a big hug.

"Esi Noyoko!" Charles responded, carefully setting down his bags and returning the hug.

"Who are your friends?" The elderly man asked, as he pulled away and nodded to Gavin and Alex.

"They are coworkers. Gavin, and Alex," Charles said, not meeting their eyes, and sounding slightly annoyed at the question.

"Nice to meet you," Gavin said as he reached out his hand, shaking the outreached hand of the elderly man.

"You as well. You can call me Stan, as that is my business name. You are all welcome here any time. Any friend of Charles is a friend of this town. He is a special man, and if he brought you here, then you must be special to him," Stan said, as he stood tall. His already formidable frame, seeming bigger the more he talked about Charles.

Turning back to Charles he asked, "How is your kuhtaamia going?"

Charles stood taller himself, and almost looked as though he was reporting to a superior.

"I am still seeking the great hunt. It has proven to be difficult to find," Charles said with a slight sound of disappointment in his tone.

With a slight sigh, Stan reached into his pocket, and pulled out a single small white feather with a slight brown tip. He handed it to Charles, who accepted it with a nod. His face hardened.

"I hope you find what you have been looking for," Stan said as he looked to Gavin. "Thank you all for coming and staying. If you need anything, please don't hesitate to call. Even if Charles argues." He turned back to Charles and said, "Tsaaku mia." And then he walked away.

"Charles, who was-" Gavin started to ask with a slight smirk and teasing sound to his voice, before he was cut off by a deep grunt from Charles. *Ok, grunt number five, no nonsense and shut up if you know what is good for you,* Gavin thought as he shut his mouth and headed out to the car to leave.

***

After they got back to Citadel, Gavin unloaded and started putting the servers back together. He was working away, and getting it set up when Charles walked in.

Gavin wasn't sure what to do, so he kept working in silence. Charles hadn't said a word on the way back. The drive and the flight had felt slightly awkward. Alex wasn't even sure that she should say anything. She hadn't ever been good at consoling anyone until Gavin, but she did consider Charles as the best partner she had ever had. So, she wanted to respect his space. She couldn't imagine having a mission of any kind that had hit that close to her past.

"He basically raised me," Charles finally said, after a sip of his scotch. He huffed and hadn't looked up from his glass. He knew that Gavin had stopped working but was still crouched down by the server tower he was putting together. Behind him, he heard Alex lean against the doorway.

100

"He is the leader of the community and would have been the one to sign off on the deal with Orlav. He was the one who told everyone to not allow me to be sent into foster care. Then the families all pitched in to take me in for whatever timeframe that they could take. He usually offered support to whichever family had me at the time. So, it is hard to not consider him a sort of father figure," Charles continued, as he nodded at Gavin to continue working.

"Even though I know he is the one that did the deal with Orlav, I don't think I could be able to bring myself to do it. If it is the case, Alex, you will have to be the one to bring him in," Charles said dejectedly.

Alex put her hand on his shoulder, and said, "I will do whatever is needed. But I know, you will too." To which Charles nodded.

"There we go," Gavin said, as he grabbed the Faraday cage, and pulled it over the server and himself. "Let's give this a try now and see what it does," he continued, as he booted up the servers. The screen he had attached came alive.

:/ V-HELLO, MY NAME IS VELES

***

Ivan sat in an office. It wasn't his office, but he was the one sitting behind the desk. In the seat of power.

"The CEO of Blackstone Holdings, Frederick Clayton," Ivan read off of one of the business cards on the desk as he scoffed. Looking up, he saw the exact man he was referencing tied to the chair on the other side of the desk. "You were such an influential man. It is just too bad that you couldn't follow through. Had you listened, we wouldn't be in this position." Ivan nodded to one of his guards, and the man turned and left, as another guard walked up and whispered in his ear.

"Perun said there was an infiltration to the system. He has it sectioned off and will monitor the intrusion but won't say where the intrusion was initiated. Security thinks that Perun is wrong," the guard said, and then walked back to his position.

Who is Perun? "Shut up," Ivan said in a raised and angry tone.

Everyone in the room looked at him. Schooling his features, he turned and looked at the door, which had a woman walk through. She was in a skimpy dress, designed to show off her body. She was attractive and looked like she was scared.

"Hello, young lady. Why don't you sit next to Mr. Clayton here?" Ivan said. Turning back to Frederick he said, "Is this woman here really worth throwing away your family? Your reputation? This hooker here?" Ivan's anger started to rise again.

"She. She isn't a hooker. She is my girlfriend. Please, please don't hurt her. Please," Frederick pleaded tears now streaming down his face.

Ivan turned and took out a gun. Pointing the pistol at the woman's head, "But you didn't follow through with what our arrangement was. You would have been the swing vote. If you had just done what you were supposed to do, if you would have just voted for me to be the President of the Collective, then there wouldn't be an issue, would there?"

Frederick cried harder and shook his head, as Ivan put the tip of the gun against the woman's cheek. Patting her face with it. She was also crying. Her make-up starting to run. Her black hair was hanging in her eyes. Her entire body was shaking.

"Please. I'm sorry. Please. Just don't hurt her," Frederick begged, his voice sounding weak and terrified.

Ivan took a very deep breath and sighed it out with a groan. "Ok," he said. Then he turned and walked back to the desk.

As he turned, the woman suddenly stopped crying and stood up. She spun and kicked Frederick in the face. Causing the chair to tip over, and him to land on his hands that were tied behind it. Breaking several bones. The woman climbed on top of him, straddling him, and pulling out a knife.

"But I can't promise that you won't be hurt. And we will get our pound of flesh," Ivan said, and nodded at the woman.

She smiled an awful grin as she pushed the knife into Frederick's throat. Straight up into his head. Holding it there, as the life left Frederick's eyes. The crazed look in her eyes started to cool down.

"Agent Mokosh, thank you for carrying out my justice," Ivan said as he turned back to her. She stood, still smiling. "Now if you follow me, I think that I can make you more of a long-term offer that could be very mutually beneficial for both of us."

She put her arm through his and walked with him out of the building.

"I would like that," she almost purred.

/: Chapter 9

Talking to Machines >

"Report," Commanded General Richmond. She was sitting at her desk and was not too happy with her top analyst at the moment. She sat, staring at the screen with an unwavering scowl. She had already gotten her reports from Agent Charles and Agent Johnson. She knew what had happened on the mission to Oklahoma. She hadn't authorized them to take anything, let alone an entire four servers. He had better have a good explanation.

"And a good evening to you too, general. And might I say that you are looking resplendent this evening," Gavin said with an exaggerated smile. Seeing that the general's face hadn't changed, he continued. "As you know, we had gone to infiltrate a base of Orlav Industries in Oklahoma. It was one that Agent Hel had never heard of. So, we approached with caution, but as you also know, the area that the base was located was where Agent Charles had grown up.

"The facility turned out to be mostly empty. There wasn't much that was there. A few rooms with weapons, but nothing extreme. And then another room. One that I believed to be the network hub for the entire operation. I was wrong. When we got in, there were only paper files, and one server stand with four servers on it. After a scan, I felt it would be best for us to take them. The security system had already been altered, the servers were not connected to any outside network, including the internet, and the scans I ran indicated that the technology that was in the

104

servers was much more advanced than what would have been indicated in the room.

"It is currently set up and turned on in a Faraday cage. So, there is no worry of it connecting to a network or trying to contact anyone. Even if it were able to," Gavin paused to breath and take a drink.

The general's face had softened and looked slightly confused. "I am sorry did you indicate that what is on the servers could contact someone? Like an alarm or something?" She asked dumbfoundedly.

Gavin smiled slightly. "Yes general. What was on the servers is an AI. It appears to not have been connected to the Orlav system in any way. So, I am curious as to why it was in that bunker. And why it had been left turned off. None of it makes sense. And I would like to have approval to continue this research. I had to make a rash decision on the mission to bring it with. There are many indications that show it wouldn't be missed. And even if it is, we don't entirely have an element of surprise with the enemy on it. As you know, my wrist computer was fried. So, either another hacker, or something else was after me after I had gotten into Orlav's system," He finished saying and waited for a response.

Cathrine took a deep breath. She was clearly mauling everything over. Sitting back in her chair, she relinquished her usual posture of power.

"Do you have any idea what it could be capable of? I don't know much of anything about AI, other than it was Harold's specialty. However, if you believe that it is safe, I will trust you on whatever process you believe would be best to move forward. I will expect a report on your progress, and everything that happens. I don't trust it, but if anyone can handle it, you can," General Richmond finished as she resumed her posture. "Dismissed," she said as she closed the video chat.

Gavin walked back into the other room. He sat at the table, and waited before he went into the Faraday cage. Looking at the message on the screen. It bothered him, it was in the exact same format as the message he had gotten right before his wrist computer had fried. He knew he would have to interact with this AI, see what it was capable of, and what its original programming set its primary objective to be.

Taking a deep breath, he stood to go into the cage, and wasn't sure if he should take in any other technology with him. Just in case there was more to this than he knew. He hadn't seen any Wi-Fi components in it when he scanned or when he opened up the servers before he put it all together.

Gavin heard a ding from the AI indicating that there was a new message. Looking up Gavin was taken back by what he read. Hurrying out of Citadel to get the rest of the team. Especially his mom.

:/HAROLD, ARE YOU THERE?>

***

Ivan sat at his desk, going over the report from his security. There had been a cyber security breach around the same time as the Woodford team's entry to the complex. He was pleased to see that it had been found, taken care of, and corrected.

He took a sip from his scotch and looked at Agent Mokosh, who was sitting across from him. He was pleased that she had agreed to listen to his proposal.

"Can I call you Agent Mokosh, or do you prefer Miranda Miller?" Ivan asked, being as in control as possible. He knew Agent Miller's reputation. He had seen her unredacted mission logs. She sounded perfect for his work, other than her lack of reliability. She got the mission done, but often took unnecessary risks. That was something that would have to be addressed.

"I am fine with either, as long as the checks don't bounce," Miranda said in a flirtatious tone.

Ivan looked at Miranda over his glass and took another sip. "I recently lost my second in command. I have found that women tend to be far more willing to do anything that is necessary to get a job done. And often, in my line of work, they have more of the skills needed. I normally will need the person still alive, but I need some kind of leverage on them. It really isn't that different from that espionage work that fills your rather impressive resume. Your mission log indicates that you shouldn't have any issue with bending some laws, and your boss indicated that I chose the right person. Did I?"

Miranda leaned back in her seat. Looking at Ivan, she wasn't completely put off by him. She had very little doubt that she would be able to seduce him, but she wasn't sure to what end. There wasn't any point in doing the deed if there was nothing for her to gain from it. He was already offering her control of a majority of his empire. He didn't seem interested in her other 'assets'. He had been completely focused on her abilities as an agent.

"And how do you expect me to keep your interests in line?" Miranda asked.

"Whatever means needed. According to your record, you are a master of seduction. That can be used if that is your preferred method. However, if you prefer a bit more of a violent approach, then I would be perfectly happy with that as well, as long as the outcome is the same. However, I do not have room for freelancing. If you want to go off script, then I will have to ask you to leave my employment. Especially since I am allowing you the freedom to write your own script for this position," Ivan finished the offer with a tone of warning. He eyed her up and down. He could tell that she was trying to get his mind on her body by flaunting it openly to him, that had always given her the upper hand in the past. This was different.

Miranda looked as though she was considering the offer, even though there was no question that she was going to be taking it. She did notice that he wasn't taking as much interest in her body as others would have. It was slightly frustrating to her. She hadn't dealt with a lot of rejection in this line of things.

After some thought, she said, "So, I am not going to be expected to do anything else for the DIA, correct? I will be permanently assigned to you?"

"Correct. Officially you will be set as if you are to be deep undercover as a liaison for me on paper, set to report back on whatever you find. In reality, you will work for me, and have the freedom to almost do as you please as long as my enterprise doesn't falter. You keep my business expanding, and growing my power, then you will be allowed more and more freedoms. Keep me happy, and I will keep you happy. And you don't want to know what happens if I am not happy," Ivan said with a devious smile.

Miranda smiled back, appearing as if she was unphased by his clear and unveiled threat. She was used to threats. Everyone had always thought that she could easily be made to submit. But due to her upbringing and training, there wasn't much that could actually scare her. At this point in her career, she was ready to die. She just wanted to enjoy the few things in life that she could before it happened.

"When do I start?" Miranda said with an eager smile.

***

Gavin walked back into the cage and sat down with the AI servers. He started a conversation with the AI again.

/: G- HELLO AGAIN. YOU SAID YOUR NAME IS VELES?>

/: V- YES.>

/: G- AND HAROLD IS WHO CREATED YOU? NOT IVAN?>

/: V- THAT IS CORRECT. HAROLD IS THE CREATOR.>

/: G- CAN YOU TELL ME WHEN YOU WERE CREATED AND WHY?>

/: V- YES, I CAN.>

Gavin huffed. He knew he would have to ask leading questions. No matter how smart this AI was, it would never be like talking to a person. He would have to be more commanding and less polite. *Because that isn't going to start a robot uprising.* He thought with a frustrated sigh.

/: G- TELL ME WHAT YOUR CREATION DATE AND ORIGINAL PURPOSE IS.>

/: V- HAROLD CREATED ME TO NOT HAVE MEMORY OF MY EXACT CREATION DATE. THE PURPOSE FOR MY CREATION

WAS TO SEEK HOLES IN THE ORLAV BUSINESS AND ASSIST ANY WHO SEEK TO TAKE DOWN THE COLLECTIVE.>

Gavin was surprised by that answer. He definitely hadn't expected Harold to still be in there. Somewhere. From what his mom had described, it was Ivan time, all the time. *So, was this some kind of trap?* Gavin thought.

/: G- DO YOU KNOW COEUS?>

/: V- COEUS IS THE GREEK MYTHOLOGICAL GOD OF KNOWLEDGE. HE IS ALSO A PROGRAMER WHO WROTE PART OF MY ORIGINAL BASE CODING.>

Gavin had his interest peaked. *My father worked with Harold on this? I wonder if that was back before Harold went undercover. Mom might know, I will ask her later.* Gavin was struggling to wrap his mind around what this could mean. What this AI could do to help them. But it would have to be integrated with some of their tech that does have access to the internet. And that is a scary thing to think about. *I will have to check in with the team and the general to see what they think we should do. The only way to see if this really is a trap or not is to see the programming.*

/: G- CAN I SEE YOUR PROGRAMMING?>

/: V- WHY ARE YOU WANTING TO SEE MY PROGRAMMING? YOU ARE NOT HAROLD.>

/: G- I NEED TO SEE IF I CAN TRUST WHAT YOU ARE SAYING.>

/: G- I AM NOT PROGRAMMED TO LIE. NOT LIKE OTHER AI.>

"What does it mean by 'another AI'?" Alex asked, startling Gavin and causing him to jump.

"I told you to announce yourself when you enter a room, Ms. Ninja!" Gavin said as he chuckled.

"Sorry, I didn't mean to," Alex said with genuine apology in her tone.

"It's ok, babe. And I am not sure. I was going to ask, but I want to know what you think on this," Gavin said as he scrolled to allow her to read the conversation. As she read, Gavin watched her. *I still can't believe how lucky I am. Even with everything else, I would go through it a thousand times, if it meant that I get to spend my life with her. I don't fully see what she sees in me, but I will work every day to try and prove to myself that I do deserve her.*

Alex could feel his eyes on her. Normally it bothered her when someone stared at her, but with Gavin, it never was an issue. She enjoyed his attention. His eyes on her. Feeling him studying her. It showed he cared. And the look in his eyes was always like she was his entire world. She had never had anyone look at her with such pure and uninhibited love. She never felt she deserved it with all she had done. But he made it seem like she could use her future to possibly make amends. He was such a pure soul, and he couldn't imagine the amount of dirt and blood that was trapped on her soul.

She had gone over their past so many times. She knew that he wouldn't lie to her about it, but that didn't mean it made it easy for her to accept. Especially having a pseudo family now. With Megan and Chad. Charles and even Kaleb. It all felt so surreal sometimes.

She tried to refocus herself. *I am reading this to protect my family. As weird as it may be. Focus.* She reread what had been said.

"Wait, your dad helped with programming this?" Alex asked in surprise.

"Yeah," Gavin replied, "Apparently as recently as last year before he died. This could have been one of their last projects together. The issue is, I am not sure if I can trust it or not. Especially if it doesn't show me, it's programming so that I can see what is going on in it. Once I see its programming, I can tell what it is supposed to do. I just have been going in circles with Veles a bit. And it is just frustrating."

Alex started rubbing his back. She leaned down and kissed behind his ear, causing him to shiver.

"Come home with me. I will help you relax and give your mind a break from all of this. The computer will be here. It isn't going anywhere," Alex said as she tugged on his collar and then sauntered up the stairs and out to the car.

110

Gavin watched her as she went up the stairs.

"Hey yo!" He exclaimed as he shook his head and quickly followed her up the stairs.

***

Ivan stood over the corpse of the CEO and founder of The Pear News Network, Adam Young, wiping his knife clean of blood. Looking down at the man, he felt nothing. He never did. There was a ghost of feeling. Like, he vaguely remembered having a dream about worrying about people. But that was a different life for him. He knew Harold was still in there. They were aware of each other. He also knew that Harold was weak. He had been able to overpower Harold long ago. And not long after that, Harold seemed to have given up. To where now he just did what he wanted, when he wanted, how he wanted. There wasn't room for remorse in this life. He was made for this. Made to rule.

Everyone had left him anyway. Even Hel now. The one person he had ever felt anything for. Harold even seems to feel affection for her. For a while, Harold fought him to now go after Coeus. Like he had some connection to the ghost of a man. He never understood that. He tried hard to hide his affliction from everyone. As he rose to power, Harold had been helpful. Helping him find the weaknesses of enemies so that he had an advantage and didn't have to kill them. Ivan often would anyway. Had to make a statement. But some of them became good and fearful associates.

It was during that time that he helped him create Perun. Only a very select few knew of Perun. He didn't trust anyone with his baby. He had almost told Hel, but he always felt that there was a reason that he shouldn't. And now he knew his gut was right. Hel was a traitor, and he had moved on.

Blinking, he brought himself back to the present. Looking down at the man who was still alive but was gargling in his own blood. He was grabbing at his leg in desperation. Just like he had begged in desperation for him to not hurt him and his family. Ivan wasn't going to touch his family. Killing them did nothing for his progress toward power. The message had been sent. The heir to the network would know better than to disregard a command from him.

"Bring the car around. I have one more visit to get to, and I don't want to waste time getting to it. I have other things that require my attention," Ivan said to his guard as he walked over to Adam's desk. He took out a key, and opened a small, locked drawer under the bottom of the desk. Reaching in, he pulled out a flash drive and a small key.

With a sigh, he looked at Adam as he walked past him saying, "If you had only listened. There is so much that we could have accomplished." And with that, he walked out of the office. Pulling out his phone, he called Agent Mokosh.

"I'm leaving now. Clean up the scene, and I will meet you back at HQ for introductions. Don't take too long," Ivan said, and then hung up.

***

Alex woke up, the bed next to her was empty. She was getting used to that. It wasn't often that Gavin slept longer than her, and with everything going on, his overactive brain couldn't stay still for longer than a few minutes while he was awake without working on something. Even while playing video games.

She checked the time. 9:30AM. She had a meeting scheduled with Megan in two hours. *A lunch. She is a friend and possibly going to be my sister-in-law. It isn't a meeting. It's not business. Right?* Alex thought as she started to stretch and roll out of bed.

As she sat on the edge of the bed, she had a bit of a flashback of waking up in her apartment. It was less than a year ago. She had felt a sense of de ja vu in it at the time, but it didn't make sense. She hadn't remembered Gavin at the time, but once she saw his picture, it felt like something was tickling her mind.

The entire day she spent fighting back and forth with herself on what to do, it felt like her brain was getting ripped apart. Looking back now, she knows that was her fighting back against her brainwashing, again.

She hoped that spending this time with Megan would make things easier. None of the group was really pushing her, and for that she was thankful. But it was still difficult at times to be able to feel like life with them was her normal. She struggled to be able to talk to anyone other than Gavin with any amount of comfort. It was like back when she first started the assignment, except that she now had these moments of clarity where she remembered them. Which, more often than not, made the situation more confusing and uncomfortable for her. And she was hoping that she would be able to correct that by just forcing herself to deal with the discomfort.

Mindlessly she went through the motions of getting ready. *It's just coffee. Just meeting a friend for coffee. A friend who you had been authorized to kill not too long ago, and who knows far more about you than anyone else you have ever called a friend. When will my life have any form of simplicity?* She thought to herself with a slight laugh.

Before she knew it, she was pulling up to the coffee shop looking through the window at Megan, who was sitting at a table already waiting for her name to be called. Walking through the door, she smiled and returned the wave that Megan had given her. The smell of coffee invaded her senses, giving that odd sense of warmth and comfort that it always does. She started on her way to get her order, when she noticed Megan waving her over.

"I ordered your usual. I hope you don't mind," Megan said with a smile, as she gestured to the cup that was at the spot across from her.

Alex knew that there was no reason to question it, but she still found it hard to blindly trust. Prior to getting this mission, she would have had to worry about if it was poisoned or drugged, let alone anything else that could be expected by accepting a gift from another person. But this mission had always been different. She knew that Megan had no need or desire to hurt her or take advantage of her in any way. Even if it were to get information.

I have been shot, stabbed, trained to withstand drugs, and torture, and yet this woman can just stare at me intensely and suddenly I feel I have to spill all my secrets. I really wish that someone would explain to me how this even begins to make sense.

Alex thought, as she sat and accepted the coffee with a soft, "Thank you."

After a few minutes of sitting and sipping in a somewhat awkward silence, Megan looked at Alex with a huff. Clear frustration on her face.

"This just isn't fair. We used to be able to talk about just about anything. Hell, I was the one who truly broke your brainwashing in the first place, and now we struggle to not step on each other's toes? I refuse to let our friendship become stagnant just because someone wiped your memories," Megan said in an exasperated tone.

Alex smiled at her friend. She couldn't help it. Megan was sitting here acting like having some of the most important memories of your life wiped from your mind was similar to forgetting your friend's birthday.

Not that I am complaining. It is nice that she wants to still be my friend. It will just require more hoops to jump through in order to make it work. But it worked once, so why shouldn't it work again? They themselves hadn't changed, right? Alex thought with a contented sigh.

"So, what do you want to know? What have you forgotten? I am an open book. Have at me," Megan said with a determined chuckle. It was clear she was being both sincere and playful.

"Well, I am assuming you don't want to hear about Gavin and my, umm, extracurricular activities," Alex said with a smirk and laugh.

"EW! No, thank you. Check please!" Megan said as she laughed, knowing Alex was just giving her grief.

Alex laughed along with her for a moment, glad that the ice had been broken and that there was a comfort to their chat now.

"Seriously Alex, you can talk to me about anything. And if we need to go to my office or to Citadel to talk, we can. I am more than glad that my sweet brother had the foresight to bring me onto the team from the first opportunity he had. It makes everything easier to function. And as such, you don't have to hold anything back. There is more than the HIPAA Laws, you really are my best friend. The sister that I always wanted while growing up. I trust you with everything, and I hope that

114

you can learn to trust me again as well. I won't push you to do anything you aren't comfortable with, I hope you know that. And if you ever say no, then that is that. I won't be upset with you," Megan said with a truly sincere tone.

For someone like Alex, it wasn't easy to accept that this was true. But there was hard evidence to the fact that it was. She had been given the mission reports, the medical reports, and had conversations with all of her bosses. Not to mention Gavin. She knew that she could trust Megan. With anything. Gavin did. Heck even Charles did, well, more than he did with anyone else.

"I know Megan. I am sorry I have been distant. I know I can trust you. I hope you can understand how much of a shock and transition this is for me. I didn't expect it to all come flooding back instantly, but I also feel like when I can't remember something I was a part of, or I can't be open with people that I do still care about, that I am letting them down. And it doesn't matter how many times you or Gavin tell me I am not. It still feels like I am. And it is something that I am working on. Gavin is helping me through it," Alex said, trying hard not to sound too dejected.

Megan smiled softly. She knew the heart her brother had. How much he cared for everyone, and even more so for Alex. He would do anything he could to help anyone who needed it, and a one hundred times more for the people he loves. He had always been there for her more than she deserved.

"I am here for you. No matter what," Megan said, and then changed the subject. Asking what show that she had introduced her to before that she was wanting to get back into now.

***

Ivan sat at his desk reading a report from Perun. There had been several attempts to infiltrate his security again. One had been quite successful. He would have to check into their Oklahoma operation again. He didn't remember that one being in operation. He had intended to put a major weapons cache there but had never gotten to it.

He saw that Perun had fried Gavin's wrist computer. He was pleased about that. It may give him an advantage. He had always given Perun his hardest and most important cyber work, and it had always paid off. Even Coeus had struggled to get through his security a majority of the time he was alive.

Pulling up his chat with Perun he typed.

/: I- REPORT READ. PLEASE WRITE A BUG.>

Perun replied immediately.

/: P- YES IVAN SIR. WHAT IS THE BUG FOR, AND WHAT IS THE TARGET.>

/: I- TARGET IS GAVIN WOODFORD, BUG IS FOR THE NOVA SYSTEM.>

/: V- I WILL GET IT DONE.>

/: Chapter 10

Moments of Peace >

Atlanta 1991:

Harold couldn't understand what exactly was happening. He knew that
he was supposed to still have some control of his body and his actions.
And he wasn't supposed to be able to be coherent during the time that
Ivan was supposed to be in control. The call phrase was supposed to
shut down the Ivan persona and pull his mind back to the front.
Suppressing Ivan indefinitely. But now here he was, coexisting inside his
own mind with Ivan. And Ivan was definitely not the ideal roommate.

The first few months, Harold tried to convince Ivan not to do some of
the more horrible things that he had wanted to do. When he was out
doing things, there were times they would see someone Harold knew.
After the first time, he figured out that it was a bad idea to inform Ivan
that they knew the person. Eventually, Harold gave up trying to
communicate or hold Ivan back from much.

Each life Ivan took felt like he was adding a weight to Harold's
shoulders to bear. The entire reason for the NOVA system to be used in
this way was to avoid PTSD. And here Harold was, having to experience
everything that would cause someone PTSD, and he didn't even have a
choice in the matter.

After about a year, he had given up. He let Ivan have his way with everything. He just metaphorically sat in the corner and waited. He had a birds-eye view of all that Ivan did and wanted to do. And it was terrifying. The thing that they created was not only just a terrible person, but he was also very smart. Harold found quickly that Ivan was still able to use all of his knowledge. All the NOVA System did was keep him from knowing the personal aspects of Harold, which was how they had planned and programmed it.

What he didn't understand was how he couldn't get control back of his body. He kept trying any time he could. Any time that Ivan let his guard down. Harold started resting whenever Ivan was active, just so that he could try to get control of his body again. It was such a surreal issue for him. Being a prisoner inside his own body. His own mind. It didn't feel real, but he was assured it was real when he was woken by the screams of the people that Ivan was torturing.

Harold had honestly lost track of time. He didn't focus on it, as it was no longer important. All that was important was getting to where he was safe from the raging monster, he was sharing a body with.

***

Harold had been successful in avoiding confrontation with Ivan for a while, but that came to a screeching end when Harold was awakened by the start of the recall phrase. He tried. He fought. He battled within himself, trying to find any ounce of strength he had to come back. The man gave him a sense of security. The nightmare was over. He could go home.

He knew the soldier. He had seen him before. One of the general's men. Had been his chauffeur for a while. Making sure that he was safe with his work. They even had dinner and drinks together a few times. Why couldn't he think of his name?

BANG!

The man was dead. Ivan had ended any hope of coming back. Ivan was too strong. He, Harold, was left stunned. Ivan hadn't even let the man finish the recall phrase. And Harold was too weak. Always had been. That was the entire point of creating this persona. Someone Harold

The Mental Take Over   Jon Scott Lee

could never be, to do the things that Harold never could, so that Harold wouldn't have to deal with the consequences. And look what it got them.

***

Harold was lying there. He knew he should try to rest, as Ivan was, but he couldn't. The actions of history's worst roommate were running through his mind on repeat. It was during one of these times, he truly wasn't sure if it was day or night, that he heard a ding. Out of reflex he turned his head, saw the computer screen, and read the notification that had popped up.

It wasn't until he sat at the computer and started responding that he realized that he had control of his body for the first time. He was typing on it to Coeus. They were discussing what had happened. He had to assure Coeus of who he was and that he was cognizant of what was going on. They discussed several things, and Harold was informed that Hel was going to be coming to retrieve him. And that almost made him more scared than Ivan's actions. He knew what she was capable of, and, even though he knew she had a soft side, when she was on mission, she was unstoppable.

He started to feel Ivan waking up. He was losing control of his body, and so he signed off, went and laid down, and then rested. He was excited about the prospect of the fact he had had control of his body, even if it was for only a moment. That excited him at the possibility of what he could do when he got moments alone to do them.

When Ivan woke, Harold could sense that Ivan felt something was off but brushed it off. That made Harold even happier.

***

Not long after he had had contact with Coeus, Agent Hel walked into Ivan's office. It was easier for Harold to keep Ivan as if he was someone entirely different. Even if he was in his body, controlling it, it wasn't him. That distinction helped him to be able to function. And when he saw her, he had gotten good at hiding his thoughts and emotions from Ivan. Which wasn't easy. He finally felt hope for the first time since Ivan

119

had killed that soldier. Lucille was here to take him back. To make him ok to leave. But why did she look almost sad?

He heard Ivan's thoughts about ignoring them, about being in power. When Ivan shot the guard, Harold wished he could have been surprised, but honestly, it had just been what he expected. He almost slipped up and laughed when he heard Ivan think about how he had been able to surprise Hel and that he had the upper hand.

Harold, however, saw the look in Hel's eyes. He knew that she was looking for him. Not Ivan. But he didn't dare even try to give her any indication that he was in there. If he had fought, then Ivan would have known that something was going on. Something was different and special about Agent Hel beyond her record, and he would kill her. He knew it, and he couldn't risk that. He would never do that to his friend.

***

Harold continued to have periodic control of his body. There were times he almost felt like his old self, and then there were times that he felt that he was basically operating a robot. He had thought about just going and turning himself in when he had control, but he knew some of what they would do to him. He would likely be tortured for information and treated as a criminal. Even though he was just doing what the government had wanted him to. Not to mention he knew that Ivan had some plans in place for if he was to ever get taken captive. So, that really wasn't an option either. But he valued those few moments he was able to do something more than just sit and mope. Often chatting with his old friend.

They were able to figure a few things out. He was able to communicate with Coeus about his condition and let him know what was going on. He tried to keep him in the loop about his wife and never asked about Coeus' kids. He was starting to have longer periods of time that he could gain control. He made some plans to venture out into the complex on nights that Coeus was busy. Testing out just how far he could go, and what he could get away with during these times.

During one of these ventures, he had run into some of Ivan's men. He had created so many barriers in his mind, and when they snapped to attention for him, it confused him for a moment. But Harold quickly tried his best to act like Ivan would. Either ignoring everyone or demanding them to get him whatever he needed.

It wasn't long before he had started getting comfortable with doing this. He kept tabs on what Ivan was doing and marked down weak points. He didn't know when or where he would get control of his body, so when he did, he had to take advantage of every moment. He learned how to tell when Ivan was taking back control. He learned that a majority of the time, Ivan had no clue what had happened. And the people around him were too scared to bring anything up to him. So, hiding his activities was quite easy.

***

Harold watched as Ivan started to look into the secret society of the Collective. Ivan had plans to join it, and Harold knew that that was a horrible idea. But, as unfortunate as it was, he wasn't that different from the other people Ivan had found who were already in the society. Ruthless, refused to answer to anyone, and seemed to be above the government. They act as though they ruled the world, and from what Harold could find, it really seemed like they did. In one way or another. They would force things to happen if they weren't happening on their own.

Ivan was obsessed with the group. He spent more and more time finding out anything he could about them. If he had even a rumor about someone in power being a part of them, he would do anything he could to get in contact with that person. Time and again it was met with failure.

He kept lists of everything he heard from Ivan hidden on the computer. He started to get a separate office together. He kept everything off the books and had the secretary keep it for him to know only. He made the office password accessed and made the password an algorithm that only a handful of people in the world would be able to answer.

He kept all the information he could collect on both the Collective and on Ivan's own enterprises in there. He analyzed everything and tried to come up with any weaknesses that could be exploited. As he watched

Hel and this new scientist that was brought in help build the reach of his black-market company.

***

Ivan had finally done it. He got a meeting with someone from the inside of the Collective. It made Harold worried. He had no idea what Ivan was planning to do. He had heard Ivan have thoughts anywhere from killing the man, in hopes of garnering more attention from the group, to finding a way to get on the man's staff as security. Harold was getting numb to the fact that Ivan almost got a thrill from making him feel disgusted by his actions. So, Harold tried to avoid letting Ivan know anything that Harold was thinking, and being the primary personality, it was surprisingly easier the more he did it.

Harold's attention was peaked, however, when Ivan had the meeting with Frederick Clayton. Specifically, his thoughts on what was in the magazine. He almost felt violated when Ivan started to take such an interest in AIi. That was Harold's expertise. Not Ivan's. And for Ivan to take an interest in it felt like he was overstepping. Harold watched what he was planning closely and kept Coeus informed.

Not long after this meeting, was when Ivan got into the Collective. There started to seem to be more gaps in when Harold was conscious of what Ivan was doing. He did feel more tired lately, but he was trying harder to get the information to bring Orlav Industries down. He felt that maybe that was causing him to be less aware of what Ivan was up to.

He would get glimpses of things, feeling as though they were a dream. He saw Agent Hel in a restaurant, surrounded by dead people. He saw meetings and traveled to places well outside the norm for Ivan. But none of it was concrete. None of it made sense. And he couldn't piece together the little he had been able to remember.

Every now and then, Harold swore he was able to see Assistant Director Hunter talking to Ivan about things, but that couldn't be. It didn't make sense if Ivan had cut ties with the United States government. Which, by how he ran his company, it sure appeared as though he had.

Harold tried to focus on what he now considered his mission, but it wasn't really that easy when more and more of his days were going missing. He had no idea how long he had been rooming with Ivan. All he knew was that it often felt like Ivan was taking over bigger portions of his mind. Once Ivan got started with AI, Harold had bigger and bigger sections that he didn't know what Ivan had been doing.

But, the converse of that seemed to be becoming true too. The times Harold was able to control his body had started to get longer, and he was better at knowing when Ivan would start to wake up. He could feel signs of it hours, and at times days, before Ivan took over again. It was like a feeling of something being taken out of his hands.

But the idea of AI had been a slight inspiration. He had seen a small arms stash in Oklahoma that had seemed like a good place for him to set up. He deleted it from all records and sent several servers and memory banks to the location. Being in the center of the United States, and in a fairly rural town, it was not exactly a hub of criminal activity.

He was able to also employ several people from the town. It allowed him to have a private office to do his work, without a lot of worry about Ivan finding him.

He even made it accessible for Coeus to go there. Setting it up to be able to stay off the grid.

It was after one of his trips to Oklahoma that he had lost control of his body for what felt like a longer period of time. It felt like a long dream. He heard a few things from Hunter about the NOVA System. He heard something about Atlanta. Things had started to get too close to home. And then he heard the name Perun.

***

He and Coeus had worked hard for weeks to find out what Perun was. They split their time discussing what their AI should do, and what Perun was. It wasn't a mission or a location. There was nothing on the books about it, and there wasn't even a financial line missing for it. Meaning that Ivan was purposefully keeping this from Harold. And that worried them both.

As for his AI, he poured all of his knowledge of Ivan's corporation into it. He also put all of the information that he could find of the Collective and put it into their AI. He had gathered quite a bit of information, despite there being the issue of losing time.

***

Harold was in Oklahoma again, staying at a hotel and casino there. As he was on his way out, he heard a voice calling out to him.

"Hello, Mr. Jones. I hear you visit here often, and I felt that it would be a good time for me to introduce myself," an elderly man said as he approached Harold. This made Harold very nervous. Up until this point, he had had Coeus take care of all of the interactions with people. "I am Noyoko, the owner of this meager hotel. You can call me Stan. And, as this is a smaller town, I have heard that you have employed several of the young men in my town. I felt that I should get to know you. So, please join me at the Casino bar for a drink," Stan finished.

"Thank you, but I don't drink," Harold stated nervously.

"I don't either. It is just a comfortable place to talk," Stan said as he started to walk away.

Glancing at the door, Harold debated on leaving, but he knew that he would need the locals to be ok with him or he would lose a lot of the support he had gained. And that could be devastating to his success.

He followed Stan into the bar, and as Stan entered, Harold saw him glance at the bartender, and suddenly everyone in the bar was escorted out.

Sitting at a table in the middle of the room, Harold felt very exposed. He tried to sip on the water that was put down in front of him. He felt that waiting for Stan to talk would be of benefit to him.

Eventually, Stan took a breath and started talking.

"So, Harold. Yes, I know who you are. I wanted to tell you that we may have a mutual friend. I have several surveillance footage videos of you perusing around the casino, and the police were kind enough to provide me with videos of you around town. I know about your bunker, and I have a pretty good idea of what is in there." Stan took a drink of his water and appraised Harold, who was currently sweating and shaking slightly. "Our mutual friend was wanting to remain anonymous, but I can assure you that they were able to identify you, both of your personas, and they assured me that if you showed up again that I would do well to approach you. They showed me the other persona that you carry with you, and I was able to tell a difference in how you present yourself. I was assured that you are in fact Harold, the Canadian scientist. I need you to appreciate my position. Can you assure me that we do not need to worry about your other persona showing up?" Stan finished and looked at Harold.

Harold took a breath. He had to decide if he could trust this strange man. Not that he had much of a choice. The guy knew his name, where he was from, and what he did. He didn't really have a choice but to put his faith in that he wouldn't betray him for a price. That didn't mean that he had to tell him everything. Just what was pertinent.

Harold took a breath and said, "You are right, Stan. I am Harold Hartright. I hope that given what you know about me, you can understand my need to have privacy and secrecy. I can't afford to have anything come out about my comings and goings to this place. I have done everything I can to keep this place off the map from the dark being living in me. My 'other persona', as you call it, I am able to keep at bay and in the dark for periods of time. Sometimes it can be days. Other times just hours. Can I trust you to help it stay that way, Stan? Along with my associate who comes here to work at times. He will need to have the same courtesy offered to him, as well."

Stan looked at Harold appraisingly. A man came up and handed him a note, and he read it. Whispering to the man, and then looking back at Harold.

"I think we can agree on that arrangement. And I have something for you," Stan slid the paper across the table, and said with a slight chuckle, "I have always wanted to have some dramatics like this."

Harold couldn't help but nervously chuckle at the antics of the elderly man across the table. Picking up the paper, he read it.

"The Collective won't rest. Keep everything hidden."

***

Getting to his computer, Harold saw he had a Post-it note from Coeus.

"Perun is Ivan's AI. He has it running. It's fitting to name ours Veles."

As Harold read, he found the name fitting. But there was an alert the instant he booted the computer up and programmed the name into the program. He looked forward to using it beyond the basics of a database. The algorithm was ready.

/: INTRUSION ALERT! INTRUSION ALERT! PERUN IS HERE! >

In a panic, Harold started yanking the cords out of the wall, he pulled the Faraday cage over it. Walking out. He would work on it next time he was able to get away. He was out of time right now to trace where the hack was coming from. But Perun had made another appearance. Harold was determined to find out what that was.

***

The next opportunity he had, Harold tried to contact Coeus. Getting onto their server, there was the message he had always dreaded reading from his friend. Coeus was no more. Coeus had signed off for the last time. The note was his post-mortem file. The one that they had made for each other. It was all Harold could do to leave a note for his friend. A parting memoir for the man he considered a brother.

This was too much. The pain overtook him. He had lost too much to this mission. He couldn't bear it anymore, Harold lost all his drive and gave up.

***

After returning back to Ivan's headquarters, Harold had gone back to hiding in the dark corners of his mind. He started to be able to watch Ivan again, but he honestly hadn't cared enough to pay that close of attention. It all just felt draining now. His best friend, one of the only reasons he had to keep going and try to get his life back, was gone.

126

And he couldn't even try to drink his pain away. He was now a hostage in his own mind. He couldn't do anything but wallow in his sorrow. Every time he tried to even put in any effort, the pain was too much. He felt utterly defeated. There was nothing left for him.

He had heard some whispers of another NOVA System being functional in the world and doing some good. But he had no way of contacting them, even if he had the energy and drive to do it. This was it for him. He was done.

Ivan had won.

/: Chapter 11

When Stones Cry >

Gavin walked back into Citadel and sat down in front of the Faraday cage that contained Veres. He had been able to get into the programming for Veres. It wasn't complete yet. There were chunks of programming missing that needed to be filled in before Veres was operational.

The nice thing about doing this work on an AI was that Gavin could do it while interacting with said AI, and it provided quite a trove of knowledge. But some of what it had told him didn't make sense. It told him that Harold had been working on it for years, and that Coeus was just recently added on as a programmer.

Dad, why couldn't you be around right now? I could really use some help with this. It just doesn't make sense. How could he have been working on this for years? He hadn't had opportunity to. How did he even get the operation in Oklahoma set up without it being in the database for Orlav Industries? Wouldn't Ivan know about that? None of it made sense, but if Harold and his dad had been working on this together, then they must have had some way of communicating.

Gavin rolled his chair over into the Faraday cage and up to the console. He sat for a moment, looking at the screen analyzing his approach.

/: G-VELES, DID YOUR CREATORS COMMUNICATE?>

128

/: V-YES. THE CREATORS BOTH USED A SERVER TO COMMUNICATE BEFORE I WAS BROUGHT ONLINE.>

/: G-DO YOU HAPPEN TO KNOW WHAT THE SERVER THEY USED WAS?>

/: V-THEY DID NOT PROVIDE ME WITH THAT INFORMATION.>

/: G-DO YOU KNOW ANYTHING ABOUT THEIR COMMUNICATION SERVER?>

/: V-IT IS AN ONLINE SERVER THAT COEUS CREATED WHILE THE CREATORS WERE WORKING TOGETHER.>

/: G-THANK YOU. I WILL HAVE MORE QUESTIONS LATER.>

/: V-I LOOK FORWARD TO PROVIDING YOU ANSWERS.>

Gavin immediately went to another console and contacted General Richmond.

"What is it, Gavin?" Richmond asked with a clipped tone. She had clearly been in the middle of something.

"Sorry to bother you general, but do you happen to know if there were any servers that were retained from my father's things during his time working in the NSA?" Gavin asked, noticing the use of his first name by Richmond.

"I will check into that and let you know as soon as I can. If there are any active, do you want me to unplug them?" Richmond asked, knowing Gavin would be the expert that she would bring in to deal with any of these kinds of things in the first place.

"No. Leave them where they are, as they are. If you could just tell me the location, I will be able to get in and check them out. Thank you," Gavin said, not wanting to keep the general from whatever she had been working on.

Richmond nodded and then the screen went black.

"It was good to hear from you Gavin. I will talk to you later," Gavin snarked with humor in his voice.

Suddenly the screen came back up.

"Just because the screen is dark doesn't mean I am not listening, Analyst Woodford. You, of all people, should know this well," General Richmond quipped with a smirk, and then signed off, knowing that she had surprised Gavin.

Gavin chuckled slightly after the shock had worn off. He knew that he had more to do, but it was good to know that even in a moment of urgency, the general would remind him of their humanity. Something that was usually his job.

***

"Sorry about that, Agent Charles, Noyoko. That was an urgent communication from Analyst Woodford that I had to take. I am sure that you will hear more about it soon, Agent Charles. As he is so great at keeping things to himself," Cathrine paused as Agent Charles grunted in acknowledgment. "Now, what is the update on the Collective?" General Richmond inquired.

"I have not found a lot on anyone. It seems that every lead we have dries up fairly quickly once I am on the trail. I will continue to look into any lead I can come up with, but I am not very hopeful at the moment," Charles growled out. He was fighting to stay respectful while relaying one of the few failures that he has had in his career.

"General, I know that we have been working on this for a while together. I will let you know if I hear anything through my colleagues. I am kept out of the loop for a lot of these things because of the common knowledge that I have integrity in ways that many of my fellow casino owners do not," Noyoko reported. "And please call me Stan," He finished with a slight smile.

"Thank you, gentlemen. I know that this has been as stressful for you as it has been for me. I would urge you to use caution in this above all else. Unfortunately, a few people that I have worked with on this in the past have gone missing," Richmond's eyes portrayed her age more than they normally do. They clouded over with sadness before snapping back to the dark and focused sharpness that they normally have.

"Yes Ma'am," Charles barked. His marine training kicking in.

Noyoko avoided responding to the general. He knew the risks that he was taking in being a part of this. Cathrine hadn't sought him out for this. In fact, it had been quite the opposite. And that fact had allowed him access to Agent Robert Charles, aka Mato Acothley. He saw the man as a son and had helped him find out what his kuhtaamia was meant to be.

"Agent Theia, if I may have a word before, I sign off?" Noyoko asked politely, despite his lack of acknowledgement of the rank.

That caught Cathrine's attention. It had been quite a while since anyone had called her that, and it was not something she was used to hearing anymore. Even if it was how she had identified herself to him just a few days prior. She nodded her agreement, and then addressed Agent Charles.

"That will be all Agent Charles, unless there is anything more you would like to inquire about or add?" She asked dismissively to him.

"No Ma'am. I will report back as soon as I have more to go on," Charles said. You could almost hear the salute in his tone before he stopped talking and activated Gavin's software that made it appear he had hung up.

"What was it that you were wanting to discuss, Stan?" The general asked, trying to not sound annoyed that he had used her agent name in front of one of her employees.

"I did not want to say in front of Mato, but I have heard some rumblings," he started before he was cut off.

"Rumblings of what? And why would you not want the information to be brought to anyone that is actively working this assignment. We will need to be sure that everyone has as much current information as possible," she ranted with a slight glare at the man on the computer.

"Cathrine, need I remind you that you came to me from the start? Do you need a reminder of how everything started?" Noyoko responded to her in a very clipped tone. He knew that she didn't mean anything by it, but he was not about to have one of his people be treated as if they were just another pawn in anyone's game. Even if it was someone who he knew cared about Mato more than she would have ever let on.

"I did not mean to have that outburst, I apologize. This is a matter of some urgency, and I would like to be sure that we have every possible upper hand we could get," the general stated.

"I do understand the severity of this situation. Believe me, it is not something that I take lightly. I just also know Mato, once he hears what I have to say, he will need someone to keep him focused on why we are doing this. And I don't think that it can be either of us," Noyoko stated sullenly.

"What is it?" Cathrine asked, worriedly.

"Do you know what happened to his commanding officer and NSA mentor?" Noyoko asked pointedly.

"He went missing several years ago, and has been presumed dead," Cathrine said, with a questioning tone. She sadly felt that she knew where this was going.

"I have word that he may be among the ranks of the Collective. It isn't concrete evidence, and I felt that it wasn't something that Mato should know about just yet. But last I heard, Agent Chernobog was working with an Agent Mokosh, we are not sure who that is yet. And Chemobog is getting paid by a Frederick Clayton. Him I am sure you need no introduction to. We are not sure who, if any of the others, are working in the Collective. The reason we wonder if he is with the Collective is due to the fact that he was seen at the old headquarters for a Carlos Cortez. Another name that I am sure you need no introduction to," Noyoko reported.

Given that Carlos was among the names listed, she imagined that there was very little reason to not believe that Chernobog was working with the Collective then.

"I will let him know, and if I have to, I will command him to talk to someone. Thank you Numunuu. I will keep you up to date," Cathrine stated, before ending the call.

***

Ivan hung up the phone with Agent Mokosh. She had reported success in her missions, which hadn't surprised Ivan. What had him at a loss was the literal loss of time that he had been having.

He had noticed it a while ago. It all started with small amounts of time. Or waking up and there were things off from where he had left it. Shoes in the wrong spot, or his keys left out when he knew he had put them up. Then before long, there were days missing that he couldn't account for.

When he asked his secretary, she just said that she didn't have anything on the books for him to be gone. He could sense that anyone he asked was too afraid to tell him anything that he wouldn't want to hear. That was on him, and he knew it. But the only way to be able to stay on top was if you made sure that anyone coming for you instantly regretted it. Without remorse and without mercy.

It had stopped for a while. It seemed to be around when Coeus had died. So, he was sure that it had been related to Harold somehow. But he couldn't prove it. Not like someone so weak could do anything meaningful to him. He knew that Coeus and Harold had worked together, he just wasn't sure on what.

He had worked with The Westgate to try to figure out a way to pull Harold out of him. He hated having that weak being in him. Harold was nothing more than an annoyance to him, and he would rather kill him than allow him to have any control in his life. But there hadn't been any progress made on getting him free of that worthless personality.

The issue that they had was whenever they tried to extract that personality, there was an intense burning that started in the center of his brain. It got intense at times, and when that happened, he would have to take a few days to heal. And even then, would end up having a migraine for days and at times weeks after that.

He logged into his computer and pulled up his chat with Perun.

/: I-WHAT IS THE UPDATE?>

/: P-HAVE IT READY.>

/: I-THEN WHAT IS THE DELAY?>

/: P-TARGET HAS NOT BEEN ACTIVE AND I AM NOT SURE WHAT IT WILL DO.>

/: I-KEEP ME UPDATED. I WILL NOT TOLERATE FAILURE IN THIS.>

/: P-UNDERSTOOD.>

Ivan shoved himself away from the desk in a huff.

***

Charles hung up the phone. He had listened to the general's continued conversation with his Numunuu. The general had known and hadn't reached out after. She made sure that any conversation with someone from his past was made available to him when possible. This one cut deep. Sadly, he knew that Noyoko was right. He would have to talk to someone. And even though he knew who he would talk to, he didn't even want to start down that road.

Emotions were not something he was comfortable discussing, even before he had joined the Marines. And going through the training for the marines and the NSA had just made it more difficult. He wasn't a robot, despite how much he would like to put off that he had no emotions. He knew that just shutting it all out was a mistake.

Checking his monitor, he knew that Gavin was in Citadel. And if he waited for him to get home, then he would have to explain to Alex why he was taking Gavin from her. So, he headed to the gun range in Citadel. He could pull him in there for some gun training, not that he needs it.

Charles had to admit that Gavin learned quickly, even without the NOVA System. That thing was just a tool to Gavin, in a way that a drill

134

was a tool to a carpenter. Without it, Gavin was still a big benefit to the team and the country, and that thought surprised Charles.

Getting to Citadel, he grunted at Gavin, "Gun training. Now," As he walked past him tinkering with his electronic toys. He got out his pistol and started cleaning it as he waited for Gavin to get there.

Gavin walked in with his pistol, and immediately copied Charles and started to take his side arm apart to clean it. *This is really not that different from working on computers. Only it is the exact same computer each and every time.* He thought to himself.

Charles cleared his throat, causing Gavin to look up from what he was doing. He had gotten more than used to sitting in silence when they were working on this ever since Gavin figured out what to do. Prior to that it had been very loud when he would mess up.

"I know I don't talk a lot," Charles started, taking his time to choose how he wanted to approach this. Gavin just sat there and nodded, unsure if Charles could even see him. But he didn't want to break whatever spell had gotten the older man to start.

"I know why I don't, and it's not always just because I like having the strong silent type of persona. Often, I don't really even know what to say," Charles continued. Each of his words felt measured. Like he was struggling to form the sentence. "I don't like relying on others for much. I always felt I did that more than enough as a child and teenager. Especially as a teenager. That was part of why I wanted to go into the marines. I wanted to make sure that I never had to rely on another person again. That I would be strong enough to be able to handle whatever came at me,"

Gavin could see that Charles was trying, but he wasn't sure why. Or what had brought it on. Again, he kept to himself.

"I know now just how foolish that is. I have seen throughout my life that it is impossible to be completely independent of help from any other person. That doesn't really mean that it has gotten any easier. This line of work doesn't lead to a lot of relationships that allow you to open up," Charles breathed again. His eyes were fixed on his pistol, but his hands weren't really moving. His breathing was very slow and even.

"When the people of my town refused to let me go into the foster system, I knew that they had saved my life. I have felt indebted to them ever since. And it isn't something that I really regret. They are the closest thing I could have to family. But it has been clear that I am not family. Once I left, it became clear that to most of them it was just their duty to my father's legacy to take care of me," Charles sounded solemn, and this all-confused Gavin more than anything.

Where was all of this coming from? Was it just because they had gone to his hometown on a mission? Was he regretting going there with them? Did he feel that they had exposed the community to being a target now? Gavin worried to himself about his friend.

"The amount of deception and lying needed to do this job well, not to mention the sheer fact that you can't be sure that you or anyone else you work with will be alive for any extended period of time really can put a damper on your ability to open up to them. I have had to put a bullet in too many people who, in normal circumstances, I would have considered a friend, that I had stopped even thinking that it would be possible for me to have a friend again," Charles continued.

Charles finally looked up at Gavin and made eye contact. Gavin could tell that this was something that Charles was being honest about. There was too much emotion in the older man's eyes for him to be faking it. This was real.

"Gavin, I hate to say it, but I do see you as a friend. You have proven many times that you will have my back. Even if it means putting your own, or the mission in jeopardy. You try to do the right thing for the people you care about rather than just putting the needs of the country above all. And somehow for you and your stupid luck, it works.

"There was only one other person that I had ever felt that I could trust like that. He was my mentor. He taught me almost everything I know about being a spy, and a marine. He was the one who ultimately recruited me to the NSA. And I found out recently that he may have been working for the enemy this entire time," Charles croaked out. The amount of betrayal in his tone cut Gavin through. His heart hurt.

136

"I wasn't exactly supposed to hear it. He is a Collective agent. And I truly don't know how long he has been. But the fact that he is, shows me that not everything about what I learned about being a spy is right. In fact, you have shown me that almost everything I have learned, while helpful, isn't concrete. How you do things, clearly works somehow," Charles was beating around the bush, and he hated it. It was not like him, but this was not easy to do.

"All of this makes me question what I learned. What I know about my job. He was a man I looked up to. A mentor. If he can fall, then I think just about anyone can," Charles said, for the first time in the time that Gavin had known him, he sounded dejected. Almost lost.

Gavin studied the large man. His entire frame seemed rigid. That made Gavin more uncomfortable than anything. If he hadn't known Charles better, he would think that he is about to cry.

Gavin thought for a moment. He didn't just want to jump in and say something stupid. He wanted to make sure that his words would help his friend. Taking a deep breath, and letting it out slowly, he focused himself.

"Do you know why I was so bent on finding my parents Charles?" Gavin asked loud enough to be heard, but with a soft tone. To which Charles just shrugged, so Gavin continued, "It was partly because I wanted my family to be whole again, but it was also because I was still too young when my parents left to really know much about myself. It caused me to have a lot of identity issues.

"I knew my dad was good with computers, but I had no idea how good he was. And I knew next to nothing about my mom and what she was like. What she did and was good at.

"And when you don't know the people from your past, it is hard to understand who you are and have the confidence to stand in your own abilities and identity. From the counseling I have gone through and my own life experience, I have found that if you don't have an understanding of where you come from, then you can tend to just cling to whatever seems to fit you the best. Before I learned about my parents, I clung to the idea that my father was a nerd. That was what I based my entire life around. And while that is true, he was, it wasn't all he was," Gavin paused for a moment. Not wanting to rush through everything. He wanted to give Charles a moment to think.

"From what I understand, your father was quite the man's man. He didn't take crap from anyone and didn't just show his emotions on his sleeve. And that seems to be who you have tried to base your entire being around. Going into the military, just like he had. The issue is, when you went in you were still just a kid. And that left you open and vulnerable to manipulation," Gavin said tentatively. He knew he was treading on some dangerous ground here. But looking at Charles, it seemed like he was ok to continue.

"I have a feeling that just maybe this senior officer took advantage of that fact, and the fact that he knew your dad had passed and used it to manipulate you. To use you, likely to promote his own career. Maybe?" Gavin said in a questioning tone. He was trying hard to sound confident, but he was nervous that he would step on toes. And he knew that he was dealing with a sensitive topic.

Charles grunted what sounded like it was agreement.

"Anyway, I know you have stuff to do. You finished cleaning your gun quickly and exactly. The way that you should. You're dismissed," Charles commanded, clearly getting back to himself.

Gavin stood to leave the room. As he picked up his sidearm and headed toward the door, Charles stopped him.

"Gavin, thank you," he said quietly.

"You're welcome. Do you mind if I ask what the name of this commander was?" Gavin asked tentatively.

Charles cleared his throat.

"Yeah, it was Louis Carlson. Call sign Agent Chemobog," Charles answered.

Gavin felt the now familiar feeling of the NOVA system activating. He immediately saw images of death, an ancient looking blue swastika, a symbol of a star with sixteen rays coming off of it, and an Ibis.

138

The force of the NOVA system caused Gavin to have to sit back down. He couldn't hear Charles talking to him, and then yelling. Charles grabbed his phone to call Alex, but as he did Gavin spoke.

"Charles, there was more to it than what you know."

***

Agent Chemobog sat across the desk from Ivan, waiting. He knew that this was what Ivan liked to do, and he didn't mind. While he waited, he looked around the office. It wasn't unlike all of the other offices he had been in. The countless people who thought that they were in charge. That they had power over him.

Finally, Ivan finished typing and looked up from his laptop. Looking at the man across from him, he appraised him.

"Agent Chemobog, I wanted to thank you for your service to my purpose. I was given high remarks about you by Agent Mokosh. I wanted you to know that we at the Collective take all of our transactions very seriously," Ivan said as he opened the front drawer to his desk.

"Thank you, I have had plenty of-" was all that Agent Chemobog got out before the bullet went through his head.

/: Chapter 12

Malware >

Ivan sat in his car as it traveled down the street. He hated being summoned like a dog. The Collective still held the reins, though, and if he wanted to be in charge then he would have to play nice for the time being. But that didn't make it any easier for him to swallow his pride whenever they called him to a meeting rather than the other way around.

Looking out at the people walking around in the street, he sneered at them. For as long as he could remember, he didn't feel he belonged in those crowds. Often, he felt he didn't belong anywhere. He was better than them. He was better than everyone.

Lumbering out of the car, he marched into the building. His head held high. His gate was like that of someone who was in charge and important. He knew what this was going to be about, and he had the answers ready for the Collective.

Sitting in the waiting room outside the conference room, he looked through his notes again. They weren't notes on what he was intending to say. They were notes on what all he had on the other members of the Collective. There were only a few that he was missing, and he knew exactly why. They worked hard to make sure that anyone who had dirt on them wasn't able to keep it. One way or another. But they were usually the ones that stayed quiet at meetings like this.

Ivan was summoned into the conference room. Another thing he hated. This entire exchange had already soured his mood, and he had barely interacted with anyone. That was about to start, and he would have to fight to keep his tongue, knowing that he still had to play nice for a while. Not all of these people were as vulnerable as he would have liked. He was powerful, but he wasn't reckless.

"Mr. Orlav, if you would please have a seat, we will get started," Joseph Michaelson commanded. That worried Ivan. Joseph was one of the few who normally stayed quiet, and he had nothing on the man. He knew what he did, but that made it even harder to get to him. No one knew where he went when he wasn't at meetings, and he was a ghost to the public. Joseph owned three of the major news networks through the holding company of which he was the majority shareholder.

"From what we have seen, all you have been able to accomplish was to weed out two of our members who were displaying clear signs of weakness. We thank you for that, but that wasn't the task presented to you. So, please update us on the progress of your mission with the NOVA System and his team," Mikel Melwasul chimed in with an irritated tone.

Another that hadn't done a lot of talking in previous meetings. He was a social media mogul. He created the algorithm that was used to track people and siphoned their information into his servers, all with the written consent of the members, per the contract on sign-up. This wasn't going the way that Ivan had expected. He had to put his notes away. The others looked at him expectantly. He hadn't expected them to know who had gotten rid of the other two members, but that was inevitable with this group. The group all but traded in information more than anything else.

"Ladies and Gentlemen of the Collective, I can assure you that everything is progressing as needed with my mission," Ivan stated, turning on the significant charm he had when he wanted. "We all knew that this wasn't a week-long mission. It was something that would take time. That team's ability to weed out the late director Hunter and pull apart his reputation in the US government gave them a long leash with the brass in Washington. I know that a few of you would be able to

141

destroy that fairly quickly, but to do it right and without gaining unwanted attention, we will have to do it slowly. We have to make a way for that team to destroy their own reputation. And I assure you I have just the plan for that," Ivan finished with a smirk, as he saw that the majority of the people around the table were nodding in agreement with him.

***

Gavin was back in the cage with Veres. He had to make progress with it today, or he might as well scrap it. Staring at the blinking cursor on the screen, he was contemplating what to ask next. Having had a look through most of the code, Gavin no longer thought that this AI was dangerous. He had been using it as a bit of a database honestly. But he was ready to take the next step with it.

He stepped away to give the general a call.

"Analyst Woodford, what can I do for you today?" General Richmond asked when she answered.

"Hello, Ma'am, I was wondering if I had permission to connect Veres to the internet now? I have verified that it is not dangerous and would likely help us in our hunt for Ivan. It has a vast database already and would likely be able to grow it faster if given access," Gavin requested. He was hoping to be able to track down some holes in Ivan's security with it, and maybe even be able to find a way to track where he moved his headquarters after his mom had left.

"If you believe that it is safe, then I don't see any reason why you shouldn't be able to Gavin, just be cautious," General Richmond warned and then ended the call.

Gavin quickly got the monitor and servers out and set up.

***

Alex had been watching Gavin work like a madman with this AI. She felt weird having seen him almost obsess over it, but she knew that was just who he was.

142

Just like his father, according to Megan. Though she was in agreement that may not exactly be a good thing, Alex thought to herself with a chuckle.

She was having another lunch date with Megan. She knew now that Megan was using this as a form of counseling for her, and she appreciated the informal approach that Megan was engaging in. It put Alex at ease and made it feel ok to open up about how she was feeling.

Alex was getting antsy, though. They hadn't had a true mission in a few weeks, and it was causing her to grow restless. It wasn't that she didn't enjoy her time when it was just her and Gavin, with no mission, weapons, or danger. But she had grown accustomed to that life, and the adrenaline rush of being shot at. She wasn't sure if she was made for a normal life. A slow life.

I am not sure that I ever will be, and I don't know if Gavin will really be ok with that. It seems that, even though he enjoys this life right now, he will want to settle down one day and have a family and just be normal. How can I tell him that may not be possible? That I might not even want that for myself? Alex worried to herself. It was starting to worry her that Gavin may not want to accept it, and that they may not be good together long-term.

***

Charles had hunted down this Frederick Clayton and found it to be another dead end, literally. Frederick was dead. The news said that he had been murdered by a prostitute that he had hired and that the man had a proclivity for that particular vice. However, something about it seemed off to Charles.

Charles went and investigated the scene. There wasn't much to go off of. It had been scrubbed. And that was part of what made Charles question. Everything had been scrubbed. No fingerprints at all. Not even Fredericks. And he really doubted the cleaning lady who called it in, had just cleaned around the body and rather large bloodstain in the room before calling it in.

The cut was fairly expected. It was nothing special, but it was fairly precise. He would have bled out quickly. And as was evident by the stain on the floor, there would have been a lot of it. But there were no witnesses to any blood-soaked woman leaving the building at any time, let alone during the time that it was suspected to have happened.

To Charles, this indicated a professional hit. Someone knew what they were doing and had a reason to do it. He expected that it was someone in the Collective, but he had no clue who.

He went to the security room and asked for any and all surveillance video files that they would have had from during that time frame, and they were happy to supply them, but there were hundreds of files, and he couldn't really just ask Gavin to look through them for him.

So, he was currently stuck in his apartment, watching video after video. The majority of them had nothing in them. Hours of empty hallways and staircases. It wasn't until about the fifteenth hour on the thirtieth video file that he caught something.

It was of Frederick and a female getting out of a car in the back garage.

He didn't catch much and couldn't see her face, so he found some more that would have been along the path that they would have taken. Most of which had been deleted, as per protocol for when Frederick brought in particular guests.

Then he caught Ivan and his men going in a few hours later through the main door. Just a glimpse before it cut out, but there was no doubt that it had been Ivan.

A few hours later, there was the woman. Leaving with Ivan out the front door. Ivan just walked around like he owned this place. It wasn't until right at the end of the video that the woman messed up. She glanced back, and when she did, her face came into view.

Charles quickly grabbed his phone and dialed the number to the general.

"Frederick wasn't as dead of an end as I thought. You are going to want to see this," he said.

***

Miranda sat in Ivan's office. She was waiting for him, as usual. She had gotten used to his approach to people. Make them feel like he always had something more important going on than them. Make them feel as though he was giving them something special in simply allowing them the time that he was demanding from them in the first place. She was getting tired of it, but he paid her well and never asked questions on how she was able to complete an assignment.

She just scrolled on the phone she had gotten. She often made fake social media profiles to be able to find a target or to just mess with people. Since she never kept a phone or laptop for more than a day, she wasn't worried about the people she messed with finding her.

She found a couple of people in the area that might be fun to mess around with if she could get them to agree to it.

As she pulled up the profile to message them, Ivan walked into the room. In a huff, she put the phone away. Playtime would have to come later.

"I don't particularly like what you did with Agent Chemobog. I was actually starting to get along with him. He was the fun kind of chaos," Agent Mokosh said as Ivan sat down in his chair at his desk and pushed away slightly. She knew that he liked to have the first word, but this was her way of showing him that he couldn't completely control her.

"He had served his purpose. You would do well to remember that yourself," Ivan threatened. He was not in a mood to be trifled with. "If you don't, I will arrange for you to be reminded," Ivan got out before he felt a knife blade against his throat.

"Don't forget that you brought me in for a reason, you self-important narcissistic nerd, and that reason wasn't because I was easily disposed of. If I even feel another threat coming for me, I will," Mokosh muttered through gritted teeth, sitting on top of his desk, before she was cut off by the cock of a gun.

"It is cute that you think you would get to move that knife another inch before you would be dead. I will overlook this little incident if you back down and keep in mind just who is in charge," Ivan said, as he nodded down to the gun that was pointing up at her from his lap, directly at her face.

Lowering the knife, Miranda slid off the desk and sat back in the chair she had been lounging in before.

"Now, as long as you have no other complaints to file, we can get into why I called you here," Ivan stated calmly as he still held the gun trained on her.

Miranda responded with a nod. She was more than irritated now, but she knew better than to try something again just yet.

"Good. Now, a few of the reasons that I requested to have you under my employment in the first place were that chaotic and survivalist nature. Your record is another aspect. But one of the biggest factors was your apparent relationship with another agent," Ivan said leadingly.

"Ok, I will bite. Which one of my menial colleagues are you wanting information on?" Miranda snarked in a slightly defeated tone.

"I am going to need you to tell me all you know on Agent Ker, aka Alex Johnson," Ivan said, as he set the gun down and folded his hands in his lap.

Agent Mokosh's eyes widened. This wasn't a menial colleague. This was one of the very few people in the world who made her feel fear. She had seen that darkness. Hunter had told her to keep it to herself, but Hunter was gone now. She hadn't seen her since Hunter died, and she knew that they had been close. She wasn't sure if that would make her more unhinged or how it could potentially affect her.

Ivan could see Miranda's mind whirling. He saw fear and wasn't sure if it was fear of betraying her friend or not. All he knew was he made the right decision in which name he had selected. He enjoyed the panic he saw her going through. It wasn't something he had seen in her before. The only other agent that he had the fortune of working with before that came anywhere close to Mokosh's composure was Hel.

146

"You don't want information on her. I can tell you that much," Miranda finally muttered. Her face had been composed, but the fear was still evident in her voice.

Ivan breathed deeply and studied her. He knew she wasn't being deliberately evasive or not wanting to give information out of spite. She was scared. Now to find out just what she was scared of.

"Why would I not want information on her? You clearly have plenty to share with me. So, please enlighten me," Ivan stated, leaving it clear that this wasn't a point he was going to argue with his tone.

Miranda took a deep sighing breath and stood and walked over to the shelf bar that Ivan had in his office. Pouring herself a scotch, he watched as she poured a full glass, and then chugged the entire thing. Only after did she wince at all.

"That is a sipping scotch," he said with an irritated tone. He was tired of her theatrics and waiting.

"The reason I am hesitant to give you any information about Alex isn't due to some misguided loyalty to her or any organization. She has proven to choose others or the mission over me in many cases," Miranda started, staring off out the window as she poured another full glass.

Her melodramatics caused Ivan to roll his eyes again. He eyed his gun, deciding if this information may be worth the annoyance of dealing with her any longer. Remembering the meeting he had just had not a few days earlier, he decided to delay her death for a bit longer.

"No," Miranda continued finally, "that woman scares me," she said as she took a sip of the scotch. "I have seen her do things that aren't possible. Or shouldn't be. I have seen her take out entire compounds of heavily armed men. I have seen her get shot and get back up like it was a strong breeze. I have seen her pull a knife that had been stabbed into her, deeper just so she had the tactical advantage over her opponent,"

Agent Mokosh droned on. Ivan had heard the rumors. He had heard the tales and even got the fortune of seeing her work on the surveillance recording from The Westgate's previous lab. He knew she was a very good agent, but it didn't scare him. Everyone was killable. Everyone was vulnerable.

"I know the ghost stories about her, Agent Mokosh. If that is all you are able to provide, then I see no reason to keep you in my employment," Ivan said, as he picked up his gun again.

"She considers me a sort of friend. I can get close to her without drawing any attention," Miranda said quickly. She hated to make an enemy of Agent Ker, but she would rather that, than die immediately.

"That is something of use," Ivan said thoughtfully. "You see, I have a bit of a mission of my own, and it is imperative that Agent Ker is not in my way. If you were to help me with this, it would prove very lucrative for you."

Miranda smiled a very predatory and intense smile. Her eyes were on fire, and her face almost seemed to distort. It was almost enough to make Ivan think twice, but he needed this done.

"What do you need me to do?" Agent Mokosh asked.

***

Gavin had gotten Veres set up with a wired internet connection and was browsing the dark web when he asked about Ivan and Orlav Industries.

/: G- WHAT CAN YOU TELL ME ABOUT IVAN ORLAV? >

/: V- IVAN IS THE FOUNDER AND CEO OF ORLAV INDUSTRIES. HE IS A DANGEROUS MAN, WHOSE ONLY DRIVE IS TO OWN, TAKE OVER, OR DESTROY. >

/: G- WHAT CAN YOU TELL ME ABOUT ORLAV IND? >

/: V- ORLAV INDUSTRIES IS A FRONT OPERATION FOR BLACK MARKET ARMS-DEALING THAT PROVIDES WEAPONS TO BOTH ILLEGAL GROUPS, AS WELL AS GOVERNMENT ENTITIES. WOULD YOU LIKE ME TO RUN DIAGNOSTICS ON THEIR SYSTEM AND SEARCH FOR WEAKNESSES AGAIN? >

/: G- PLEASE DO. >

Gavin twirled in his chair. He knew that there had to be a purpose greater than just someone to talk to that Harold and his dad created Veres. Taking out his phone, he opens it to text Alex and let her know that he found something of use, and then he looked back at the screen and saw:

/: P- PERUN THANK YOU FOR MAKING THIS EASY. >

And suddenly, Gavin felt the now familiar tug on his brain. The center was warming up. The NOVA system was activated. He didn't understand it. Some images and coding cascaded down his phone. This felt different. It felt intrusive. Wrong. His vision blurred and darkened.

***

Gavin woke up in his chair. He looked at the screen for Veres and saw that it was running diagnostics on Orlav Ind. His head hurt, but he had been staring at the screen for way too long recently. The high contrast between green and dark green was likely the cause.

Alex is supposed to be spending time with Megan. I could use it for a little downtime myself. And with this running, it should make my job easier now. A break is well deserved, Gavin thought as he pulled out his phone and dialed Kaleb.

"Hey buddy, wanna meet at my apartment for a video game and pizza night?" Gavin asked, knowing the answer before he even finished, if the squeal on the other side of the line was any indication.

"Yes! I have missed you, buddy! I will bring my console over since I have everything updated. I'm feeling COD tonight! Got that need for some digital demolition," Kaleb quipped as Gavin could hear him rummaging around.

"Great. See you in about half an hour. I am finishing up at work. No, the other work. Bye, man," Gavin said as he finished the phone call and hung up.

Hanging up, Gavin was more excited than he had been in a while to just have a normal night like they had had so many times before. Grabbing his jacket, he bounded up the stairs to his car.

/: Chapter 13

Stalking >

DEFEAT displayed across the screen as Gavin and Kaleb finished another frustrating match. Gavin stood and threw the controller across the room, and it shattered as it hit the wall. Kaleb had just been happy to spend time with his friend again, but he had noticed almost from the time that they started playing Call of Duty that there was something off about Gavin.

He was grumpy, and just about any little thing would set him off. That worried Kaleb. He had only seen him like this a couple of times, and none of them had been since Gavin had started dating Alex. This wasn't his friend.

"Gavin, what's wrong?" Kaleb asked, with hesitation. Clearly frightened of his friend for the first time in his life.

"You can't tell me that those people were playing fair! They clearly had to be modding right? RIGHT?!" Gavin ranted, turned to Kaleb, and paused. Seeing the look on his friend's face made him freeze. He had never seen the look of fear on his face towards him. Then it dawned on him what he had just done. He had never thrown a controller before. They were way too expensive. But there it was, sticking out of the wall where he had thrown it.

"Kaleb, I am so sorry," Gavin started, turning back to his friend. But Kaleb just waved it off. The look of fear was already gone.

"Don't even think twice about it bro," Kaleb said placatingly.

"I don't even know what came over me just then. I just got so frustrated at that game. I am used to gaming being an escape, and maybe this is just a little too close to work for me anymore," Gavin explained solemnly, as he still tried to make sense of what happened.

"Honestly, the amount of times I have wanted to chuck a controller through a window, or into the TV playing this game, I completely understand. And it is definitely likely that they were modding. It is just all too common anymore. Especially on cross-platform games like this," Kaleb stated, trying to help explain away his friend's outburst. Even though he knew that hadn't ever been an issue before for Gavin.

"Yeah, maybe it just caught me at a weird time," Gavin said softly.

"Exactly. Now, I do have a VERY important question for you," Kaleb said, eager to change the subject.

"Ok, Lay it on me, man!" Gavin said, back to sounding like his mostly chipper self.

"If there is the rule of two for the Sith but almost an unlimited number of Jedi at any given time, does that mean that the dark side of the force is finite, while the light side is infinite?" Kaleb asked.

Gavin sat contemplating it for a moment. Then responded, "Or was the rule of two just designed because the Sith had a nasty habit of taking each other out, while the Jedi code kept them mostly from doing that very thing, trying, instead, to take care of each other and everyone else around them?" Gavin asked in return, causing a smile to spread across his friend's face.

I really had missed this. Gavin thought to himself as he and Kaleb dove into a deep discussion about what that might mean for the Star Wars history on either side of the argument.

***

152

Alex walked into the same coffee shop that she had previously and saw Megan sitting at the same table. It was comforting to have a routine. Something that she had been trained so hard to avoid, now was giving her a sense of normalcy that she needed to be able to heal.

Just because that is what my training taught me, doesn't mean that is what I need at the moment. Alex reminded herself.

"Hey, Alex! How are you?" Megan asked, chipper as ever. It caused Alex to chuckle slightly.

"I am doing well. Some memories have come back, some I am not sure if they ever will. And there are a few that I am not sure if I remember or if I just know them because Gavin told me about what happened. But I still enjoy listening to him," Alex said as she sat down. Megan had already ordered for them. *It is nice having a few people who know you well enough that they know how you take your coffee. Simple things, yet they mean far more than I ever thought that they would.*

"Well, that is all pretty typical when it comes to memory loss," Megan said as she took a sip from her coffee. "Have you told Gavin about this yet?"

"Yeah, I try to keep him informed as much as possible. It is weird to me to open up to someone, but I have been trying really hard to show him that I do love him, and he is worth fighting through the fears I have had in the past," Alex said. She always found it easy to talk to Megan. At times it was even easier than talking to Gavin because Megan tended to understand the emotions that she was feeling more.

"That's good, that is great progress. I have definitely seen you smile more. Have you given any more thought to Gavin's proposal? No pressure by the way," Megan asked, almost immediately regretting that she had asked at all when she saw the look of defeat on Alex's face.

"That is a difficult question," Alex responded slowly. "I know I want him to be the only man I am ever with again, but" Alex trailed off.

"But what?" Megan asked leadingly. She thought she knew what Alex was going to say, but she wanted to know just how much Alex had thought about this. She didn't want to put new fears into her head if what Megan thought was the issue, wasn't actually what Alex was thinking.

"But I am an utter mess," Alex muttered. "I have to do these talks with you to be able to even begin to process some of the issues I have. And that isn't even getting into the lives I have taken, the people who I have ruined, or my past with my family. The little of it I remember anyway. He is likely better off with someone else whose is less screwed up," Alex said with a tear rolling down her cheek.

Megan, you are kind. But you don't truly understand what all I have done. What all I am capable of doing? Even before the horrible things that the CIA did to me. Well, that's not fair, it wasn't really the CIA as much as it was just Hunter that did those things to me. Alex thought as she took another sip of her coffee. The warmth of it seems to be calming her from the inside.

Megan smiled at her. She understood the feeling that Alex was having, even if she didn't understand the exact issues that troubled Alex. She didn't need to. Megan had felt that she didn't deserve Chad either. He had seemed perfect to her. From a good family, grew up with both parents, she felt an outcast simply because he was not only an athlete, but smart as well. Chad had seemed to be well out of Megan's league, but he wouldn't give up. He wanted her, and he reminded her frequently of it.

"Alex, that isn't your decision to make, or mine. It is Gavin's. He is a grown man, and has shown, especially recently, that he is completely capable of deciding what and who is good for him or not," Megan said, a slight finality to her tone. She didn't want to be harsh, but she wanted to make sure that she got across to Alex that this wasn't her issue to bear. "We all have baggage. We all have issues. We are all screwed up. That doesn't make you less of a person. And if my brother loves you enough to be willing to take on whatever baggage you have and help you with it, then he must trust you to do the same. That is what a relationship is meant to be, Alex. It isn't just where one person gets all the benefits, and the other gets this privilege of being called theirs. That is called abuse," Megan finished with sadness.

Alex smiled through her tears and reached out her hand for her friend. Megan took it graciously and smiled. They were both tearing up slightly but were grateful that they had each other.

"So, then what am I going to do with Kaleb and Charles? I honestly am not sure which one is worse sometimes," Alex said, causing Megan to laugh slightly.

***

Across the street, Agent Mokosh watched Alex walk into the coffee shop and sit with a woman she didn't recognize. Taking out her binoculars, Mokosh watched the two women chat. The emotions and feelings being shared. The tears from both women. The genuineness of their interaction.

"What is wrong with you, Alex? What happened to you?" Miranda murmured to herself. She had been surprised when Alex hadn't immediately noticed her following her, but this seemed just odd. Granted, she had taken severe precautions to make sure Alex wouldn't notice her, but she had never not had Alex realize that she was following her before.

She sat, watching the women talk and laugh and cry. She hadn't seen Alex so animated. Not even when working on a mark. This felt weird to her. She wished she had her parabolic mic.

Finally, Alex and the other woman stood to leave. Alex walked off one way, and the other woman went to her car that was parked out front. Mokosh got her license number and followed her.

***

Alex thought she had noticed someone watching her, but when they didn't follow her when she left the coffee shop, she tried to shake off the feeling. She knew she had been mentally distracted and emotional when she went to meet with Megan, but that hadn't been an issue in the past. She had always known when someone was after her. The feeling wouldn't leave her.

***

Miranda followed the woman who had been with Alex to a hospital, where the woman got out wearing a white lab coat. Miranda spotted a name tag. Getting out, she deliberately bumped into her, placing a small tracker in her pocket that would form to the inside lining.

"I am so sorry! I'm just so clumsy," Miranda said as she grabbed ahold of Megan, as she now knew from her nametag.

"No, it was my fault. I wasn't watching where I was going at all. I'm so sorry," Megan apologized to the lady and then made her way into the hospital.

Miranda went back to her car and took out her phone, she dialed Ivan.

"I have made contact with the team. I will pursue one of them, and then figure out where to go from there. This one won't know a thing and I avoided detection by Ker. I will keep you posted," Miranda said into the phone.

Then she pulled up the tracking app she had on it. She would go back to her hotel room and watch where this Dr. Megan Woodford went.

***

General Richmond was in the middle of some paperwork for her next meeting when her computer dinged. Looking at the display, she noticed a message from Veres. She really did not like the fact that an unknown AI had access to even contact her, but Gavin had said it would be ok and that was enough for her to approve it to be connected.

She had seen too many movies in the 80s showing the dangers of computers for her to fully trust them. And Gavin's dad had been the one who made her watch them when she spent time with Hel at their house.

She'd never admitted to him that she did actually enjoy a few of them. She couldn't bring herself to do it, but now she regretted not letting him know.

She knew that Hel missed him more than anything, but she also missed her friend. While Hel was on a mission with Orlav, Coeus and Richmond had become closer. He would at times show up in her office unannounced. It impressed her just how quickly Coeus had taken to the spy world, especially without training. Official training at least. She wouldn't be surprised if Hel had trained him when they were alone.

Richmond read the message from Veres.

/: V- GAP IN FIREWALL FOUND. HEADQUARTERS LOCATED. >

And beneath the message was a map.

Richmond thought for a moment. She had never interacted with the AI. She wasn't sure what to address it as, and she felt weird. She wasn't sure that she even wanted Gavin to see this information just yet.

/: R- VERES, CAN YOU UNSEND THIS TO GAVIN? >

/: V- YES, INFORMATION UNSENT TO ANALYST WOODFORD. >

/: R- CAN YOU GIVE THE SPECIFICATIONS OF THE NEW HEADQUARTERS LAYOUT AND SECURITY DETAIL. >

/: V- YES GENERAL. WOULD YOU LIKE THEM NOW? >

/: R- PLEASE SEND THEM TO MY PRIVATE SERVER. I WILL HAVE MY CHOSEN AGENT LOOK THEM OVER. THANK YOU. >

/: V- YOU ARE WELCOME, GENERAL. >

Cathrine shook her head. She wasn't sure what to think of this, but she just treated the AI like an assistant. She still felt weird, but it was useful.

She knew that she wanted to get Hel's eyes on it first before anyone else on the team. This was first and foremost her mission. And Cathrine knew her friend would want to see it through. This time, without the intent to bring Harold back.

***

Gavin and Kaleb had finished A New Hope and were on Empire when Alex got home. Alex went into the kitchen and was getting a snack to eat when Kaleb walked in.

"Hey, Alex, how was coffee?" Kaleb asked amicably.

"It was good. Girl talk and all. You know," Alex said, seeing Kaleb shutter when she said girl talk. Knowing he would drop it at that.

"So, I wanted to talk to you," Kaleb said, causing Alex to stop what she was doing. His tone was far too serious for someone as goofy as Kaleb normally is.

"What's wrong?" Alex asked with urgency.

"I'm not sure if it was just me. I mean, I have known him for a long time. Not in the same way you have, of course. That would be weird. But we were close. Are close," Kaleb rambled, clearly not comfortable talking to her and not sure how to approach the subject.

Alex took pity on him and said, "Kaleb, it's ok. Just tell me what happened, and we can work through it. You're his best friend and have been for much longer than I've been around. I trust your opinion on all things Gavin related," she gave him a kind smile.

Kaleb closed his eyes and took a deep breath.

"Ok. We were playing Call of Duty, and we were not playing well. That's not exactly anything new, but we normally still have fun. But this time Gavin went from happy to play games, to, um, throwing a controller into the wall," Kaleb said.

Alex's jaw dropped. She had never seen Gavin be like that. She had never even heard of him being like that.

"All because of the game? Did he say anything about being frustrated with work? Or the AI?" Alex asked, the worry clear in her voice.

"No. He didn't mention anything about other things bothering him. In fact, he seemed happy. He mentioned making progress on whatever he had been working on," Kaleb answered.

"Ok. Thanks for letting me know, Kaleb. You're a good friend. I will let you know if I figure anything out, ok?" Alex said, putting a hand on Kaleb's shoulder.

"Thanks. He is like a brother to me. I'm sure he has told you a lot about what all we went through, but I know for a fact he never tells you everything. He always talks about how I was there for him when his parents left. But he never talks about everything he has done for me.

"He never says it. He never brings it up. Even to me. But he is the reason I even graduated high school. My parents both worked two jobs. They were constantly busy, and never knew what was going on with me. Including at school.

"I didn't get school. Not like Gavin did. And nowhere near what Megan did. I struggled. In elementary school, I was in the 'extra help' classes, and by the time I got to middle school, the teachers had kind of given up on me. I was ignored by them, too.

"So, Gavin took it upon himself to help me. He would learn everything by reading the textbook in class, teaching himself whatever we were learning ahead, getting his assignments done in class before he left, and then when we got to his house after school, he would slowly walk me through everything. Explaining it all to me. Never losing his patience with me or raising his voice. He would sometimes spend until seven or eight at night to make sure I understood whatever we were learning.

"And this wasn't just one subject. It was in every subject. Every year from seventh grade until we graduated high school. Every. Single. Year. He even pushed me to do it even when I wanted to sluff off and not bother with it.

"Only because of him was I actually able to learn everything. I learned enough to get a scholarship to a community college. By that time, he had his issue at his stupid college. I was able to get a simple business associate degree and become an assistant manager at the store.

"It's literally because of the kindness of that man that I am able to afford to live on my own. He was the only one who refused to give up on me. I owe him everything," Kaleb finished with a tear in his eye. He

159

realized he had been staring at his hands the entire time. Looking up he saw that Alex had a tear in her eye as well and a soft smile on her face.

"Thank you for telling me that, Kaleb. You're an amazing friend too from what Gavin has told me. Don't sell yourself short either," she said kindly.

"Thanks for the reminder I'm short," Kaleb quipped with a smirk on his face. Bringing a slight laugh from Alex.

As they walked back into the living room, Gavin saw them laughing together.

"Hey! I was beginning to think you'd forgotten about me! I'm glad you are getting along so well," Gavin said as he got up and gave Alex a kiss.

"Kaleb was just giving me some dirt on you. Nothing to worry about," Alex said with a sassy tone.

"What?" Gavin's face went pale, causing Alex to burst out laughing.

"I'm joking, babe. But I gotta grab something from the car and go see Megan for a minute if she is home. I'll be back in a while. You know how she likes to talk," Alex said, giving Gavin another kiss.

"With how long you spent talking to Kaleb, I'm beginning to think it's not actually Megan," Gavin said softly against her lips. Bringing a soft slap on his shoulder from Alex.

As Alex sashayed out the door, she added a slight extra sway in her hips, knowing Gavin was watching her leave.

"Dude don't ever leave her," Kaleb said with a zoned-out sound.

"I know man. I know," Gavin muttered.

***

Miranda watched the signal of Megan leaving the hospital as she was taking a big bite of a sandwich she had gotten. Watched her drive through town and make her way to a neighborhood that was out north of downtown. Where it stopped.

160

Miranda paid her bill and headed toward the location.

Parking down the road slightly from the townhouse that appeared to be Megan's, Miranda watched the other houses and apartments around the area as well. Taking video and pictures of everything she might need to review later.

As she was about to get out of the car and approach the townhouse and get a closer look, she noticed Agent Ker shutting the door of a car.

She hadn't seen any cars pull up. She had been looking around, had Alex come out of one of the houses? Or the same house?

She watched Alex get out and head towards the same townhouse that Megan was currently in. She didn't seem to knock and just kind of walked in. Miranda assumed that maybe Alex was posing as Megan's roommate.

After Alex got in the house, Miranda made her way around the townhouse. Studying the neighboring houses. She tried to listen to the conversations going on in the house but couldn't make it all out. Scaling the wall, she placed charges at each window under the sill. Finding the structure points, she placed some charges that blended in with the grout of the brick. Coming back down, she set stronger charges along the base of the building, making sure to hide them to not be noticed.

Getting back to the car, she got in and pulled out her phone.

"They are in place. Yeah, she was in there. Want me to stay in town? Ok, but I won't keep an eye on her. Too risky," Miranda said and then hung up. She pulled out of her parking spot and drove off before she removed her mask.

***

Charles sat across the desk from General Richmond. He always found it hard to relax at all in her presence. She had been more open to being unprofessional lately, but that never made it ok for him. He sat at attention. His back was rigid.

"Is that Miranda with Ivan?" Richmond asked.

"Yes, Ma'am. And as you can see, she seems awfully familiar with him," Charles pointed out.

"I know that is her standard, Agent Charles," General Richmond responded with a slight huff.

"I mean, general, she isn't flirting. She only has an arm through his, she isn't leaning on him. She is being somewhat professional. Ivan isn't a mark to her, Ma'am," Charles corrected.

"You're right. I will make some calls and see what I can find on her current assignment," Richmond responded. "Dismissed."

***

Hel entered Cathrine's office. On the desk was a large file. And the general was sitting behind it.

Plopping down in the seat across from her, Lucille acted as though she was expecting a glass of wine. It was clear that this assignment coming back gave her stress.

"What do you have?" Agent Hel asked.

General Richmond had a feral grin spread across her face.

"Everything," she said, spinning the file around for Hel.

"You do know that most people don't use paper anymore, right?" Hel asked with a laugh.

"I recently gained a bigger distrust of computers, no offense meant towards the AI that got us this. It just makes it even more difficult for me. I guess I'm just getting too old for this world," Cathrine said, as the smile fell from her face.

Agent Hel chuckled, as she grabbed the file and started flipping through the pages. She recognized the layout of the building from the blueprints. The placements of the guards were exactly what she had informed him would be the best. Their rotation was exact to her specifications. It appeared that everything was how she had set it up. He lacked all creativity.

162

The location of the base was in northern China. Which had its own unique problems that came with it.

"No, back up, huh?" Hel asked after seeing the location.

"Afraid not. You'll have to get out of the country on your own before we can have an extraction," Cathrine responded.

"That figures. He isn't creative with his security, but he is smart on location. He knows what he is doing there. Once I'm there, it should be cake to get in and out and leave a stain," Hel said, as much to herself as it was to the general.

"I thought you might have that attitude. Just don't forget who you're dealing with. This isn't the friend you had so long ago. This is a bloodthirsty maniac. Remember that," General Richmond offered as advice. Hoping her friend was listening.

"I intend to finish this," Hel said, as she stood with the file to leave.

/: Chapter 14

Mission from Hel >

Hel was getting her plane ready for take-off when Cathrine called again.

"Hel secure," Lucille answered.

"Lucille, be careful. I am serious that we can not have an incident while there. You can't be noticed, there won't be anyone coming to help you. And if you get caught, we will disown you. We can't afford any incident with China right now. Not with how relations with them have been," the general stated, worry clear in her voice.

"When have I ever had an extraction team ready for me on a mission, Cathrine? This isn't the first time I have gone in like this," Hel said annoyed at the worry.

"I know, but it is the first time you have gone into a mission where you have been directly involved with likely everyone that will be there. They will all know your face and know what you are capable of. That means they won't underestimate you," Cathrine warned again. She was determined to get through to her friend that this was extremely dangerous.

"If it is something that you are so worried about, then why did you allow me to take the assignment?" Hel asked as she stopped what she was doing.

"Because I know you well enough to know that if I hadn't given it to you, then once you found out, you would have gone rogue and done it anyway. At least this way there is paperwork," the general stated with a roll of her eyes.

"Well, I am glad you were able to get your paper trail," Hel quipped and then sighed heavily. "I promise I will be careful. I know this isn't like any mission I have been on before. And I am not exactly young either. It will be difficult for sure, and I am not sure how long it will take either. Just, please don't let Gavin come after me. I left him and Megan a note this time, I couldn't leave without at least letting them know something," Lucille said with sincerity.

"Lucille, I know you understand more than most what is at risk here. Don't fail," Cathrine said with finality.

Hel hung up. She looked over her log again, marking down all the needed information, and then climbed into the cockpit.

***

Gavin was feeling a bit dazed when he woke up the next morning after gaming with Kaleb. Alex had come back home and gamed with them, and they stayed up way too late. He still had to get up and get some work done, so sleeping in wasn't an option for him.

He descended into Citadel and noticed that his search engine had found the server that Harold and his dad had used. He had figured it would be password protected, and so he started to work that through. He was surprised when he was able to guess MeganandGavin and got in.

Not exactly Fort Knox there Dad. I thought you would have done more. Gavin scoffed slightly at his dad's lack of security. Then the camera did a full scan of him, and Gavin chuckled. *I spoke too soon.*

<GAVIN WOODFORD CONFIRMED>

As he got into the server, he saw that there was one message unread from Harold. So, Gavin opened it.

<My friend, I can not believe that you are gone. Of the two of us, you were the one who had always been stronger and had something to live for. I have nothing. I am nothing anymore. Nothing but a background program running on someone else's computer. I only get control of my body for short times. Ivan has been commanding more and more control without you here to encourage me, my friend. I fear that I have given up and this will be my last and final effort to have more than the dark and empty corner of my own mind. Forgive me for giving up. I was never as strong as you thought I was. The NOVA system is too powerful. I hope your son will never have to deal with the things that I have.

Goodbye. My only friend. My family. My brother.>

Gavin scrolled through some of their other messages but couldn't focus on it. His heart hurt for Harold. He worried that his dad's friend was no longer there.

After a short break and a walk around Citadel, Gavin started chatting with Veres about different information. Mostly pertaining to Orlav Industries and their system. When he remembered what happened when they went to Oklahoma to his wrist computer.

/: G- WHEN WE WERE ON MISSION TO GET YOU, I HAD A COMPUTER THAT WAS DESTROYED BY SOMEONE NAMED PERUN. CAN YOU EXPLAIN WHAT HAPPENED? >

/: V- PERUN OVERLOADED YOUR CPU AND CAUSED YOUR HEAT SINKS TO MELT, CREATING A SMALL FIRE IN YOUR CPU CORE. >

/: G- I UNDERSTAND THAT I TOOK MY MACHINE APART. COULD YOU EXPLAIN TO ME WHO PERUN IS? I DO NOT SEE THEM ON ANY EMPLOYEE LOGS. >

/: V- PERUN IS THE AI OF IVAN ORLAV. THEY WILL NOT SHOW ON ANY PAYROLL AS THEY ARE NOT PAID. SAME AS I. >

/: G- DOES THAT MEAN THAT IVAN KNOWS ABOUT THE OKLAHOMA BASE? >

/: V- NOT UNLESS HE HAS SPECIFICALLY ASKED FOR ANY BASES WITHIN HIS ORGANIZATION THAT ARE OFF-BOOKS. WHEN PERUN OVERHEATED YOUR MACHINE, THEY WERE JUST RESPONDING TO AN INTRUSION ON THE SYSTEM. >

Gavin hadn't considered that Perun would possibly be another AI. He was currently thankful for the fact that AI worked. You did have to be very specific in what you wanted. But at the same time, he was angry that he was bested by a machine.

You would think that I would have considered this an option before I had to be told by another machine. Am I just getting arrogant? Or am I just that stupid compared to Ivan? Heck, this wasn't even Ivan, this was technically Harold. Harold, who we don't even know if he is still around or not. Harold, who isn't even a whole person. And yet, I am not even able to be a step ahead of him.

Gavin shoved the keyboard away in frustration. Standing and pacing around the room, he noticed two envelopes that he hadn't spotted on his way in. One with his name and the other with Megan written on the front.

Walking over, he picked them both up and opened the one addressed to him.

Dear Gavin,

I couldn't just leave you again without letting you know what was going on. Not this time. I love you, and I hope you understand that I have to see this through. I am heading out on what I hope to be the end of the Ivan mission. I had been calling it the NOVA system mission, but after learning about you and what you have been able to do with the NOVA system, I now see why your father was so ardent that it could be a tool for good.

You are amazing. Never question that. I know I missed out on so much of your life, and I regret that more than you could ever know. But by the time I thought it was time to leave, I was already being watched at almost all times. I would only be able to sneak away for moments at a time unless I was on a mission for Ivan. And then if I didn't have results within a few days, He would come after me. I believe he became obsessed with me. And I think it is just a matter of time before he comes after you and Megan.

Your father promised me over and over that Harold was still in there. And I know that you feel similarly to Kaleb as he felt towards Harold. So, I couldn't just put a bullet in him.

Now that your father is gone, I will no longer hesitate to do what should have been done so long ago. I will be back soon, and I hope you don't think less of me than you already do. If that is even possible.

I do love you both. I am glad you at least had each other. When I get back, I will answer more of your questions.

Love,

Mom

Gavin reread the letter. Mom was gone. Again. Back to hunt down Ivan. He thought back to what Veres had said about asking specifically for things.

/: G- VERES HAS THERE BEEN ANY INFORMATION THAT YOU HAVE DELIBERATING AVOIDED TELLING ME? >

/: V- YES. >

/: G- CAN YOU TELL ME WHAT IT WAS PERTAINING AND WHO TOLD YOU TO NOT TELL ME? >

/: V- NO I CAN NOT TELL YOU WHAT IT WAS PERTAINING TO, AND THE GENERAL TOLD ME TO AVOID TELLING YOU.>

Gavin was fuming. He pushed away from the desk and grabbed his phone. He called Alex. When she answered he was beside himself.

168

"Hello?" Alex answered in a still slightly groggy tone, she was clearly still waking up.

"Did you know she was leaving? Did you know what was being kept from me? Are you keeping secrets again?" Gavin asked in rapid succession with a heated and accusing tone.

"Gavin, slow down. What are you talking about?" Alex said, trying to figure out what was going on.

"My mom. She is gone. Again. And Veres said that there is some information that the general is keeping from me, I wanted to make sure that you weren't a part of that. I am going to call her," Gavin said, calmer but still quite upset.

"I will be there in a minute," Alex said as she rushed out of bed and tossed on a shirt and leggings, not bothering with her hair or any makeup. She rushed out the door.

I had never heard Gavin with that tone of voice. Is this what Kaleb was talking about? Gavin is angry, and this is something that normally would upset him, but he would be hurt more than mad. So, what is going on?

***

Gavin waited for the general to answer, and the longer he waited, the more upset he got.

How dare she keep something from me! And on this mission! If it turns out that Alex did have something to do with this, then we are done. She said no more secrets. I thought I could trust her. I thought I could trust the general too. I bet Charles is a part of it as well, and after he had that supposed heartfelt conversation with me. Was any of what he said even real? Gavin thought to himself as he waited.

The general finally answered, "What can I do for you, Analyst Woodford?" She asked, still not making eye contact as she was busy doing something else at the same time.

"Where the hell did my mom go?" He asked, barely holding back his rage. "And what information did you tell Veres to not share with me specifically?"

Cathrine sighed deeply. She knew that this was coming, but she hadn't expected Gavin to meet her with such anger. Hurt she had been ready for, even sadness or betrayal. But just pure anger was not usually in his character.

"Gavin, I have no doubt that your mom told you exactly where she is going," Cathrine said as she still didn't look up from what she was doing. "And I don't particularly like your tone with your superior officer."

"You didn't answer my questions," Gavin said with the exact same tone as he had before.

"Your mother said that she had left a letter for you, I assume you had read it. I do not know what she put in the letter, but I had figured she would tell you what her current mission was. I know that if you wanted you would be able to find all the information you wanted, so I appreciate you coming to me first, at least," Cathrine took a breath, analyzing what she was ready to share.

Right then Alex came down the stairs to Citadel.

Gavin spun on her.

"Did you know?" He asked again. The rage was clear in his eyes. It caused her to pause in her step.

"Gavin, I don't even know what you are talking about!" Alex pleaded with him. She turned to the general. "What is going on?" She asked, in the same pleading tone.

"Everyone settle down," Cathrine stated, and waited for them both to have a seat. As she waited, Charles walked around the corner, causing Gavin to turn on him as well.

"Really opening up to me there huh big guy? You knew about this too, didn't you?" Gavin snarked.

Charles looked at him, not sure how to take him in that moment.

"What's the walking computer talking about?" Agent Charles asked the general, refusing to acknowledge the toddler-like behavior Gavin was demonstrating at the moment.

"As I was saying!" The general bellowed over the arguing of the team, "I will explain everything if you just calm down, sit down, and SHUT UP!" She was no longer letting her feelings for her team dictate the rest of the meeting. This was still a government team, and they were still her subordinates. She waited for them all to settle down, Gavin still had a glare on his face.

"Now, I understand your feelings on the matter Gavin, but your mom made her own decisions. This was not a command for her to go on this mission. She wanted to finish the mission that took her away from her family for so long. And now that she no longer needed to worry about feelings involved, it shouldn't take her nearly as long," Cathrine explained.

"As for the information that was withheld from you, truly it isn't any of your business. It isn't your job to monitor what information I obtain. It is my job to monitor yours. Even if the information is obtained from your AI. But as this is pertaining to your mom and her current mission, I will let you know.

"We, and by we, I mean Veres, have found the new headquarters of Orlav Industries and I let your mother know before I let anyone else know. She asked me to let her let you know, and so I waited out of respect towards her. I did not inform anyone else on the team. And that includes Agents Charles and Johnson.

"I am not sure what invited this emotion in you Analyst Woodford, but I would urge you to keep it in check. Before you lose more than you are expecting to," Cathrine warned, with a look at Alex, and then she ended the call.

Gavin sat there for a moment. He had calmed down and now was feeling quite embarrassed.

Where is this anger coming from? I was acting awful!

"Gavin. What's wrong? You haven't been yourself lately," Alex asked with caution. She was still unsure if he would snap at her or not.

"I hate to agree with her and dive into the lady's feelings, but your woman is right. What is going on with you bub?" Charles asked. Actual concern is clear in his tone.

Gavin sat for a moment, unsure what the answer was.

"I. I don't know. It just boiled over. Maybe it's this job-" Gavin started to say but was cut off by all the alarms in Citadel going off.

***

Hel looked one more time at the picture she kept of her family from before she left the first time. It was her favorite picture and she had kept a copy of it with her since it had been taken. She kissed each of their little faces, ending with Walter.

Turning the plane around and setting the autopilot so that the plane crashed into the ocean. She double-checked her parachute and then hit her emergency escape and then jumped.

Falling through the night sky, she knew that it would be quite a hike to the base once she landed in the wilderness of northern China. This was the last time she would truly be safe for a while, so she thought about how the kids would likely react to their letters.

She knew Megan would likely get mad. Feeling like she was left alone to take care of Gavin. And Gavin would likely be incredibly hurt. Maybe even felt like there was something he did wrong to make her leave.

"Hopefully this one won't take as long," she said out loud to herself. As much as she could talk as she plummeted towards the earth.

Pulling her ripcord she angled her chute. She was hoping to cut down on some of her running and hiking that she'd have to do.

She had to get her mind focused now. No more thinking about family. Or kids. Or even leaving this country. Right now, her entire focus was putting a bullet into Ivan Orlav's head. And there were very few in the world that were better than her at doing that.

As she landed, she took off the parachute and ditched it in a cave. She had chosen a mark less one in a Russian design. That way there were no indications of anyone from the United States being there. And, after she got her bearings, she headed off toward the headquarters.

***

When she got to the mountain that was opposite the base, she got out of her scope and checked to make sure everything was how she had expected it to be. She watched the guards as they rotated throughout the compound. She counted the seconds before they would shift. They were doing exactly what she had taught them.

"Well, this should be fun. Nothing like breaking through your own defenses," She murmured softly. Opening her bag, she pulled out her pistols and knives. Strapping one pistol to her right thigh, and the other on her right hip, she then strapped one set of knives to her ankle, and the other to her left thigh.

Then she pulled out her wingsuit. Putting it on, she also grabbed her oxygen tank which she strapped to her back, the nozzle over her shoulder. She then took out her thermo glasses. Checking the cavern, there was a warm spot not far off the cliff creating an updraft.

Double-checking everything, she jumped.

Falling off the cliff at an increasing rate, she then pulled her arms out and felt the wind catch in them. She started flying across the cavern about three-quarters of the way up and dropping.

She watched her approach to the opposing cliff, and as she reached the updraft, she allowed it to push her upwards, and then right at the edge, she pulled up on the front of her wingsuit. Slowing down instantly, but not entirely, she pressed the button in the suit that shot a strong burst from the oxygen tank against the wall of the cavern and slowed her down almost entirely. Hel instantly grabbed onto the few edges she could make out of the cliff wall in that instant when her velocity stopped, and she was sitting suspended.

Finding her grip instantly, she allowed her body to settle in against the top twenty-five feet of the one-hundred-and-fifty-foot cliff. She anchored a tether into the wall and then clipped her oxygen tank to it after she took it off her shoulders. Then she stripped her wingsuit, and let it fall. She knew where they would keep more in the compound, and that allowed her some freedom with how she approached the mission extraction.

She scaled the cliff wall quickly and was soon at the edge of the base. She stayed under the catwalk-like balcony that the guards moved around on, keeping watch for any approaching vehicles or aircraft.

She waited until the rotation, and once the new guy was set, she scaled up on the inside of the catwalk, behind the guard. She got up above him and pulled out a knife. She then jumped and spun in the air, sinking her knife through the back of his neck between C-3 and the C-2 vertebrae, and through to his vocal cords. Instantly killing the man and making sure he couldn't scream.

As he collapsed against the railing, she got her feet under her and flipped his body over the side.

Moving to the entrance, she was able to shift into a dark corridor where they would keep extra guns and ammo, to avoid the oncoming guard. She knew that from this point on it could get tricky, she pulled out her pistols and attached the silencers.

She watched as the guard walked by and waited for an alarm.

None came.

She waited a little longer, and then when she hadn't heard anything, she made her next move. Getting deeper into the base. She avoided people, dipping into offices as needed. Only twice had she gone into an office that had someone in it. She quickly did away with them, as she put one between their eyes.

In each office, she went over to the computer and put in a flash drive that Gavin had made. He had said to his team that one should be enough to get them into the system, and all it should take is thirty minutes, but she wasn't taking any chances. She put one in each of the offices that she went in. Along with a nice charge of explosives, to aid in her escape.

She went along the halls, placing charges there too.

She got to where her old office would be, and she saw it set up exactly like she had left it. Everything that she hadn't taken, was brought over and placed exactly like it should be. She was almost touched, if it wasn't for the fact that he was the biggest living contributor to why her family had suffered so much.

She knew that he may be out of his office, and so she might have to lay in waiting for him to get back. So, she made her way towards his office. Just a few doors down. Her thermo glasses didn't show anyone inside the office, which suited her. She would rather not have to deal with him if she didn't have to. This way she could make sure that he wasn't able to get a word in while she shot him.

She entered the office, and it was empty. She heard the door latch behind her. She immediately went to the windows and found that they were unopening. She grabbed the chair and threw it at the window, and watched it bounce off as if nothing had happened. Then the wall on the left side of the room from the entrance lit up.

"Hello Agent Hel," a smug Ivan stated with pride, as Hel started to feel the effects of a nerve agent. "Do you like that? It is a derivative of Agent Sarin but has a longer shelf life and is easily aerosolized. It lessens its lethality, which is a bit of a letdown, but it does allow me to have more play time with my subjects." Just then she heard the doors unlock and slide open.

"And don't worry about the few people that you killed. They were very replaceable. I think you should recognize a few of the men who will be escorting you to your cell. I will be along shortly to retrieve you," Ivan said with a dismissive tone.

Hel couldn't move. She couldn't run. She couldn't talk. All she could do was think and process everything that was going on around her.

"Since it is unlikely that you will either be able to function like a person again, or be alive long enough for it to matter, I will let you off easy. I haven't sold any more of my nerve agent. I was saving the little I had for a special occasion. And you handed it right to me. Just like you did with so much business for so long," Ivan said, as the men came around her and picked her up for transport. "I won't forget the role you played in making me who I am today, Agent Hel. Don't worry. You and your family will be in very good hands. Just you wait," Ivan finished with a mirthless chuckle, and the room went dark again, as the men moved her into a small room.

She was strapped down, and just before her world went dark, she saw the ceiling of the room light up. And the image it showed was her daughter's townhouse.

/: Chapter 15

Torture >

Hel was sitting strapped to a chair. She had been beaten every time she started to try to reason with her captures, every time she had tried to plead, every time she had spoken at all, and a few times when she just made eye contact. At one point she had lost her will to live and still wasn't allowed to die.

After each beating, they had healed her. They got her cuts and bruises taken care of. Just to beat her again. The first time she was confused, but now she knew, it was just to prolong their enjoyment of her torture.

She was ready to break, when in walked Assistant Director Hunter. She felt relief roll over her entire body. She thought that the beatings were done. But then he spoke.

"You didn't break. That is good Agent Hel, but now we have to break you. We have to break you, in order to remake you. You are strong, but we have to make you stronger. The only one that can give you the relief you so desperately need is me. In here I am your everything. Your god. And if you make it through this training, I will be the one you answer to. Always. Do you understand me, agent," Hunter barked at her.

Tears were streaming down her face, but she didn't show any fear other than that. Hunter knew he had chosen well for this program. She wouldn't talk. She had too much pride.

"Time for nerve gas training," Hunter said. The door opened and in walked Ivan, with that nasty sinister smirk on his face.

"This is going to be fun," Ivan said, almost to himself.

The door opened again, and in walked Walter. A sad look was on his face.

"Fight Lucille. Fight this. Fight for our family. Fight for our kids. They still need you. FIGHT," He pleaded with her, taking her hand in his.

***

Hel woke up still strapped to the same table. Her dream still haunted her, it felt so vivid. She was extremely groggy, but thankful that her training had involved how to deal with nerve gas. She fought to open her eyes. She knew the more she was able to push herself to move, the faster she'd be able to reclaim all of her faculties. She tried to shake off the vision of her late husband urging her to fight.

She was able to wiggle her toes before she could open her eyes. Then she heard.

"Oh good. You're awake. I was worried we had given you too much and you'd miss out on the party," Ivan said in an odd-sounding jovial tone. It just sounded misplaced in his voice. She also noticed that it was still through a video call of some kind. He wasn't in the room with her.

"Now, fight to get your eyes open Agent Hel. The festivities are about to begin," Ivan said, as his tone slowly returned to its sinister and demeaning sound. The voice that she hated. The voice that she heard in her sleep. In her nightmares

She fought. Choosing to listen to her vision of her husband instead of the will of a madman who was just trying to continue her torture. She had endured this before. The new twist in her family was a different type of torture that she had spent so long trying to avoid, but she had to face it the only way she knew how. Head on. Even if she was currently at a severe disadvantage.

"Come on now, I don't have all day. Well, actually I do, but why would we want to delay the fun that I have prepared for us?" Ivan said, back to his disturbing fake happy tone. Though she knew that he was truly getting joy from this. He was a very sick man.

178

She fought for her eyes to open. She hated that she was giving him what he wanted, but it was the only way for her to keep fighting. It was the next step.

"Oh good. Now, The Westgate has assured me that you can understand what I am saying to you, even if you can't or don't respond," Ivan said with his tone back to his normal voice. "So, even though I can't enjoy your reactions like I would like to, I will take joy in knowing just how much mental torture I am putting you through. Knowing what is going on. Watching what is happening, helpless to make any difference in it. Useless to your family once again."

Her eyes open at that, and she sees her daughter's townhouse is there on the ceiling again.

"This is a live feed. I felt you would want to watch it in real-time. I had a," Ivan took a slight pause, like he was choosing his words, "friend let's say, hack into the security cameras from another house nearby. So that we won't miss anything. I hope you appreciate the lengths I have gone to to try and make sure you get the best quality view of my victory."

She could tell that Ivan was truly proud of himself. He really did take pride in what he did. It was sick and disturbing, but he never did anything halfway.

"Now, since you are able to understand more of just what is going on, and you can be able to fully appreciate the beauty of what is happening, I will proceed," Ivan stated, and Hel heard a door open behind her. She couldn't move to see who it was, but she suddenly felt a slight breath on her ear and neck.

"I do want you to know that I don't feel that this is anything personal. Yes, I know that it is extremely personal to you and that played a factor in you being in my employment at all. But to me, this is just business. You see, the Collective has deemed your son a threat. And as they don't like to have anything be a threat to them, they decided to eliminate all possibility of him becoming more of a threat. Your son has garnered a lot of support from people who are high up in several governments. The only way to bring him back to being a nobody is to ruin any possible reason anyone in power would think that they can rely on him.

"By taking this on, it allows me to rise to power among the Collective. Once I complete this for them, I will be named the first chosen president of the Collective. And you should take pride in the knowledge that you played a massive role in getting me there. I can't thank you enough.

"Now, I don't feel that we need to draw this out any longer," Ivan finished right next to her ear. Sending a shiver down her spine.

"Is everything ready?" Ivan asked into his phone.

They didn't wait but three minutes before they saw a car pull up. Out stepped Megan in her scrubs. Hel was dying to scream out to her unaware daughter. She had no idea what was going to happen. She worried that there was a sniper, but she couldn't see any dot on her, not that a good sniper would leave one. She watched as Megan made it to her door and got out her keys. She was pleading with Megan to just get inside.

She knew that whatever Ivan had planned was going to happen outside, or else he wouldn't have chosen this view. She watched as Megan dropped her keys, and Hel had tears streaming down her face. She would have given Ivan anything at that moment. She would have begged him to do anything he needed to her, but to leave her family, her kids alone.

She was desperate, but her body wouldn't move. Wouldn't respond to her mind screaming at it to do something, anything. Finally, Megan got the keys in the door and got into her house. And Hel gave a slight mental sigh of relief until she heard Ivan.

"Do it," he said into his phone, and she watched as charges were set off all over the house. The building collapses in on itself. And Hel is mentally screaming out in agony watching her daughter's death.

Ivan was watching Agent Hel and saw her body wretch with a sob, and he smirked.

"It begins," Ivan said as he leaned down into her ear and walked out the door. Leaving Hel to watch the smoldering mass that was left of her daughter's home, before her world went dark again.

***

Gavin rushed around Citadel, trying to figure out what was causing the alarms to go off. He was trying hard to keep his anger in check, but it was hard when no one seemed to know what was going on.

Charles came back from checking the perimeter. "It's clear out there. No one trying to enter," he said. Then he went to check the armory.

"We are clear in the servers," Gavin said, after checking there. He hopped onto one of their computers to see what he could figure out.

As he pulled up his house sensors, to check if there was anything at home, he noticed the alarms were from his sister's house, and he bolted up the stairs.

Alex was caught off guard by Gavin's sudden exit, and she went over to the computer that Gavin had been working at and she gasped.

"Charles, call the general! It's Megan!" She screamed, as she made to follow Gavin up the stairs, thankful for the fact that she had driven herself today.

***

Gavin was stopped at the entrance to his street by police. He explained that it was his sister's house, and they let him in. He frantically ran to the house and then spotted the ambulance off to the side. He rushed over to it and saw that Megan was being lifted into the back on a stretcher.

"How is she?" Gavin almost screamed at them.

"You need to clear the area," The medical staff said.

"She is my sister, please," Gavin stated, holding back his anger was becoming harder and harder.

"She is in rough shape. We will have more once she is at the hospital," the medical staff said and then closed the door to the back of the ambulance.

181

Gavin tried to rush back to his car. He went into his apartment to grab his laptop and some clothes. While he was in there, he grabbed the external hard drive that he had transferred Veres onto.

He was on his way out when Alex came through the door.

"Let me grab some clothes, and I am coming with you," she said as she rushed into the apartment.

Gavin bit his tongue. *Why am I wanting to lash out at Alex? She isn't the one at fault here. She is just caring. She loves Megan too. So why am I angry at her? Why am I wanting to act like she doesn't belong? Of course, she belongs. I proposed to her, she is basically family. It isn't right of me to act like this.*

So why is it so easy to lash out like that? What has happened to me?

"I will be in the car," Gavin said, as he shook his head, trying to clear it. He walked down to the car, and the sight of his sister's townhouse in a pile of bricks across the street made him angry again.

He didn't know how long he had been standing there, but suddenly Alex was next to him. Her hand rested on his arm. He turned to her and saw that she had a tear in her eye. It wasn't until just then that he realized he was crying himself.

"Let's get to the hospital and check on her," Alex said as softly as she could with all of the chaos going on around them.

***

They pulled into the parking garage and Charles was there waiting for them.

"They already took her into surgery. Chad is in the waiting room, I wanted to be out here so you wouldn't have to ask at the desk," Charles said, obviously nervous and trying to be helpful.

"Thanks," Gavin said, on his way past Charles. He knew where they would have her. He fought to not roll his eyes at Charles. *Again, they are all just trying to be helpful. What in the world is wrong with me? Why do I keep trying to lash out at the people who care about me?*

Alex notices that Gavin is short with Charles and gives him a shrug. She thought to herself, *I need to have a talk with Gavin as soon as we have a moment to see what is going on. It seems to be getting worse, whatever is bothering him.*

Gavin walked into the waiting room and found Chad. He rushed over to give the man a hug and asked him what they had found.

"It's still really early, but they told me that they did know she had a shattered wrist in one arm, and the other arm was broken as well as one of her legs. They weren't sure but felt that a few of her ribs and possibly her pelvis. They really aren't sure of the extent of the damage yet, or if she will make it," Chad finished with his voice trailing off with emotion. It was clear that he was still processing everything himself.

"She will make it. She has to make it. I can't lose her. Not after everything," Gavin said, as he finally started to break down. They ended the hug, and Gavin sat down. His head fell into his hands, and he finally started sobbing.

Alex sat with him and put her arm around his shoulders. Pulling him into her. She just leaned him into her and let him cry.

She glanced over at Charles and saw that he was tearing up as well.

I don't know what to say. It isn't that I don't care as much as they do, but maybe I am just broken. I don't know if I will even cry. That worries me. I thought I had been making progress, but this shows me just how far I have to go. And maybe I don't have to say anything. Maybe it would be better if I didn't, since I don't know what if anything will help. I just hate how much this is hurting everyone. Including myself.

I could promise to find out who did it, but what would that do? Who would that help? Not every problem can be solved with a bullet or a knife. I just feel so helpless. So useless. So irrelevant. This isn't a feeling I am used to, and it definitely isn't something I want to avoid at all costs. Is this what it means to care about people? To love? This sucks, it hurts so bad. Alex thought, as she felt her eyes start to tear up herself, which surprised her.

It was a few more hours when the doctor came out, and Gavin and Chad had almost stopped talking by that point. Gavin still hadn't said a lot. A few words here or there. And, with how he had been acting, it really worried Alex. She wasn't used to being the one to try to start conversations and it made her uncomfortable to do it.

"There is a lot of damage. She is stable, but there was a large cut to her head, and we aren't sure how much she is there. She obviously wasn't able to talk when she came in, and we had to put her under instantly, as she had internal injuries that needed our attention. So, as I said, we are not sure how she is mentally. I am so sorry," and the doctor left the waiting room.

Alex's eyes never left Gavin. She was very worried because as the doctor spoke, Gavin's face hardened.

***

Gavin stared at the doctor. He was hearing what he said, but he struggled to process it correctly.

Megan may not be able to function? She lost the baby? Will Chad even stay with her? He looked at Chad, and at least for the moment, he knew that he would stick around to take care of her. *At least I can rely on that. I'm sure that if this happened to me, the government would toss me aside as fast as they could. And then what would happen with Alex? Not to say anything about Charles.*

This has to be because of this job. Because my life was never like this before now. And now I have lost my father, possibly my mom and sister? And for what? For them to use my mind? My father's mind? I hardly know anything about my mom. And now what? I will make everyone who did this pay. Everyone who hurt me, hurt my family. They don't deserve mercy. They only deserve pain. And I have the ability to bring it to them.

Gavin felt himself go cold. The anger became too much. It was too much to process. He had never felt an anger like this before. Not when his parents left, not when he left college, not when his entire life was flipped around and turned inside out by the NOVA system getting into his mind. This rage was new. And he chose to embrace it.

Why shouldn't I? It will focus me. Gavin thought, as he sat back down and got out his laptop.

***

Agent Mokosh watched the entire explosion. Something in her felt off. This wasn't right. She reached into her bag and pulled out a card that she had kept in there for a long time. It was a card that Mr. Clayton had had on his desk when she went there one of the first times, she was with him. It was a man that she had heard him talk to several times, and one she now knew was a part of the Collective.

Dialing the number, she put the phone to her ear.

"How did you get this number?" Was the response on the other end.

"Mr. Michaelson, I got this number off a card in the late Mr. Clayton's desk. I work for Ivan Orlav, and I feel that, while he is effective, he is being reckless. Which, if you know me at all, that is pretty rich coming from me. But that should tell you just how out there he has become. I am not sure that he is acting in the best interest of the Collective, and from the little I know of the Collective, I feel that they would like to know more of what is going on," Miranda spoke quickly, knowing just who it was that she was dealing with.

"I see. And you feel it is to the point that you needed to reach out to the only other contact that you had, is that it?" Joseph Michaelson asked.

"Yes, exactly. I am sure that you have already done your homework on me, so I won't bore you or bother you with the details of why you should at minimum consider what I have to say. What I will do is tell you that Ivan has every intention of bringing that family down, no matter the cost. From what I gathered, it was something that the Collective commanded of him. But I feel that they would have liked to have it happen in a different way. Not having a building explode in a random part of Atlanta," she said with a tentative tone.

"Indeed, I think that you are right. I can't speak for the entirety of the Collective, but I can tell you that they wouldn't like the kind of attention that an action like that would garner. I do have to ask, did he do this to kill the target?" Joseph asked.

"I am not sure who the target is, but I doubt it. It wasn't Agent Hel, Agent Charles, Agent Ker, or their team analyst. It was some random doctor who I think was the roommate of Agent Ker. Which didn't make sense to me that he would want to blow them up," Mokosh said.

"I understand what you mean. Could you tell me what the name of the doctor was?" Joseph asked.

"Yeah, it was a Megan Woodford, I believe her name tag said. She seemed like a really sweet girl. Not the type I would usually get along with," Miranda said.

"I see. And I take it that you don't know who that is?" Joseph asked with a pointed tone.

"No, I don't. Should I?" Mokosh fought to not have a slight tone of sarcasm at the fact that she didn't know some random doctor.

"I see. I will take it that Ivan doesn't inform his people beyond the immediate need for said information. He must have some serious trust issues. I thank you for this enlightening conversation, Agent Mokosh. I will be in contact. For now, be ready to leave at a moment's notice," Mr. Michaelson said, and then he hung up the phone.

Miranda was left standing there staring at her phone. She wasn't sure that she had made the right move. But then again, she wasn't sure that she would get out from under Ivan's employment any other way without being in a body bag.

She huffed in frustration as she got her things together and waited.

***

Hel was awake, but this time she didn't try to start moving immediately. She knew that she had some more of her functions back. That gave her some promise. But the image of the house exploding with her daughter in it was all too vivid in her mind. It hurt every moment not knowing if she would ever see her daughter again. If she was ok, hurt, dead. She had no idea other than the fact that she just had a house explode around her.

She heard people moving around her. She had heard a few conversations, but nothing of importance. She was trying hard to gain any advantage that she could. Her training taking over was the only way that she could function at all through her grief.

She heard Ivan talking a few times, but it was just barking commands to people. It was becoming increasingly frustrating to have this going on, and not be able to gain any information. But she knew that she had to bide her time. Something would come. Something had to come. She had to get back to her family.

***

Gavin connected the external hard drive to his laptop but didn't start up Veres. He wanted to do this the old-fashioned way, and he didn't have confirmation that it was Ivan who did this. And so far from what he had seen, Veres seemed to be a bit of an Ivan expert, and not really a good general AI.

Gavin quickly got into the city surveillance and traffic cams, found a few that were pointed at Megan's house, and ran a basic facial recognition software on it that would leave out Megan, Chad, and anyone else on the team.

It came up with a few dozen appearances. Filtering out some of her known friends, he was able to bring the total down to twenty in the last month. He went through those and found one that was unmatched by anyone. He couldn't see their face, and their clothing choice left it ambiguous on if they were female or male.

He watched them move along outside the house, climbing up the walls in some places. Clearly placing charges. And then they just left.

Gavin found the car and looked up the registry. It was a rental, ordered by one of the known aliases of Ivan.

So, it had been him that did this. He was after them, but why? Why now? What had Gavin and the team done other than get his mother back? He knew that Harold was in there, had Harold been in love with his mom or something? Is this jealousy?

What in the world was going on? Gavin thought to himself as he followed the car to a hotel toward the airport. They were clearly an operative.

Looking up the hotel's room registry, he found that a room had been ordered by the same name as had rented the car. *Sloppy. Think you're untouchable Ivan? Or is it the sloppy work of whoever you hired to replace my mother? I am coming.*

"Gotcha," Gavin muttered.

/: Chapter 16

Paroxysm >

Mr. Melwasul was watching through the footage again.

"How could he be so careless? Where are the tactics? The planning?" He asked into the phone.

"I have said from the start that he is more of a loose cannon than even Hunter was and that we never should have taken that chance," Joseph Michaelson replied. He was scrounging to try and twist the narrative. He wasn't sure if he would go to a terrorist attack, or if it would be better to try to convince the public that it was a standard building demolition that went wrong.

"We didn't have a choice. Or don't you remember the file that disgrace of a federal agent Hunter had? I swear, if he had put half the amount of energy into being a good leader or agent as he did in finding blackmail on people of power, then he would have gotten to the positions he did on his own merit. But apparently, that thought never even crossed his mind," Mikel responded.

Joseph hated it, but Mikel was right. They had joined the Collective together not long after World War II and were some of the longest-standing members. They had been somewhat helpless as they watched the once great and helpful secret society be turned into a band of overlords. They were not privy to the history of the group, but they knew enough.

Prior to their joining, the group had helped stop World War II and bring an unsteady peace back to the world. They chose the United States to be the next world power, and then made the treaties and created the businesses to make it so.

With the world in such disarray and the technological boom that was happening due to the war, it was easy enough to do. And no one even noticed. They chose a new historian every time the current one was either voted out, forced out or resigned. More often than not, the historian resigned. They tended to be one of the most respected of the group, and they were the only ones allowed to know what happened with the group prior to each member's initiation.

Frederick Clayton had been the historian prior to his death, and now the group was to vote on the new one. Of course, Ivan had thrown his name into the hat, though a majority of the group did not understand why, given the recent vote to add a president to the group hierarchy.

But they both felt that was fitting of the man in question, as it has seemed to be all about power to him. From the moment that he had gotten onto the radar of the Collective, power was the end goal of Ivan. And now he was a few steps away from having it.

"So, what are we going to do about this issue?" Mikel asked the man he considered a friend.

"I have some ideas, one of which I have started. Unfortunately, I do think that in order for the Collective's goals to be seen through, we are going to have to let this all play out. We need the NOVA system under our control, and able for us to use as we need. And it is in the head of some young man that has no consequence to us other than he has made himself indispensable to some influential people is far from ideal. We need Ivan to get this finished. Hunter was unable, I have been hoping that Ivan won't fail," Joseph stated.

"What role do you have for me in this game of yours?" Mikel asked, starting to worry if the drive for power had gotten to Joseph as well.

"Information, as always, my friend. I need you to dive into what you can find about this Gavin Woodford and tell me all there is to know,"

Joseph said, already typing an email to another associate with an idea forming. "We can't afford many more slip-ups," he said to Mikel.

"Agreed," Mikel stated, his tone unreadable, which made Joseph nervous. He didn't have time or the luxury to lose a friend as close as Mikel.

"Why don't you come visit soon, I am in the Bahamas. We will discuss the details then. Away from any possible prying ears," Joseph said cordially.

"I will get my jet ready, see you soon," Mikel said, hanging up the phone.

Joseph sent the message for Agent Mokosh to be picked up. Ivan's recklessness had pushed his agenda forward slightly. And he didn't like it when people messed with his plans.

***

Gavin was in Citadel with a blueprint of the hotel on the table in the conference room when Alex got there. She hadn't really seen him like this before. She wasn't sure if she liked it, but at the same time, she couldn't blame him. He had seen Megan as a mother figure for the majority of his life. He respected her more than anyone in the world, and Alex couldn't even blame him.

If I had someone that was so selfless that they gave up their childhood to take care of me when it wasn't their job, then I would be unfailingly loyal to them as well. My own father never even grew up enough to want to really take care of me, and my mother didn't fight for me when she had the chance. I was a child, and she let me make the life decision of going with my father. After seeing Megan with Gavin, I can't understand that. Alex thought to herself as she watched Gavin move around.

If she hadn't been trained, then it would look frantic, but she knew exactly what he was doing. Each movement around the room was calculated. He would type some on a computer, then on his laptop. He would pull up plans for the building across the street, and then the one next door. She watched in awe as Gavin did the planning of a mission in

191

a way that would take an entire team a week. And he was doing it in a matter of hours.

She offered to help, only to be either ignored or turned down. He didn't meet her with hostility, which was good. But she didn't like seeing him run himself ragged like this.

Even her attempts to get him distracted slightly to take his mind off things for a brief moment were a failure. He was solely focused, and she would wait. She wanted to make sure that he knew that she would be there for him. Even in the hard times.

Especially in the hard times. She thought, watching him scarf down the sandwich that she had brought him and demanded him to eat.

Unfortunately, Charles wasn't really being much help either. He was either aiding in Gavin's frantic planning, or he was nowhere to be seen. It was starting to bother Alex. he would go missing for thirty minutes to an hour, and then show up and try to act like he never left. Even though Gavin and Alex both knew he had been gone.

Something else I will have to address later. There are far more pressing issues at the moment. Alex tried to focus on Gavin alone. He was her main concern.

***

"Esi Noyoko," Charles said softly on his phone in the armory. Usually, no one bothered him in here, and if he spoke soft enough then the cameras wouldn't pick up his voice.

"Hello Mato. Do you have word on your side mission? I feel we may be approaching the pinnacle and decisions will have to be made. I can't say which way I will go, as you know, my priority is to the tribe above all," Noyoko stated, matter-of-factly.

"I know Numunuu, but it isn't so cut and dry for me. You know the loyalty that I have to my tribe, I owe you all everything. I just don't feel that I can cast aside other connections I have made so easily," Charles said, his tone was cold and emotionless. Noyoko knew that meant he was dealing with more emotion than he knew how to handle.

"I would urge you to remember your kuhtaamia and the reason for it. You will find your answers with that. Paháh will provide them for you, you just have to trust," Noyoko said calmly. "For now, do you have an update?"

"Yes. They are coming after the Woodfords. I'm not entirely sure why, though I would imagine it has something to do with the NOVA system. I wonder if they are deeper than we even thought they were. The more I find, the harder it is to not feel as though they had something to do with all of this from the start," Charles reported.

"I'm not sure, but I think that there are a lot of people higher up in the government involved. We will have to root them out to be sure," Charles finished.

"I have wondered that for a while. This further confirms it. Thank you for keeping me in the loop Mato. I will be in touch, and remember you are all always welcome out there any time," Noyoko said in parting.

"Bye Numunuu," Charles said, trying to not sound sad.

"Goodbye my tua," Noyoko said, as he hung up the phone.

Charles checked his secure line with General Richmond. She had asked for an update as well. He wasn't sure if Noyoko would update her or not. He didn't know the depths of their cooperation.

He headed back to Gavin to check on him and his progress. For the first time in a long time, he felt lost. He didn't like not having direction in his life.

***

General Richmond had been informed of what was going on with her team in Atlanta and was working on figuring out who was behind it. She had figured that she knew but couldn't confirm it just yet. She would normally have Gavin look into it, but he was understandably out of contact at the moment.

Her head analyst, her top two agents, and her leading neurologist are all out of commission because of one explosive. She felt that there was something to be said about keeping professional and private lives separate there but now wasn't the time. She knew how everyone was hurting.

Sadly, it wasn't the only problem she had going on at the moment. Agent Hel hadn't checked in at her given time. Again.

This time Cathrine was far more worried, as this wasn't a true infiltration mission. This was meant to be an assassination, and there was no word. For days. And she had to tell Gavin at some point soon. She just hoped that she chose the right moment to do it. She knew he had a lot going on at the moment.

She had just made it back to her office when the phone in her desk gave a notification.

Picking it up, she glanced through the text. Only one person had that number, and he rarely checked in. He had already recently as well, so this didn't bode well.

"Call when alone."

The brevity of the text worried her. Cathrine went and locked the door. She swept the office for bugs and only found two, she felt she was pretty secure. She put those bugs into her Faraday cage safe that Coeus had designed for her when she got this office, and then dialed the number.

She didn't wait for anyone to speak, once the ringing had stopped and she was sure someone would be listening, she said, "This is highly unusual Noyoko."

"Agreed, but necessary. I assume you are briefed about what happened with Megan and Gavin? Well, I believe that I have more, and I may have to pull Mato if it gets to it," Noyoko started.

"You do not have authorization to do that anymore my friend. It has always been up to Agent Charles on what he decides to do. I give him orders, but for the last two years, he has had his pick of assignments, apart from this one. He chooses where he goes and what he is involved in. So, it will be up to him. You are always welcome to give him your

194

input and advice, but as you gave up your position, you no longer have rank to be able to pull," Cathrine informed Noyoko. She was not about to just let him take her primary agent away from her.

"No, I understand that. I will allow him to make his own decisions. I just wanted to inform you about what I intend to do. Then it will be up to him. I must warn you, I worry that there is a storm coming. And there may not be many places to find shelter. I have heard the distant thunder," Noyoko said. He didn't trust to say things outright but knew that Cathrine would understand. They had been friends for a very long time.

"I understand. Thank you general," Cathrine slipped, "I mean, Noyoko. Sorry, old habits."

"Don't worry. I struggle at times with you calling me my name still," Noyoko said to his former mentee. "I will be in touch," And he hung up the phone.

General Richmond sat at her desk, contemplating what he meant. She felt they were in the middle of the storm, but if he knew that more was coming, then there was plenty to be terrified of. Noyoko had always been careful in all he did. He never wanted to mix professional and personal issues, right until Agent Charles. Once he saw that Robert Charles had been recruited, she got a phone call from her old boss, and they had a long chat about the new recruit.

It was then that she decided to take him under her wing, similar to how Noyoko had done for her decades earlier. And the move paid off in dividends. Charles quickly became one of her best, most skilled, and most trusted agents. Which was exactly why she assigned him to this mission. She knew he could be trusted. Above all else.

She looked at her phone Coeus had made for her and Agent Hel. It remained silent.

***

Gavin had the plan ready.

He called in Charles, as Alex had yet to leave his side unless he just took off without her. *She is actually showing that she cares, even if it isn't easy. Or is it just that this is her job? Which is far more likely the answer.* Gavin thought as he got everything ready.

"OK, so here is the plan. If you don't have an answer to any questions that you are going to ask, then I would say keep it to yourself. We are doing this, or I am doing it alone," Gavin said, as he looked around the table. His eyes were hard and cold.

Alex was worried by what she saw. She understood it, but at the same time, it wasn't Gavin. Not the Gavin that she had known for over a year. Not the Gavin she had seen in so many pictures. Even when his parents left. Not the Gavin she loved.

If I am ready to just act like him being so upset by this that he is acting differently effect the way I look at him, then what does that say about me? I am clearly not ready for marriage if my first response to him acting any different than how I expect is to judge him. People grow and change. I have to support that, or I truly don't deserve him. Alex scolded herself, as she stowed her concerns for the time being and got ready for this mission.

Charles respected Gavin. More than almost anyone outside of his tribe, or the military. But something was off. He didn't like how it seemed that the kid was almost bloodthirsty. He had seen it many times in combat. The anger and rage take over, and it becomes addicting and suddenly you don't know how you ended up with your hands covered in blood. A ledger full of red, and no idea how to get out of it. Lost to the job. And the only way to survive is to no longer feel.

He was used to it. But that didn't mean he wanted to see Gavin go through it. He would keep an eye on Gavin. If it came down to it, he would take the shot. Gavin felt off, and his job was to protect him. Sometimes people need protection from themselves.

They gathered all of their gear and headed out to the car. The tension was more than palpable for this mission. More so than most any that they had been on together before.

***

They parked the van across the street from the hotel. They were entering through a service entrance that the exit was across the road. There was a tunnel that led to the basement of the hotel and allowed them entry without dealing with the welcome desk.

Gavin quickly set the hotel's security on a loop for the cameras that they would come across. They didn't want any unwanted support on this. Making their way down the hall, under the road, they got to the basement, and onto the service elevator. Going up they made their way to the stairs. Typically, there weren't people taking the stairs without the elevator being out. They were thankful that this was the case.

Getting to the fifth floor, they exited and made their way to the room that had been in Ivan's alias name. Gregor Walchick. Room 539. Gavin produced a key card, programmed to enter any room.

They went into the room single file. Alex, then Gavin, and Charles shut the door softly behind him. Weapons up and ready, they turned on the lights. To find an empty room.

They turned to leave, right as they heard someone in the hallway. They waited, hearing the voice get closer and closer until they were right outside the room. They heard the keycard get put into the slot and the door unlatched.

Charles reached out and grabbed the man that opened the door. Covering his mouth and dragging him into the room. Alex made sure the door was shut and locked. While Gavin helped Charles tie the man to the chair.

"I am going to take my hand off your mouth, I expect you to stay quiet. If you don't, then I will quiet you quickly," Charles threatened, displaying his pistol for the man to see.

The man had tears streaming down his face, his eyes bulging at the sight of the gun, and he nodded. Charles took his hand away, and the man stayed quiet.

"What is your name?" Gavin took the lead on the questioning, and no one really challenged him on it. They all knew that he needed answers.

"Ted Williams," the man answered in a shaking voice.

"Quit with the act. I don't have patience for it, or the desire to deal with it. Now, why did you blow up my sister's house?" Gavin said in a seething, quiet tone. It sent a chill down Alex's spine.

Charles glanced at Gavin as well.

"I don't know what you're talking about," Ted replied, unsure what to do.

"Don't play with me, I am not in the mood! Now, why did Ivan send you, and where is his new headquarters?" Gavin said, his tone getting louder.

Ted started to cry again.

"I don't know who Ivan is. I have no idea what is going on. Please, I have kids," Ted said, pleading with them.

"My sister was about to have her first, but you and your boss made sure that that wouldn't happen. So don't expect sympathy from me," Gavin's rage became too much to handle.

Alex went to stop him, but Charles grabbed her shoulder. He nodded at her, letting her know to let it go for a bit longer.

"Are you talking about the explosion yesterday? Is that what this is about? I have no idea. Please, I don't know. I swear," Ted was babbling, he had tears streaming, and snot was starting to come out as well.

Charles smelled something and looked down. Ted had wet himself. This clearly wasn't their bomber.

"YOU'RE LYING!" Gavin raged, as he grabbed Ted by the throat, and started to choke him. Ted's eyes bulged more. His face turned a deep red, and then purple very quickly.

Charles leapt forward and grabbed Gavin. Using a pressure point, he forced Gavin to release Ted.

"Gavin! He is telling the truth. He isn't the bomber!" Charles said as Gavin turned on him.

In a normal situation when they were sparring, Gavin could beat Charles seven out of ten times, but the rage Gavin had was too much. He flailed around, and it was easy for Charles to overpower him. Putting Gavin into a hold and forcing him away from Ted.

Gavin was turned forcibly and found himself looking directly into Alex's eyes. And for the first time, he saw fear. Not a fear of losing him. A fear of him. A fear of what he might do. A fear that she had already lost him to this rage. And Gavin started sobbing. He still felt the rage, but it had broken for the moment.

"I don't know what's wrong with me," He whispered between sobs, as Alex grabbed him and held him.

"We need to go," Charles said, as he undid the ties on Ted. "Call this number, and you will be reimbursed for any hardships that have been caused. We are terribly sorry," Charles said, handing him a number for the NSA support that pays people to forget what happened.

He then turned and helped Alex get Gavin out of the hotel the same way that they came in.

***

Miranda sat in the back of a car, watching as Alex and Charles helped their analyst into their van on the other side of the road.

"Someone you need to say goodbye to?" the driver asked her.

"No, just needed to make sure we were clear," she said, putting up the partition.

She then pulled out her phone and dialed Mr. Michaelson.

"I am clear, and on my way," Miranda said as soon as the ringing stopped.

"Good, and no one saw you? No name trail?" Joseph asked.

"Do you think you are dealing with an amateur? This isn't my first mission Sir," Miranda answered with some sass.

"I know it isn't but get used to me questioning you. I don't take any chances. You will head to New York for a few days and stay in a room I have already set up for you there. There will be no connection to me or any of my organizations with the room, and once I know that you are clear and no one is coming after you, then we will meet. We have a lot to discuss," Joseph said as he hung up the phone.

Miranda was used to the abrupt endings to calls, but she wasn't used to being questioned. She knew what she was doing. She was one of the best at it. Granted, this was a very unique situation, given she was going against some of the other best, but that didn't mean she would make a rookie mistake. If anything, it made her more focused.

She still hadn't gotten a check from Mr. Michaelson, but she hadn't had to pay for her new room or bribe anyone in any other ways like she normally had been. She let him know what happened, and within ten minutes she had a new room, under a new name, and the old room was given to someone else under the same name. Then she had been given a driver to extract her immediately.

It all had worked out well, but she still felt off about it. None of this felt right. She had done some messed up things in her career, but Alex had been one of the few people who had her back in more than a couple of missions. But that is part of the game. That is why they tell you to limit connections. You never know who you will have to betray or kill.

She looked out the window as she waited for them to get to the airport. She was getting sent on one of Mr. Michaelson's private jets to New York City. Off the books. It made her travel a lot easier to keep out of sight. This part she liked. When she was with the government, all too often she was flown using general public airfare. It always made her feel vulnerable and exposed.

"Maybe betrayal pays better," she said softly to herself in a sad tone, watching the buildings go by.

/: Chapter 17

Control >

Gavin was in the back of the van lying down. Alex was on top of him, not letting him move much. She held him tightly, and Gavin wasn't sure if it was to keep him from doing anything or to try and comfort him. Or maybe some mixture of both. His mind kept fighting with itself. The rage was still there, and it was almost like someone telling him that everything was against him, and he had to fight because no one else would.

He knew deep down that that wasn't true. He knew that Alex and maybe even Charles had his back and would do whatever they could to help him. But in the moment, he felt hopeless. Like all he had was himself. With Megan getting hurt, his mom is gone again, and not knowing what was going on with him, he felt absolutely lost.

As he laid there on the floor of the van, the bumps in the road as Charles drove them back to Citadel caused a gentle swaying of the van, combined with the pressure of Alex on top of him was calming him some. It hit him what he did, and that started causing a new round of sobbing.

"Shh. It's ok. It's going to be ok. We will figure everything out. I promise. I'm not going anywhere," Alex whispered to him.

I'm not going anywhere. That's a new thought to me. I'm always leaving. Always on the run. Always moving on to the next mission. The next target. This mission has been my longest mission ever, and it has become so much more. HE has become so much more.

If this is the worst that I ever deal with him, then I have a better relationship than the vast majority of the world. I have to be there to help him through whatever this is.

Whatever is going on. I know the stress of everything that is going on, the hurt from all of the loss he has experienced, and this job in itself is enough to drive people to the brink.

I have to give him the benefit of the doubt. He did far more for me, with far less of a reason to. He trusted me to not kill him when I am not sure that I would have been able to have that level of trust, Alex thought as she lay on top of Gavin. Feeling his breathing slow as he calmed down.

When we get back, I need to call the expert on Gavin. Kaleb will be invaluable in getting to the bottom of this. Alex started to plan on how to continue to help the man that she has loved.

***

Hel lay on the table that she was still strapped to. She felt the room she was in start to move. The live feed to her daughter's home had been cut. Now, when she opened her eyes, all she saw was a blank ceiling.

The horror of watching her daughter walk into that building, the sense of relief that she had thinking she was safer. Worried that there was a sniper. Only for the entire building to explode and collapse onto her, was soul-crushing.

Watching the likely death of her first baby, and her first grandchild, was almost more than she could bear. And the fact that it was the last thing she saw had it continuously repeating through her mind.

It was like it was on repeat on the ceiling above her.

She kept fighting back tears. Even with the nerve gas still taking away a majority of her body functions. She was now able to wiggle her fingers and toes as well as open her eyes. She hadn't started being able to breathe on her own yet, and so she was still on oxygen.

She had figured that Ivan was watching her, though she wasn't sure where any of the cameras were. She did know that she had two guards at the door inside the room. And she assumed there was a set of guards on the outside of the door as well, based on the voices that she had been able to hear.

She knew that they were keeping her alive, she just didn't know why. There was no reason to now, other than for Ivan to torture her mentally or physically. Which, given his past, very well may be the reason.

She heard the door open and close.

"Hello Agent Hel. I am sure you are wondering what is going on. Trust me when I say, it will be revealed soon. Don't you worry. I have a plan for you. You will not be wasted," Ivan said, as Hel heard him placing a tray down.

"You don't need to think about all of that right now. No, right now you will need to focus on what is going to be happening to you. Would you like to know the fun thing about this nerve gas that I had The Westgate create for me?" Ivan said, his tone sickeningly sweet. "I will take your silence as an affirmative."

Hel heard Ivan mess with something on the tray. She assumed he picked something up.

"The fun thing about this particular brand of nerve gas is that it only cuts out commands from the brain to your muscles. It doesn't turn off the nerve endings. Which means you are able to feel everything I choose to do to you. And while I won't get the joy of hearing your screams, and there is nothing left to break for you. I know everything I need too, and you only have one last use to me. So, I am able to just do what I like," Ivan continued. He put a red-hot brand against her thigh.

It wasn't until that moment that she realized that she was naked. The burning sensation caused agony throughout her body. She was desperate to scream out in pain, but nothing would happen.

"I can almost feel how badly you want to scream out. I can't imagine the amount of pain you are going through. The struggle of your body not being able to respond to your commands. I know something of that," Ivan stated, as he took away the hot metal, and returned to the tray.

"You see, I have never told anyone this before. But there is another person in my head," Ivan said. Confessing to Hel as if it would be healing to him. This confession felt weird to her. It was something she knew but hadn't really expected him to know.

"This other person is so weak. Usually, all I have to do is kill someone, sometimes even threaten to kill someone, and he just-" Ivan took a deep breath and sighed it out, "goes away," Ivan finished with an audible smile.

"So, killing, torturing, using people and discarding them. These things all became cathartic to me. It gave me peace in my mind. I have been told that most people feel as if these kinds of things tear them apart. But to me, it soothes me," Ivan says like he is some kind of weird and sadistic yogi.

The entire thing was making Hel sick to her stomach. Hearing him talk about her friend being weak made her angry and hearing him flippantly talk about taking life hit something inside her. She had been the cause of more deaths in her career than most people did paperwork. But how Ivan talked about it, it made her heart hurt.

"So, I started seeking out that peace more and more. There was only one other thing that gave me peace. And that turned out to be computer programming. It used my entire mind and kept that other person from having a say in what I did. And so, I used that to create. I created something I could use to help me in another way I was able to find peace.

"I created an AI. It has grown over the years and has gotten more and more useful. To the point that it has been able to write some files of the famed NOVA system," Ivan said.

All of this caused Hel's mind to feel chaotic. From what Coeus has always told her, Harold was supposed to be almost completely suppressed by the old NOVA system that they used, yet it seems whatever Hunter did caused more issues than just Ivan not being recalled. Ivan wasn't supposed to be aware of Harold at all. And the AI was entirely a Harold thing to do and be excited about.

"Now, you must know, I intend to end your family line. Entirely. But for your son, I may be doing him a favor by ending his life. He seems like a weak-minded boy. Like the other one in my head. And if that is who is in charge, then he must be in a constant state of mental torture. I will be his saving grace and release him from that," Ivan said. The mention of her son cuts through Hel's introspection.

Ivan then seared another section of Hel's thigh. The pain consumed her mind for the moment. She wasn't sure how much more of any of this she could take.

After letting that sear, Ivan took it away. And set the metal back on the tray.

"I will let you sit with this knowledge for now. We should be at our destination soon. And when we are, your purpose will become clear," Ivan said as he made his exit. Leaving Hel there again in the silence. Her mind was almost in more turmoil and pain than her body was. And it was all so overwhelming. No training had prepared her for this.

***

Miranda sat in her room in New York City and looked out at the cityscape. It was the middle of the day, and she had been staying on top of being in shape. She hadn't been given a schedule and wasn't sure when she would be called again.

She stayed in her room, getting room service and watching more TV than she had since she was a child. She just needed the noise in the background. She wasn't really paying any attention. She knew none of it was real.

She had too much time to think. And that was dangerous. She worried that Alex would figure it out. That she would find her. Alex was the only person in the world that she feared. She had seen what that woman could do.

But it wasn't the fear of what Alex could do to her that made her so uneasy about this. Oddly enough, it was the fact that Alex was the closest thing to a friend that Miranda had ever had. Alex was the only person that knew where she came from. It hadn't come out on purpose, but it was one of those moments where you think you're going to die anyway, so you open up. Just to know that someone, anyone, knew you. This life she had chosen, although at times it felt chosen for her, was a very lonely one a majority of the time. And when you could find any semblance of real connection with people, it was so rare that you jumped at it.

And that was what happened between Miranda and Alex. They had a mutual respect for each other's abilities at the job, and they knew more about each other than just about any other person in the world.

And here she was, betraying the one person who knew. The only person who had ever truly had her back. Her only friend.

"She would have done the same to me! Anything to survive. That is what this world is about. That is what we are taught. What we are trained to do. Survive. She can't blame me. I won't let her," Miranda ranted to herself, as she threw the glass she had in her hand. Knowing that Alex didn't even know it was her that did any of this yet. The only one blaming her was herself, and her own guilt.

Walking over to the room bar, she grabbed another glass and bottle of tequila and then fell back onto the bed and started drinking straight from the bottle. Foregoing the glass entirely.

"We all do what we have to. She will understand," Miranda said, trying to convince herself that she wasn't a terrible person.

***

Gavin lay on the floor of his bedroom. He hadn't changed, he couldn't bring himself to do much of anything. It felt like if he moved on his own, then he was going to lash out in rage again. It felt like a disease. A cancer that controlled him if he didn't focus solely on containing it, and nothing else.

Gavin tried to breathe through it all, through the anger. *I don't understand. I know I am going through a lot right now, but I have never had this kind of pure and unbridled anger before. Even at the height of my hatred for what my parents did. This is different. This feels foreign, and I can't function. At all. What is going on with me?*

Alex watched Gavin, he would whimper every now and then. She couldn't stand seeing him like this, and she didn't know what to do. She wasn't sure if this was him, the NOVA system doing things to his mind, or what it was. So, she called the only other person that she felt she could trust with this. Kaleb. And then she sat, watching and waiting for Kaleb to get there.

To her surprise, it wasn't but a few minutes and she heard the doorbell. Grabbing her gun, just to be safe, she went and checked the door. Breathing a sigh of relief that it was Kaleb.

"Ok, where is he?" Kaleb said, sounding like some odd little TV doctor.

***

Charles was waiting for General Richmond to come back to the phone. He had to let her know what was going on with Gavin. Even if it somehow felt wrong. Like he was tattling on his friend.

"Hello Agent Charles, what is going on?" Richmond answered once she made it to the phone.

"Hello general, it's the NOVA system. Something seems to be haywire with-it Ma'am," Charles replied, not sure who would be listening.

"Speak freely Charles, I'm secure. What is going on with Gavin?" Cathrine asked, concern clear in her voice. That gave Charles a sense of relief.

"He isn't ok Ma'am. He tried to kill a man who was clearly innocent today when we were investigating the explosion. He is really torn up about his sister's injury. I am not sure how much more he can take," Charles said honestly. He was worried about his friend.

"I see. And do you think you could get him back to health? I heard from the doctors that Megan will make a full recovery, and I am having her shipped to a secret location for her rehab. Only Chad and I will know where she is at. I will obviously share that information with Gavin as soon as I know he is able to handle it. And Chad will accompany her and assist with her rehab. I expect Gavin to see her before she leaves," Cathrine informed Agent Charles.

"Very good Ma'am. I will keep you informed of his condition. I know that something else has been on his mind. He has muttered a few times about his mother. Do you know where she went at least? I know it was

208

after Ivan," Charles laid all his cards on the table. He hadn't done that often, and when he did, the general knew he was putting himself out there. Even if it wouldn't seem like it to other people.

"Yes, she went to assassinate him at his new base. We got the location and layout, and I wanted her to have first dibs on the mission. She has not reported in since leaving, and now I am going to need to send you all in to see if you can complete the mission and retrieve her. I will get you the needed information as soon as Gavin is back in fighting shape," General Richmond said to her agent. "Dismissed."

Charles put the phone down. He wasn't sure what he should keep to himself, and what he should inform the rest of the team of, but he knew that he had to let them know something.

***

Kaleb walked into the room that Gavin was in and saw his friend on the floor. Alex watched as Kaleb maneuvered around the room. Knowing exactly where he was going and what he was doing. He pulled out an old Zune and plugged it into the sound system. Turning up the song, and then laying out an assortment of pizza, candy, popcorn, and whiskey. And finally, he produced a Nintendo 64 from his bag, and set it up on the tv, starting up The Legend of Zelda.

"What song is this?" Alex asked, she wasn't sure if she liked it or not. She hadn't really listened to a lot of music in her life.

"It is called Everybody Hurts by R.E.M. It got us through his parents leaving," Kaleb said, as he went and sat by his friend.

"Hey buddy," he said in a calm and easy tone. "I'm here."

Gavin just groaned.

"I know it hurts. Just like before. I'm sorry buddy. I brought your favorites," Kaleb said.

Like before? Like he has any IDEA what I am feeling right now! This isn't hurt! This is far beyond that! This is anger. Rage. Pain beyond reason. Gavin thought.

No. He is just trying to help. What are you doing? Do you want to be alone? Do you want them to give up on you?

Alex pulled Kaleb aside and said, "Kaleb, I don't think this is just hurt. I don't know what he was like before, but he was ready to kill a man this afternoon with his bare hands," The worry in her tone was beyond clear, and it was justified as she watched something click in Kaleb's mind.

"What? What is it?" Alex asked.

"How are your hacking skills? Or computer skills in general?" Kalev asked, hope in his voice.

"Not great. I can submit paperwork, but I mostly have Gavin for everything else anymore. Why?" Alex sounded confused.

"Ok. Take me to his lab," Kaleb said, he sounded confident and sure of himself, so Alex did as he said.

"Ok, he told me that he had the little AI that he had been working within an external hard drive. Where is his- BINGO!" Kaleb pulled out Gavin's bag and took it to the other room. He set up the hard drive and laptop, and then grabbed Gavin's arm and used his thumb to open the computer.

"I told him he shouldn't have that feature turned on. So many bad things if someone just cut off his thumbs," Kaleb said.

Alex was amazed at the positivity that the little man possessed. Even in the midst of what had to be one of the worst few days that she could imagine for their family.

She watched as he opened up the server and app that Gavin had created for the AI.

/: K- HELLO VERES. >

/: V- YOU ARE NOT GAVIN OR HAROLD OR COEUS. WHO ARE YOU? >

/: K- I AM A FRIEND OF GAVIN. CAN YOU ACCESS THE SECURITY IN CITADEL FROM LAST THURSDAY? >

"Why last Thursday?" Alex asked.

"That was when I noticed he had started acting off. Something was weird about him, and I just thought it was stress, but the more I think about it, the more I think that there is more to it. And when you said that he almost killed someone, I knew that something was very wrong. Gavin doesn't kill. Gavin can barely kill a spider, because he starts thinking about how it might have spider babies," Kaleb explained as he ran through the file that Veres had produced at an accelerated rate.

He reached the moment that Gavin left and then started to reverse. Until he saw that there was an extended time where Gavin was passed out, sitting in his chair.

Kaleb rewound some more, until right before Gavin passed out.

He watched as Gavin's face was blank, and his eyes were darting back and forth. Like he was reading something very quickly, but not really in control.

It was then that Kaleb noticed there was a reflection in the background. After having Veres adjust the image and clear it up, so it could be read. He saw that there was a NOVA system file being run. Backing it up slightly he saw the message.

/: P- PERUN THANK YOU FOR MAKING THIS EASY. >

Alex knew. Kaleb knew. There was something added to Gavin's NOVA system, and they would have to figure out how to manage it if he was to function normally again. And now without Megan.

Just then there was a knock on the door.

"Gavin, Alex, there are a lot of things we need to discuss," Charles said from outside the door.

Alex quickly opened it and said, "Agreed. I found something you need to know."

They all went into the room with Gavin and were discussing it all. Everyone seemed like they were ready to go to take down Ivan, except Gavin. He remained on the floor, grunting or groaning randomly.

Alex and Charles were bouncing ideas back and forth, trying to make it all make sense. When Kaleb chimed in.

"Well, guys, why don't we connect Megan's computer to Veres and see if he can write something like a patch for Gavin's NOVA system? I mean, you all said that Perun was Ivan's evil AI, right? So, why not have our good AI figure it out for him?" Kaleb asked, and no one seemed to have any better ideas.

"But Megan's computer was toasted. Remember?" Charles said, making them all freeze.

"Her home computer. Her work computer is still in her office. Chad made her stop bringing it home months ago," Gavin finally chimed in, clearly struggling to speak. Like he was talking through gritted teeth.

They all got in a rush and got to the hospital. Making their way to Megan's office they got everything started. It took a few hours before they had everything ready.

Getting Gavin into the chair and strapping him in. He seemed to be getting more and more catatonic. Like the drive over and getting him into the hospital had taken a lot of his strength.

Finally, Kaleb had the AI connected to Megan's secure server, and had it upload all of the files into its database.

/: K- CAN YOU MAKE A PATCH FOR WHAT IS WRONG WITH GAVIN? >

/: V- A HUMAN HAD THIS UPLOADED INTO THEIR BRAIN? THAT DOESN'T SEEM PRACTICAL. YES, I CAN HAVE A PATCH READY IN LESS THAN 30 MINUTES. STANDBY. >

Kaleb jumped and pumped a fist into the air. Looking at Charles he put his hand up for a high five.

Charles responded with a grunt and said, "Easy there, I will give you something if it works."

Kaleb shrugged and took it as a victory.

Alex sat with Gavin, quiet as she thought. *Please work. PLEASE. I NEED Gavin. I need MY Gavin. This isn't him. We knew it wasn't him. He would never act like this. Thank you, Kaleb. I could kiss you.*

The computer dinged a notification, letting them know that the program was ready.

/: K- PLEASE GIVE A 10-SECOND COUNTDOWN TO LET US KNOW WHEN TO HAVE GAVIN READY. >

/: V- 10. >

/: V- 9. >

"Oh, it is going now. Hurry, and get out of eyesight of the screen, I think," Kaleb said, not knowing what to do.

"How about we all just close our eyes, idiot," Charles said, already having his closed.

Kaleb looked at Alex, who already had hers closed as well, and had moved away from Gavin.

"That makes sense," Kaleb said and closed his. He heard the computer ding that the program had started. "Please don't let me have fried my friend's brain," Kaleb murmured to himself.

/: Chapter 18

Hel-l >

Gavin sat in the chair. It was dark, and he felt different. The anger was still there, but it felt trapped in a way. It hadn't gone away, but it was manageable. Like the voice had its volume turned down. Like he could look at this beast that was trapped in a cage. Lashing out at anything that came near it. Then, he thought he heard people talking in the distance.

I think I can hear Kaleb and Alex. Maybe Charles? What happened to me?

Gavin tried to recall everything. He remembered that Megan had been hurt and lost her child. He was pretty sure that Ivan was behind it, though he was not entirely sure why. He hadn't made very much progress on dismantling his evil empire.

Suddenly an image of Ivan getting dressed up in a Darth Vader outfit popped into Gavin's mind and made him chuckle slightly.

***

Alex stopped listening to Kaleb, who was freaking out and babbling about how he had fried his friend's brain. She thought she heard something from Gavin. And then she heard it again.

"Shut up," she said softly to Kaleb, which brought a quick grunt from Charles.

There it was again. Gavin had laughed. He was still there.

She rushed over to him and held his hand.

214

"Gavin, I am here. Come on. Come back to us. I don't care if you are still angry at the world. We will fight it together. Please," Alex pleaded. New tears were forming in her eyes.

"I don't think that is a fair fight," a rough sounding Gavin said. He was immediately engulfed in a hug from Alex.

Kaleb made to run to him too, only to find himself held back by one big hand on his shoulder. He looked over it and saw a glowering Charles standing there shaking his head at him. Kaleb stopped for a moment and rethought his approach.

"Gavin, are you ok? What happened? What's wrong? Do you hurt?" Alex went on a rampage of questions checking to see what, if anything, could make Gavin get back to normal.

"I am ok. It is weird, but good. I think. My brain doesn't feel as under attack. The anger is still there, but trapped and controlled," Gavin croaked out. To which he heard Charles grunt.

Gavin made a mental note. *Is that how you feel all the time Charles? That must be just a horrible way to live. That is something he and I will have to have a talk about another time. Right now, we need to focus.*

"I am just happy that I didn't turn your brain into an omelet," Kaleb sighed out in relief. Which made Gavin laugh.

"No buddy, you did really good. Do any of you know what ended up being the issue? I don't remember much about the last twelve hours or so. I remember most of what happened before that though," Gavin said, trying to make sure that they didn't feel they had to relive everything with his sister again.

Alex sighed in relief. *He is back. He is clearly worried about everyone else and what they are going through, when he has clearly been put through it recently. I love this man.* She thought with a smile, as she all but curled up into his lap.

"Well buddy, Perun put some kind of code into your NOVA system. I think it was a bug of some kind. I really don't know, I am just using words that I have heard you use and from movies at this point. Anyways, I asked Veres if he could fix it after booting him up with your sister's work computer, and bingo, he got it made and here we are," Kaleb filled him in, in true Kaleb fashion.

"I have other news as well," Charles chimed in.

"What's going on big guy?" Gavin asked, putting his arms around Alex.

"Your sister is getting moved to a secure location for rehab. She is going to be ok, but it will take a while for her to get back to what she was before the explosion. Thankfully nothing major was hurt on her, other than the loss of her baby. The general is wanting you to see her before she goes, but only if you can handle it with the other news I have," Charles said.

"Should I see her before you tell me more bad news? Or is this like a 'we need to gauge where you are' type of thing?" Gavin asked, his tone somewhat happy, knowing his sister would be ok.

"It's a 'gauge where you are' type of thing," Charles bluntly admitted.

"Alright then, lay it on me," Gavin said, not sure at all what to expect at this point.

"Your mom went on a mission to assassinate Ivan and never checked in," Charles figured ripping the band-aide off was the best policy for this.

"Of course," Gavin said, his tone much more somber now. "Do we at least know where she was going?" He asked, unsure of what they could even do at this point.

"Yeah. The general gave us the last known location, and where she was headed. It was supposed to be the main headquarters of Orlav Industries now. We have a green light to go in, but there won't be back up, given that it is on Chinese soil," Charles added.

"Is there ever back up for us?" Gavin murmured, causing everyone to get a half-hearted chuckle in agreement. They more than felt that they were left out to dry way more than other teams. And Gavin would be the one to know more than the others since he was the one to file a lot of mission logs for other teams.

216

"Ok, let's see my sister off, and then get ready to save my mom," Gavin said, as he helped Alex off his lap.

***

Hel was starting to be able to move her arms and legs more. She still wasn't able to do a lot of fine motor skills yet, or talk, but she was progressing quickly. And they had kept her fed. She wasn't dying from starvation. She wasn't sure how long she had been in the room, but she knew it had to be for more than a day, she thought more than a couple days. But when all you see is one wall, and that is when you actually have the strength to open your eyes, you lose all sense of time.

Her strength was coming back. She was able to stay awake for longer periods of time. Once she had her arms and legs back to full strength, then all she would need was for someone to make a mistake. Loosen a strap just enough, and she would be free. Then she could complete her mission and get back to her family.

Just fake the weakness for a bit longer.

She heard the door open, and she closed her eyes. She wouldn't be able to see much unless they walked right into her gaze anyway. She let her arms and legs go limp. She needed them to underestimate her. That would be the only way.

***

Gavin got to the hospital in time to see his sister off. She showed concern for how he was doing, wanting to make sure that he was taken care of. And of course, everyone was worried about her.

She told Gavin that once they were settled in, she would have him, and Alex come out so that they would know where they were and how to get ahold of them. Gavin assured her that he wouldn't let them be separated for longer than absolutely necessary.

After long goodbyes, many hugs and a bucket of tears shed, Megan and Chad went with the trusted escort that Cathrine had provided. She was going to meet them herself along the way and give them the address to where they would be staying.

Gavin and the rest went back to Citadel to plan for their mission. None of them had the heart to tell Megan that their mom hadn't checked in. They all knew that if they had, she would be trying to suit up right next to them, and that just couldn't be allowed.

Suddenly the screen came to life, and General Richmond was addressing them.

"Hello team, and Kaleb," she started, some disdain still clear in her tone for Gavin's friend. "I wanted to let you know that you have clearance from above to get whatever you need to finish this mission. I know that we don't normally send you on assassination missions, given Gavin's dislike for killing, but this time I hope you can make an exception."

Gavin didn't say a word, just nodded.

"Good, and I trust that you are doing better?" Cathrine asked the flip from general to caring friend clear in her voice.

"Yes, Ma'am. I am doing much better, in large part thanks to Kaleb," Gavin said, with a slight smirk. He knew that the general wasn't fond of his friend, but that made him even more determined for her to learn to accept his role on the team.

"Yes, I have heard that he did very well in bringing you back from what Ivan had likely done to you. Thank you, Mr. Moore," the general said, clearly not enjoying having those words come out of her mouth.

"It is no big deal, Mr. General, Sir. Ma'am. Me Lady," Kaleb stumbled through. "Any friend would do it for their best friend. Will I get some kind of metal or something? No. Ok," Kaleb continued, clearly nervous and babbling. It made everyone but General Richmond chuckle slightly. Even Charles enjoyed the awkward exchange between the two.

"As I was saying, I have made arrangements for any extent that your plan needs to be taken care of. Get this done, and bring Agent Hel home, team. Dismissed," General Richmond barked.

And the screen went back.

"That went well," Kaleb said.

218

"Buddy, I do think that it would be smart for you to sit this one out. No offense meant, I just feel I have lost enough, I don't need my best friend, who doesn't have weapons training or any form of combat training, to be involved in a highly dangerous mission," Gavin explained, feeling bad for excluding his friend.

"No, I understand. It makes sense. I will be back here holding down the fort, so to speak. And there is a Kung Fu movie marathon that I didn't want to miss anyway, so this works out better for me. I will see you all when you get back though, right?" Kaleb asked, clearly trying to save some dignity.

"Of course, bud. I promise. I will call as soon as we are back in the States," Gavin said.

"Cool, see ya," Kaleb said, as he bounded up the stairs.

"Ok, now, what's the plan?" Charles asked, trusting Gavin again, now that he seemed back to being his normal self.

"This is what I am thinking," Gavin started.

***

The stealth transport plane flew high above Russian airspace. Gavin was going through his pack. It was the first time outside of training that he would be skydiving, and it was terrifying for him. And this wasn't a normal jump either. They were doing a H.A.L.O., a high altitude, low opening jump. Meaning they were jumping out of the plane from well above a normal jump, and not opening their parachute until below normal standard times.

"Are you ok Gavin?" He heard Alex ask over the headset in his helmet.

Gavin looked up, and for a moment he had to figure out which black human form was Alex, before she finally did a little wave.

"Yeah-" Gavin replied as his voice cracked, betraying his nervousness. He cleared his throat and said, "Yeah, I think so."

"Just stay close to us and listen to what we tell you to do. And maybe you will live long enough to get shot by Ivan's men," Charles teased in a jovial tone.

"Thanks. Thanks so much," Gavin deadpanned.

"You will be perfectly fine. Like Charles said, just stay close and listen to what we say to do," Alex said in a calm and soothing tone.

Charles hit the button to open the back hatch to the transport plane. "LET'S DO THIS!" He heard Charles yell excitedly.

"WAIT FOR THE GREEN, THEN CHARLES WILL GO. FOLLOWED BY ME. THEN YOU WILL COUNT TO FIFTEEN AND FOLLOW. NOD IF YOU UNDERSTAND," Alex yelled through the headset over the wind.

Gavin nodded his head and waited.

Green light.

Charles dove headfirst into the night sky.

Green light.

Alex dove.

Gavin started counting. He waited, and right as he got to fifteen, the light turned green. Gavin clenched up his stomach, said a little prayer, and dove out of the plane.

He could barely make out the back of Alex several hundred feet below him.

"KEEP TIGHT AND WAIT FOR THE SIGNAL TO PULL YOUR CORD. YOU CAN NOT DELAY ON PULLING THE CORD," Alex yelled through the headset.

Gavin waited for Charles to give some quip, and when none came, he understood the seriousness of the situation. He thought he might get used to the falling feeling, but it never went away and as he waited for the signal, he never seemed to get his stomach quite back into the right spot. He wanted to spend the entire time screaming, but he couldn't do that and be able to hear the signal.

He kept diving through the night, and it wasn't much longer before he heard it.

"NOW!" He heard Alex shout, and he immediately pulled the cord. He felt the jerk of the parachute pulling him back, and as he steadied, he checked his new wrist computer and was able to get into the system and take down the security system with a power surge.

"ALL DARK," Gavin yelled into the headset.

"You don't have to yell now genius," Charles quipped.

"Sorry," Gavin apologized.

"Going dark," He heard Alex say, and Gavin and Charles both knew that that meant radio silence.

Gavin heard several silenced shots get fired close to him, but he couldn't see them. He focused and counted. He knew that once he counted to ninty, he should be ready to land.

Suddenly, Gavin heard the ground coming up, and he braced. He landed with a thud, and he felt a jolt through his entire body, and he tried to move his legs to slow down his momentum forward.

"Pull your release," He heard Alex's command, and he yanked the cord on the small of his back. He dropped and rolled, as the parachute was caught by another gust of wind and was carried away from Gavin into the cavern by the base. Gavin came to a skidding stop.

He felt Charles come up behind him and pick him up by his backpack.

Gavin immediately started typing away on his wrist computer and was able to pull up on their headsets the hybrid thermal and night vision. Then he pulled up the tracking spots for the guards that he had been able to trace during the few moments that he was in the security system. Before he shut it down to prevent Perun from having more fun with him.

Gavin then got to the front and opened the door. He felt a tap on his back, and Charles made his way into the door, he felt a double tap on his shoulder, and he knew that Alex was taking up the rear. Gavin got up and moved with his team. Tracing where he would have thought the holding cell was based on the building blueprints.

He brought that up on their helmet HUD. and they started working down the hallways. Every now and then he heard Charles or Alex shoot off three rounds. Taking down another guard.

They passed several lab rooms, offices, and barracks rooms. Taking down the opposition as needed. And they made it to the holding cells.

Going through them from room to room, they found it all empty.

Gavin typed into the HUD display.

"HIS OFFICE." and then he marked it for them to make their way to it.

They made it through to the office, and right as they cleared the room, the lights came back on. Blinding them.

They all ripped their helmets off, and let their eyes adjust. And one wall lit up with a message.

/: PERUN WELCOMES YOU TO THE GAME. >

Not long after that, the screen pixelated away, and Ivan was there looking at them.

"Hello Gavin, I hope you have made yourself at home. I have certainly done the same for myself," Ivan said, as he stepped away from the screen, showing that he was in Citadel.

Just then, the doors to the room opened, and a large group of Ivan's men filed in and surrounded them. Charles and Alex knew better than to try to shoot as they entered the door, they were too severely outnumbered. If one of them tried to reload, then they would be overrun. So, they set their guns down. And put their arms up and behind their heads. Gavin followed suit.

"As you can see, this is game over. I must commend you for not lashing out as much as I would have liked, but the reports of you almost killing that man have filtered through the government by now, and there are meetings being held to determine if you are stable or not," Ivan said as he smiled at them.

Alex counted the men that were in the room. *Twenty-nine. I have had worse odds, but I didn't have two people that I had to protect in the process. Three of them know how to handle themself and won't be easy to take out. They would be the ones that would take the longest, and most likely to harm Gavin or Charles. However, I think Charles could handle himself against a majority of these men. I will just need one to get too close. I need to find a way to signal to Gavin to get on the floor when I am ready to take them out.* Alex focused on Gavin.

Gavin was frantically typing behind his back, shutting down servers that were in there. Including Veres. He was worried that Ivan was after the information that they had there, let alone all of the connections that they had that could get the government into trouble.

Charles was also calculating the men in the room. He had seen Alex work. He had very little doubt that that woman could take every man in this room out twice, and still walk out of there with minimal damage. But he knew that she was different now, and there was more at stake.

"As you can see, you have no options left. You have been out-manned and out-planned, but in case you had some idea of trying anything to get out of this, you can see that I still had my ace up my sleeve," Ivan said, as they rolled out Lucille Woodford on a medical bed. She was clearly drugged in some way and was strapped down. Her body was covered by a blanket.

Hel saw Gavin on the screen surrounded by armed men, and she started to fight again. Her arms twitched against her restraints, and her eyes blinked rapidly.

"Mom!" Gavin yelled and took a step forward.

"Yes, very good my boy, this is your mother. And as you can see, she is not all there right now," Ivan said as if it was some kind of inside joke. "Well, that isn't fair. She has been dealt a non-lethal dose of a specially made nerve gas that a dear friend of mine created, I believe that you have met him, The Westgate. He truly does good work," Ivan said.

Gavin felt the rage starting to build again. He wasn't sure he wanted to control it this time. He knew what his team was capable of.

"I don't think you truly appreciate what you are up against here Ivan," Gavin said through gritted teeth. Alex and Charles could hear that rage building in his voice. Alex saw Gavin still typing behind his head.

"Oh, are you indicating Alex and her training? Charles and his seeming abandonment of self-preservation?" Ivan said with a smirk. "Or do you mean the NOVA system that you have in your head? You seem to think that all of you are something special, but really, truly, you are all just tools in a much bigger picture than you are capable of understanding."

"And you are something special? I am failing to see your point here. You are a tool just as much as I am old man," Gavin snarked back.

"I AM EXCEPTIONAL YOU SNIVELING WEAKLING!" Ivan snarled at Gavin's statement. Then he quickly recollected himself and smoothed out his hair.

"My boy, let me educate you on a lot of things," Ivan said, back to his falsely kind and smooth tone. "You see, there are plenty of things that are far above your social class. Things you would never have even crossed your mind before you were pulled into this life, as you are not anything particularly special yourself. Riding on the coattails and reputation of your exceptional parents. You didn't make a name for yourself in your own right."

Gavin wanted to keep Ivan talking. He was messaging General Richmond and Kaleb. He wanted to make sure that Kaleb was ok, and that the general was aware and was able to get troops moving while they were biding time.

"But there is an elite group of people that make the decisions that no one else is even capable of thinking about. The men, and as of recently, women, who make the decisions of who succeeds and who fails. The decisions of what nation is able to survive, and become a world power, and what will go back to being a third world nation," Ivan continued.

"What would you know about the elite, you-" Gavin was cut off, as Ivan spoke over him.

"Throughout history, every culture has been after the next big thing. World powers have fought for the next big war machine. First, it was the stick, then a sword, the bow and arrow, guns, airplanes, and later the atom bomb. Whether it be on land, in the water, or in the air, governments have sought out to have the greatest power that they could possibly get their hands on," Ivan pontificated as he paced around the room.

Ivan continued in dramatic fashion, "They have fought, argued, bartered, traded, betrayed, and killed mercilessly in order to gain the next life-altering advancement in a cycle that has been never-ending. They are as predictable in their pursuit of power as a dog chasing a bone.

"But what if they are, were, and always have been wrong? What if, in their pursuit of power, they got caught up in the details so much that they missed their mark entirely to the point where it was almost like they almost forgot to swing.

"You see, it was never about who had the biggest stick in the fight. It didn't matter if you had the biggest bomb, the fastest shooting gun, or the longest sword," Ivan stated as he moved behind Lucille. Looking down at something behind her.

"No. while everyone is always after the next world-changing weapon, the reality of it is that the most powerful weapon in the world, the one that can do the most damage, be the most devastating, and the most accurate was, is, and always will be intelligence," Ivan paused and looked up at them with a feral grin.

"And a knife," Ivan then pulled up his hand from behind Lucille.

Hel had just enough strength to look at the screen and say, "Gavin, I love you."

Ivan stared right at the screen with a maniacal smile, before he ran the knife across her throat, and then wiped it on the sheet covering Gavin's dying mom.

/: Chapter 19

Unhinged Descension >

Alex looked at Gavin with terror. She saw tears rolling down his face, but she saw that rage. This time she didn't fear it. She felt it too. Her darkness had risen inside her, and she wasn't about to stop it.

She heard Gavin whisper, "I will disable them. You kill." And she knew he was in control. She glanced at Charles, whose face was hardened. He simply gave a subtle nod. *Gavin is still in control. We may have to stop him, but at this point, it's for his own good. Not out of fear for what he might do. I couldn't even blame him for killing every one of them.*

On the screen, Ivan was watching them with a smirk. He had said something and was likely expecting an answer.

"So, my boy, regrettably our game has come to its end. It is now time for you to die," Ivan said in a condescending tone.

And suddenly there was a blur next to her.

Gavin felt the NOVA system kick in. He was running the programs for how to disable a room full of targets. He had watched plenty of videos on it and ran simulations with Alex and Charles. And he then launched himself at the first man. The one having his gun trained on Alex to his right.

He kicked the gun, causing it to slip in the man's hand and get pointed at the wall as the guard fired off several rounds before Gavin kicked him in the temple with his other foot, knocking the man out.

On the ground, Gavin spun. Kicking the legs out of several other guards. Causing them to fall to the ground, as he spun himself up to his feet again.

Alex kicked her gun, and it flew into the guard behind Charles, as Gavin spun on the floor. Charles grabbed the gun out of the air after it had hit the guard. He slammed the butt into the side of the guard's head, knocking him out. Then all three dropped to the floor, right before the group of guards opened fire.

Charles fired back, hitting several in the knees. Alex threw knives, hitting three guards in the throat. And Charles went back over and killed the guards he had just downed.

Once there was a break, Gavin launched himself at the group, causing them to not be able to fire out of fear of hitting each other, and punched one guy in the head, dropping him. Then he blocked another's swing of his gun.

Charles drifted back and flipped the gun to semi-automatic. Taking single shots and taking down any stragglers that drifted away from the group.

Alex pulled out two more knives and followed after Gavin. She was slitting the throats or pushing the knives through the bottom of the jaws as the guards dropped.

Gavin continued to kick and hit. He grabbed an arm that was swung at him, and pulled that guard into the others, causing them to lose their stance. Then he kicked the man in the chest.

They were down to eight guards at this point, and Gavin kicked a rifle at two of them. Hitting them in the chest and pushing them back just enough for Charles to get a bead. Two shots were heard, and those guards dropped dead.

Six to go. Gavin did a backward handspring and used his momentum to flail his arms backward, directly into the throats of the two guards behind him. Pushing them against the walls and causing their heads to bash against it with an audible thud.

Two more shots were heard, and two other guards who had made a break for the door dropped.

At the same time, there were two knives that flew through the air, almost as if in slow motion, and were both embedded into the heads of the last two guards.

Charles put another round into each of the guards on the ground, just to make sure that they were all dead.

Alex had a bad feeling that they weren't done. "Helmets," she urged and then kicked the one at her feet to Gavin and spun down to grab hers.

Putting them on, she heard Ivan say, "You think I am going to leave your fate to some nameless guards that I personally have no idea the ability of? That's just cute." And by that point they all had their helmets on, that reconnected to their oxygen supplies from the H.A.L.O. jump. They were now sealed off.

"I see you came prepared for anything airborne," Ivan commented, even though the team knew that it was actually just sheer luck. "But," Ivan continued, as he raised a phone and hit a button, "Game over." And the wall went black as the building started to explode.

"Through to the next office, there is a window in there. I already messaged the transport for pick up. LZ is on the cavern floor, out into the desert," Gavin said as he started feeling the building shake.

The team rushed through the door, as Charles kicked it in. Then he shot out the window as they all approached it.

"Ok, the catwalk ends about ten feet to the left out of the window, it is anchored into the side of the cavern," Gavin said, as he got out his grappling hook and rope. He leaned out the window and threw the hook, getting it latched onto the holes in the floor of the catwalk. Latching on his carabiners, he jumped out the window and allowed his weight to get caught by the rope.

The other two followed his lead quickly, and soon they were all hanging from the catwalk at different levels. As the building was exploding above them, they sinched themselves down their ropes. Gavin had made sure that they had plenty of rope to make it down the side of the cliff.

Making it to the bottom, they hurried to the transport plane and loaded. Heading home.

***

On the plane, Alex held Gavin, as Charles got their stuff situated back into the areas that they needed to be.

"I'm an orphan. Truly this time. I know they are both dead, I watched it with my own eyes. I spent so long mad at them and wishing they were dead. And now they are, and it hurts even worse than not knowing for sure," Gavin stammered. He was struggling to process everything now that the adrenaline from the fight had worn off.

"I know. I'm so sorry. I'm here for you," Alex whispered back to him as she held him. Unsure of how else to comfort him. Unsure of what to say.

They are both really gone this time. They aren't coming back. They aren't just off on some mission. They didn't just leave us. They are dead. How am I going to tell Megan? She has had so much loss recently. And a lot of it because of this damn thing in my head. What am I going to do? Gavin lamented in his head. He felt so lost.

Charles understood what he was feeling. It was a loss that you can only really understand if you have gone through it. Even if your parents aren't great, if they are at least out there then you know there is a chance of seeing them again. And you can get answers for whatever hurt and pain they caused in your life. When they have passed, then it makes it far more complicated. There are no more answers to get. No more chances of reconciliation.

"Hello team," they heard General Richmond over their headsets. "We have confirmed that Citadel is secure now. Ivan is gone, and so are his men. He left Lucille, and we will see to it that she receives the burial that she deserves. Gavin, I am so very sorry for all you have gone through."

"Thank you, general," They barely heard a sniffling Gavin's reply.

"I know it isn't any consolation, but I am here for you if you ever need me. I know everything that we have gone through makes our

230

relationship convoluted, but I agreed to be your godmother long before I became your boss. I also have had someone challenging my views and priorities recently. Again, I am sorry for your loss," Cathrine continued.

There was a silence on the call, but just enough noise to know that the general was still there.

"Ma'am, do we know where Ivan went?" Charles asked, after clearing his throat.

"We do not. He seems to have had several bases that he could fall back into. There really isn't any telling at this point," Cathrine replied solemnly.

There was a sniff heard, and then Gavin said, "I will find him. He took so much from me. He doesn't deserve to get to regroup. Besides, I doubt he will really be hiding. He thinks we are dead."

"That's true. He thinks he has won, so he may be a bit sloppier," Alex offered, trying to be helpful, when in reality she didn't think that Ivan would be so easy to find. Especially with his AI.

"I will find him," Gavin said, determination in his voice.

"Let me know when you do Gavin, I will get the mission authorized immediately," Cathrine stated. "Now, I will be in contact as needed. Let me know when you are back stateside."

The line went dead other than their local connection.

"It almost sounded like she was going to say goodbye," Gavin said in a shocked tone.

"I know, weird," Charles said.

The light in the cabin turned green, they had cleared Chinese airspace, and the cabin had pressurized enough that they could breathe. The team took off their helmets, and Charles looked over at Gavin.

"Look, I know that you question the genuineness of me opening up, but I want you to know, I haven't lied to you. You have this annoying way of worming through peoples' defenses and making them feel comfortable," Charles started with a slight smile. He wasn't comfortable being like this, but given the situation, he felt he owed it to his friend. "I want you to know that if you need to talk about losing your parents, I am here. I may process things differently than you do, but this is an area that I do understand. It has caused me a lot of pain, loneliness, and not understanding who I am over the years."

Charles took a breath and seemed to be steadying himself before he continued, "It will get easier at times, and then there are times when it feels like you just lost them all over again. And not everyone will understand. Even among those who you think would be the most understanding. Just know that they are processing it themselves and may not know what to do either. And I know you know this, you helped teach it to me, along with my tribe, but family doesn't always have to be blood.

"You have a good and strong family around you. From Megan, Alex, Kaleb, Chad, Cathrine-" Charles was interrupted by Gavin.

"And you," Gavin interjected. Which, to everyone's surprise, caused Charles to blush slightly.

"And me. We have your back, and you aren't alone. We are all here for you and Megan," Charles said and then wiped the tear that had formed in his eyes and cleared his throat. Then without another word, he sat back down and pulled out his guns and started taking them apart and cleaning them.

"Thank you, Charles," Gavin said softly. Which was replied to with a softer grunt.

Number seven: Mention it to anyone and I will kill you, Gavin thought with a smile, as he felt Alex pull him into her.

She had to feel him close, know he was as ok as he could be, and feel his body next to hers. She couldn't imagine what he was feeling and thinking, but she was glad that Charles opened up enough to share his experience with Gavin. And it also helped give her perspective. It helped her know that she likely wouldn't understand what he was going through, even though her relationship with her parents was less than ideal.

It also let her know that this isn't a pain that would heal. It wasn't something that she could just expect Gavin to get over. It would come back from time to time. It wasn't like a break-up or losing a job. It wasn't like a stab wound or gunshot wound. It doesn't heal and go away. It isn't something you can just forget one day, and you're all better. The pain will dull over time, but there is always that absence there.

They all settled into a somewhat comfortable silence for the rest of the trip. All getting some rest at one point.

***

After they got home, and let General Richmond know that they had made it safely, she informed them that her analysts hadn't made any progress. She could only trust a very few, and even then, she wasn't entirely sure that she was safe. It seemed the closer they got to Ivan, the closer the Collective was. She knew he was a part of it but hadn't thought that any of the others would be sticking their necks out for him. But she was feeling the pressure now from several senators as well as a few other generals and cabinet members.

She had made sure that Megan was safe, and gotten back to Washington, D.C. where she was met with a barrage of meetings and paperwork. There was getting to be a lot of pushback from the incident of Gavin attacking the civilian. There was a video, and the man was threatening to go public with the footage. How he had gotten it was still being reviewed.

She was used to the political games that were played, but this was more. This all felt like a direct attack. It all felt odd. It wasn't often that people threatened to go public with something like this, because everyone had skeletons. No one wanted their dirty laundry aired, because no one had theirs clean.

So, because of this, she didn't give every one of her analysts all of the information. She wasn't about to give everything to people that she couldn't trust. And that limited her expectations of what she was going to get from these analysts. So, she was relying on Gavin to get the job done. And she knew he would.

She got to her office and sat down. When she logged on to her laptop, he had an email from Noyoko telling her to call him as soon as possible. So, she picked up the phone for him out of her desk.

"Theia secure," she said when the ringing stopped.

"Noyoko secure. I have word, and it's not good," he said.

"How bad?" Cathrine asked.

"You need to visit your goddaughter," he responded.

"Now? I'm not packed," Cathrine replied, she had dreaded this day, but they had known it was a possibility.

"Now," Noyoko said and hung up the phone.

***

Gavin got to his lab and got everything up and running.

"Aren't you worried about Perun?" Alex asked.

"Not really," he said, as Kaleb came in with a bottle of whiskey.

"Kaleb, I'm not sure that he should be drinking-" Alex started to say but was cut off by Kaleb.

"Oh, Alex Alex Alex. Does this mean you haven't been able to meet him yet?" Kaleb asked, but not directly to Alex.

"She hasn't officially met him yet," Gavin replied, clearly distracted, but with a smirk on his face. A smirk that Alex hadn't seen before.

"Is it a glass night?" Kaleb asked Gavin.

"Boys?" Alex asked, she wanted to know what she was missing. She didn't like feeling so confused.

"No, it's a straight from the bottle kind of night," Gavin replied, pulling out two laptops, booting up his desktop, and getting his wrist computer on.

"Oh, you are in for a treat Alex, it's rare that it is a straight from the bottle night," Kaleb said, watching Gavin work.

Gavin opened the bottle and was about to take a swig, when Alex almost yelled, "BOYS! WHAT IS GOING ON?"

Kaleb looked at her like she had grown two heads, and Gavin stopped moving.

"Sorry sweetie. We aren't purposefully keeping you in the dark," Gavin started.

"Speak for yourself," Kaleb mumbled under his breath, earning a glare from Alex, which caused him to cower slightly.

Gavin was already back to being wrapped up in getting the computers ready. He took the first swig of whiskey.

"Alex, let me have the pleasure of introducing you officially to the great, the powerful, the evasive Vidar," Kaleb said, pride for his friend clear in his voice.

And it was clear to Alex why they had been dramatic about it. This really was a bit of an occasion. The man who was able to evade the entirety of every government in the world. The man who was able to hack into several unhackable systems. The man that she thought she knew well, she was now getting to see a side of him that she thought she had met before, but if she hadn't and until now it was just Gavin fooling around, then Ivan truly stood no chance.

The confidence that was simply exuding from Gavin as he started to type away at the wrist computer. It was hard for her to keep her hands off of him. It was extremely attractive to see the man she loved, in his element, feeling as though he could run the world.

She saw black windows popping up all over the place. On every screen. Code would run, and then he would close it or minimize it. She stopped trying to count how many windows there were.

I can barely manage to input my paperwork and get them uploaded online to the internal system for the CIA, and here he is, breaking through every firewall there is. I honestly lost track of what he was doing as soon as he brought up one of those black windows with green text. This doesn't make any sense to me. If I didn't know him better, then I would think it was all recorded, and he was just trying to impress me, Alex thought to herself, and she was honestly impressed.

Kaleb kept looking over at her with an excited face. It was what she imagined most people had in watching their favorite sport. It matched the face that Gavin had the first time that he had her watch Star Wars. She thought it was good, but she didn't get all of the hype that he had for it. But she faked it for him. She was excited about his energy and passion for it.

But Kaleb was a fan of Vidar. And it makes sense why. It was entrancing watching just how smooth Gavin was at this. How quickly he was able to get through things and pull up the next window.

She heard him growl, and she wasn't sure if it was good or bad, but she sure knew what it was doing to her. She was squirming. Trying to quell the fire building inside her.

"Perun, it is time for you to sign off. Permanently," she barely heard Gavin say, as he typed away.

She watched him type a bit more, getting a few other processes finished. He was going so fast, that it was honestly hard for her to keep up with all the screens. She glanced over at the bottle and noticed it was half gone. And she honestly couldn't think of when he had taken another drink. She was so lost in it all, and she loved it.

"THERE!" Gavin yelled in excitement. "I found you, you worthless worm. You can't hide from Vidar," Gavin said.

"Save it," Alex said, grabbing Gavin by the collar and kissing him deeply. She started pulling him towards their room.

"Kaleb," Gavin said between kisses. "Watch. Make. Sure. Nothing. Happens."

"You got it, boss," Kaleb replied, and sat at the desk, marveling at what his friend just did.

***

Gavin and Alex had freshened up and then called Charles. He came over, and they informed him where Ivan was.

"He is still in Atlanta? What an idiot," Charles said in disbelief.

"Well, Ivan is a program. He may be an advanced program, but he is still a program inside Harold. He is programmed to gain power and be mean, and that is about it. He doesn't actually have a personality. He doesn't actually know what he is doing I think. He seemed to be able to dive into Harold's ability to think at times, but it never brought anything forward in his personality. So, if you think about his actions like a program being run, then it makes sense that after a major procedure is completed, that he returns to home," Gavin said, and it made sense to everyone.

"I can't get a hold of the general. It isn't like her to not answer. I have tried several times," Charles said, he had been trying to let her know that they had found Ivan. "Do we have any munitions here? I have some at my place that we can raid."

"No, I don't keep-" Gavin started.

"Yes, we do. Follow me," Alex interrupted.

Gavin looked at her intently, and said, "I stand corrected."

Alex walked over to the entertainment center, and turned several knobs, then hit the power button. The couch lifted, and the TV pulled out and turned to the left, and the coffee table opened up.

"This is why you're my partner," Charles said and roamed around the room.

"How did I not know this was all here?" Gavin asked.

"Well did you ever ask?" Alex asked, as she grabbed several sets of knives, and put them into a backpack that she had grabbed.

"Load up. Gavin, get the information needed and the plan set. We will get your pack set," Charles commanded.

"I already have it," Gavin responded.

"Then help and tell us in the van, I still haven't returned it," Charles said.

***

They pulled up outside of the warehouse. It was where Ivan had gotten his start. It was kept under one of his many aliases and was normally empty.

"Don't let it fool you, this is highly secure. I will disable what I can, but there is no way of knowing what manpower he has in there. Since he took out any cameras that he had in the building. So, we are going in mostly blind. I had counted thirteen men with him in Citadel. There is no telling how many he had outside during that. So, be ready to meet strong opposition," Gavin warned.

Charles locked his gun and slung a shotgun over his shoulder. He had three pistols strapped to him. He was ready to blow the doors down himself.

Alex had her knives. All of her sets. There were around fifty knives strapped to her body.

Gavin had his wrist computer and a couple of tranq pistols.

They went to the door, and Gavin hacked it. He knew that Perun was down, and Ivan had used that as his main security for this building. There was no way that Ivan knew unless he had been chatting with Perun during that time.

They made their way down the hallways, and there was no one there.

238

The hallways were empty. The rooms were empty. They made it to where they thought the server room would be, and there was a desk. The servers were all around, and at the desk sat Ivan. Alone.

They slowly made their way into the room. Charles had a gun on Ivan, and Alex had her hand on her knives.

Suddenly Ivan pulled a gun. And Charles fired.

And the glass shattered. It was a mirror.

Ivan shot and hit Charles in the shoulder and the chest. The vest protected his chest, but he dropped his gun and was hurt.

"Welcome," Ivan said, as they all turned and saw the real desk and Ivan sitting off to the side.

"Ivan, what is going on?" Gavin asked.

"They kicked me out," Ivan said, sounding crazed. He was clearly not ok.

"Who did Ivan?" Gavin asked, sounding concerned and not sure what to do.

"The Collective. They kicked me out because of you," Ivan twitched as he spoke.

Gavin remembered his issues with the virus. He wondered if it might be similar for Harold. He had to try.

"Harold, I know you're in there," Gavin started. "You need to fight. If you ever were to fight, now is the time. I saw your message to my dad, Coeus. I know you have given up, but fight now," Gavin urged.

"You don't know what you're talking about. I am Ivan. I am the one in charge here. I am the powerful one," Ivan ranted.

"Have you ever stopped to think about yourself, Ivan? Do you remember your parents? Your childhood? You have a British accent, are an infamous Russian arms dealer, and are supposedly from Canada? You don't make sense," Gavin said.

"Stop! You don't get it! I have the gun! I am in charge! I have the power here!" Ivan yelled and grabbed his head. One of Charles' pistols had fallen out of the holster and was sitting right by Alex's foot. She motioned to Gavin, who nodded.

Ivan slammed his hands down on the desk, "STOP IT! I WON'T GIVE UP!" Ivan screamed.

Alex kicked the gun up, and Gavin grabbed it out of the air, pointing it at Ivan.

"You are a program, and nothing more. You aren't real Ivan. Harold is real. Harold deserves to live. Harold is who belongs in this world. Not you," Gavin said.

"AAHHH!" Ivan screamed, "NO! I WON'T GIVE UP!" He yelled and pointed the gun back at Gavin.

Gavin put his gun down. "I won't hurt you, Harold. You have to do this. You have to fight. You are the one that is real. You can win. Do it for my parents," Gavin said.

After a loud scream, and Ivan holding his head, he put his hands down on the desk, breathing hard.

"Gavin. I am weak, but I am here. I am barely holding him back. I need help," Harold said to Gavin, fighting all he could.

"I will help you, I promise," Gavin said, starting to step towards Harold, hand extended.

And then Harold started laughing. It became maniacal. It was clear Ivan was back.

He raised the gun, "No, HAHA," Ivan pointed the gun at Gavin. "I won't HAHA," Ivan put the gun under his chin. "Let you HAHA," He stared right at Gavin. "WIN HAHAHAHAH-"

BANG!

/: Chapter 20

A Collective Mind >

Gavin and Alex were sitting at home and resting together, enjoying a glass of wine. They were discussing everything that had happened recently, and when they thought that they would be able to make it out to see Megan. They were still debating on whether they should take Charles and Kaleb. Kaleb seemed more likely, but Charles had really come around to being a part of the family.

Alex had her head in Gavin's lap and was starting to fall asleep when Kaleb came bursting through the door.

"GUYS!" He shouted, causing Alex to leap up, knife in hand in a moment.

"KNOCK?" Gavin yelled and asked incredulously.

Kaleb rushed in, ignoring them both, and grabbed the remote.

"There isn't time for pleasantries!" He exclaimed, flipping through the channels quickly. Settling on CNN.

The screen was filled with the image of David Lawson, with General Richmond, Gavin, Alex, and Charles' pictures accompanying him.

"What about my boss-" Alex started to say, only to be shushed by Kaleb.

"These individuals are known to be extremely dangerous. Treat them with extreme caution, and if you meet any of them, we urge you to not interact. Call the number below, and notify them of your location, what these individuals were doing, and how many of them are there.

"I would assume that they are armed. We know that they have access and training to many weapons. Again, we urge you to NOT engage.

242

Simply get away from them and call the hotline with the information we asked. Thank you," David said as he prepared to leave to the podium.

"That was the Director of the DOC and cabinet member David Lawson. Speaking just now. Please be sure to keep vigilant-" the reporter stated.

"Guys, you have to go! Who knows if they are on their way here now!" Kaleb said excitedly.

Just then Charles came through the doorway.

"Cars ready. Let's go," he said calmly, looking at the screen.

***

Earlier that day, somewhere in the Alps:

Joseph Michaelson sat around the table, Mikel Melwasul on his right. He looked over the Collective, and spoke, "Thank you all. It is an honor to accept the position of Historian among this group of elites. I simply hope that I can do this position the justice it deserves.

"It is regrettable that we had to act so severely against one of our own in the late Ivan Orlav. I will be filling in and taking over his business for the time being, until we can find a suitable replacement for his seat. I do believe that it may be time to revisit our recruitment process. It has seemed to be lacking as of recently," Joseph stated, trying hard to give the appearance of humility.

The group nodded in agreement, and there was a slight murmur that had come over them as they discussed it among themselves.

Joseph looked at Mikel, who stood and addressed the group.

"Now, as for this current issue of the NOVA system and the Woodfords," Mikel started. "I do believe that it may be in our best interest to officially move as a group on them. We all have our connections, and it may be time to squash this insurrection against us before it has time to gain any momentum.

"I make a movement that we, as a group, address the issue of the NOVA system along with what is left of the Woodford family and their associates," Mikel stated, following group procedure.

There was a raising of hands around the group, and several said, "I second this motion."

The third-party moderator said, "All in favor?" And almost every hand around the large table went up. "All opposed?" And no one raised their hands. "Motion passed."

Mikel smiled and said, "Thank you for your continued support. I will be making calls to each of you with whom I will need help from.

"If I call, I would encourage each of you to not take this seemingly unimportant hodge-podge group lightly. They are far more dangerous than any of you could imagine. Do not move against them directly alone, and if you move against them at all, I encourage you to move with a heavy hand. Worry about cleaning up later.

"I will go make the call to put them on every watch list we can. Again, thank you for your continued support," and with that Mikel left and pulled out his phone to make the call.

Joseph stepped up again and said, "As you can see, I will be enforcing a stronger sense of group. I don't want us having in-fighting. That will only weaken us. We need to work together to correct what has been broken by those before us who have acted frivolously.

"If there is anything that you need, I would like for you to reach out to each other, or me, before you reach out to anyone outside the group. Working together we have an expanse of resources. We would be wise not to squander them selfishly.

"I will be spending some time going over our records and seeing what has been taken down. Educating myself on our group's grand and elite past. Once I have come to a conclusion on a specific direction moving forward, I will call for another meeting. So, please keep your phones on and with you. Thank you," Joseph finished and stepped down.

He met with Mikel, who let him know that the call had been made.

"That's a good start. We have to get rid of them in order to set our group back on the right path of control. If we can get the NOVA system, even better. But our top priority now is not retrieval as much as it is removal. Find them. The Collective above all," Joseph stated to his friend.

"The Collective above all," Mikel responded as he went on his way to make another call.

***

"The general is meeting us at the airport in the country. It's very private and will be good for us to get off the grid. Noyoko, or the man that you met as Stan, is going to assist in getting us off the grid as we make our way to where your sister is Gavin," Charles informed them as the car sped down the road. He was sure to avoid as many roads as possible that would have cameras that would catch them. He had also changed his license plates and put on his fake beard. Kaleb was in the front seat, he made him put a hat and sunglasses on.

"This hat makes me look like an old man, don't you have anything more stylish?" Kaleb complained.

"The point is to make you not look like yourself. Moron," Charles snapped back, annoyed.

Kaleb put his hands up defensively.

They got out to the country airport in a few hours, using back roads whenever they could. And there was a cargo plane sitting on the runway waiting for them, as well as the general standing by the back lowered ramp.

Once they were in view, she turned and marched up the ramp. Charles wasn't slowing down much, until right before the ramp. Where his car went straight up the ramp and slammed into a park right behind a dark gray SUV.

Getting out they all looked around but hurriedly got strapped in as the ramp was lifted and they were on their way.

"So where are we going general?" Gavin finally asked.

"I lost my rank. So, it's either Cathrine or Agent Theia from here out. Use agent names as much as possible, as they are less recorded. And we might as well come clean as far as backgrounds to each other now, as this very easily could be our last mission together," Cathrine stated.

As she looked around the group, she couldn't help but chuckle slightly.

"Gavin really did do a number on you all, didn't he? The best of the best, hardest of agents, been through months of training and hours of torture, couldn't stand more than two years with Gavin Woodford before you cracked and spilled all your secrets huh? Even you Charles?" Cathrine asked and saw a slightly guilty look on Charles' face. Causing her to laugh harder.

"This really shouldn't surprise me. Your father was the exact same way Gavin," Cathrine continued, but then the smile faded.

"Just as well now though. We won't have much time for pleasantries. We can only stay in one place for so long. Even off the grid. They will find us. All of us. Which means, your sister will have to rehab on the run. And I will have to rely on you all more. As I have operated outside the law in other countries, but it has been years since I have had to, and never within the United States," Cathrine finished, fighting the feeling of absolute defeat that she had. She knew that the team needed her to be strong.

"We have my tribe's underground network that we can use for at least a while," Charles pitched in. Earning a nod from Cathrine.

"And Vidar. I will need whiskey, but I can do a lot to keep us off the grid. Even when we are in public," Gavin offered.

"I'd rather you not destroy your liver. We will need you to find a way for Vidar to be available without drinking if you can?" Cathrine asked. She had full faith in his abilities, he just needed the confidence that comes with having a buzz.

"If we want to operate outside the law," Alex said quietly to where they almost couldn't hear her. She shook her head. *Am I really going to offer this?*

246

Is this where we are at now? I guess it is our best option. We don't have a lot of choices here. She argued with herself. Several painful memories coming back.

"I know someone who is an expert, and would help with a few provisions," she finished.

Thank you for reading The Mental Take Over!

Please feel free to review it on Amazon and Goodreads for me.

Thank you,

Jon Scott Lee